C000102183

TRANSIT OF ANGELS

A NOVEL

DESNEY KING

PILYARA PRESS

Copyright © 2020 Desney King
All rights reserved.

No part of this book may be reproduced in any form or by any electronic or
mechanical means, including information storage and retrieval systems, without
prior written permission from both the author and publisher named below, except
for the use of brief quotations in a book review.

This book is a work of fiction. Any references to historical events, real people, or
real places are used fictitiously. Other names, characters, places and events are
products of the author's imagination, and any resemblance to actual events, places
or persons, living or dead, is entirely coincidental.

 A catalogue record for this
book is available from the
National Library of Australia

Transit of Angels
Version 1.0
ISBN: 978-1-925827-27-9
Cover design by Megan Montgomery
Cover photograph by Daniel Cassar

Pilyara Press
Melbourne

For my earth angels – Annie and Sam

In the icy brilliance of ICU lights, I am pinned to a beige vinyl chair. Nothing makes sense. How can this body on the bed be Bill? My husband, my anchor, my devoted partner for the past thirteen years. His shock of dark hair is gone, replaced by swathes of bandages, and his eyes have disappeared behind bruised, swollen lids. The plastic tube between his lips is attached to the ventilator that is breathing for him. Other tubes drip fluids into his veins, or drain fluids out of him. Wires monitor vital signs. Without the warmth of his skin through the coarse hairs on his arm, there would be no way of knowing if he were alive or dead.

At five o'clock this morning, kitted out in heavy leathers and state-of-the-art bike helmet, my darling roared away into the darkness. The Kawasaki's fading rumble licked across my belly as I snuggled back into the cosy nest of our bed. At the truck stop on the Pacific Highway Bill would meet his mates, Steve and Sean, for their ritual Sunday ride.

* * *

A white-clad man approaches. 'Just checking readouts,' he murmurs, and jots something on the pages clipped to the end of the bed. I can't hear his footsteps. Only the faint hum of the ventilator and the muted beeps from Bill's bank of monitors.

Time disappears in this brutal white world and I sit, breathing in and breathing out, holding Bill's limp hand, watching his chest rise and fall. Ghosts drift by – doctors, nurses, people pushing trolleys or carrying clipboards. Who are these people? Some of them shockingly familiar with Bill's vital signs, his catheterised penis, his tubes and wires and bags and dressings.

Essie rushes in. Hugs me tight, sobbing, breathless. Time snaps back into line as she whispers urgent questions, strokes my hand, swipes her tears. I look at the readout on one machine and recognise it as a clock. 'I've been here three hours and seventeen minutes,' I say. And still he hasn't stabilised.

I speak as in a dream. 'We should try and find Neil. Last time Bill heard from him, he was over in WA.'

'That was years ago, Angel. He could be anywhere. Do you even have a number for him?'

I don't. All I know is that Neil doesn't like to be tracked down.

'He's Bill's brother,' I say. 'We have to tell him …'

But it's hopeless. I don't know the name of the mine he was working at, the company he worked for.

Essie eases me back into the chair. For a while, both of us – myself and my twin sister – concentrate on breathing in and breathing out, intent on keeping Bill alive by sheer will.

Essie tells me Sean and Steve have been giving statements to the police. Telling them about a patch of oil on a downhill bend near a river, describing the details of their nightmare. They'll visit Bill later, she says. So will Liz. And Sage is on her way. She's already sent an email to Aunty Fran, although no one knows exactly where in South America she is.

As the hours pass, white-clads come and go, padding on pale-shod feet, reading numbers, making notes, murmuring to me and Essie and to each other. Not to Bill.

At some stage during the afternoon, two senior medicos arrive and ask us to leave. 'We need to do some detailed tests,' one says. 'Please take a seat in the family lounge. Have a coffee, perhaps.' I refuse to leave Bill's side, but they insist, saying they'll send someone to get us as soon as they're finished.

'Why is he in Westmead?' Essie asks, as we sink into a floral sofa. 'RPA would be so much closer to home for you. Easier for visiting.'

'The chopper brought him here,' I say. 'I think it was the closest major hospital. They keep saying his condition is critical.'

Essie wraps her arms around me as I rock and sob, oblivious to the other people taking refuge in this strange room.

After an eternity, a nurse tells us we can return to the intensive care ward. 'Make sure you wash your hands thoroughly before you go in,' she says, 'or use the hand sanitiser.'

Bill looks exactly the same as when we left him, and I wonder what the doctors did. Why is he not awake? Why aren't they helping him? Why are his clothes and boots and helmet still in the pink plastic bags on the tray beneath his bed? Again, I take his hand in mine. Essie sits silently beside me, holding back tears.

At 16:23 the curtains open and two men and a woman walk in. I think I've seen some of them before. The woman speaks. 'Could we have a word, Angelica?'

Essie closes ranks beside me, nudging us closer to the cold metal railing on the side of Bill's bed. They must have good news, I think.

My cottonwool feet are feeling for the lino floor and my face hovers over Bill's. I grip his hand very tight. 'I love you, darling. Essie's here with you, and I'll be back soon. I love you!' They want Essie to come with me but we both know we can't leave Bill alone again, and so she stays.

They take me to a room that is not white but soothing blue, with ugly patterned sofas, a blue plastic water fountain, a column of plastic cups, a low coffee table and a Matisse print slightly crooked on the wall. They invite me to sit, and I prop on the edge of a hard wooden chair in the corner closest to the door. I'm desperate to hear what they have to say.

All of them sit on the sofas but nobody looks comfortable.

The tall gaunt man with greying hair and glasses leans in my direction, looks down at a set of papers in his hand and starts to speak.

'You know your husband has sustained traumatic head injuries, Mrs Jameson? And fractures to most of his cervical vertebrae?'

'I know he might need further surgery and that you're doing everything you can to stabilise him,' I recite. I don't know, now, why they've brought me here, and I want to escape back to Bill. My spine is rigid, every muscle in my body ready to spring.

'Angelica, there's no easy way to say this,' says the woman. 'Professor Ingleside is telling you that there's nothing more we can do for Bill. His injuries are too severe.'

My body tries to move but I am solid stone, my mind slipping in and out of midnight fuzz.

The woman stands and comes towards me, slips an arm around my shoulders and holds me upright on the chair. Her voice drones on.

'I'm afraid the only thing keeping your husband alive is the ventilator. There is no evidence of brain activity. I'm so sorry, Angelica.'

Unearthly keening filters down to me and I see the people

moving, very slowly. The two men shift and stir on the sofa and the woman pushes a tissue into my clenched fist. Ice pulses dully through my veins. From a long way away I hear angelic voices whispering but there is nothing in them I can understand. Then everything goes dark.

2

When I open my eyes, I am lying inside a curtained cave. Voices drift through its walls. A warm hand is holding mine. What the ...?

I turn my head. It's Essie. But I feel so drifty, as though I might float off this crisp, white bed.

'Angel! Sweetheart, it's okay – I'm here.'

'But where are we? Am I in hospital? What's going on, Ess?'

Wait a minute. Isn't Bill in a hospital? Did I dream that?

Gently, Ess explains that I've had a shock. That I fainted. That a nurse has given me a mild sedative to help me settle.

And then I begin to remember.

'Oh my god! Why am I lying here? We should be with Bill. We need to be there when he wakes up.'

I notice Essie looks pale. And as I grip her hand, the details of my meeting with the doctors begin to return.

Bill isn't going to wake up. Isn't that what they said?

'He's on life support, Angel. As soon as you're feeling well enough, we can go and see him.'

My face is wet. I didn't realise I was crying, but Ess is dabbing my cheeks with a tissue. Leaning over, hugging me. Holding me the way she used to do when we were little and I'd hurt myself.

The intensive care unit is a vast, white space, windowless, with a high-tech console at its heart so that all the beds, arrayed around the walls in separate glass-fronted rooms, are visible to the nurses and other medical staff. It's like something out of a space movie. Except that the whole ward radiates pain, anguish, grief.

I'm sitting beside Bill's bed with Essie, holding his hand. Deja vu. But not. Now my mind is racing, trying to absorb and assimilate information. Swinging wildly between unreasonable hope and cold, harsh facts.

'He's a registered organ donor, Ess,' I whisper. 'We talked about it when we made our wills, and he was adamant. What should I do? I don't want them to cut him up.'

Sobbing. Rocking. My thumb stroking Bill's oh-so-still hand.

Why am I whispering when they say he can't hear?

'You have to tell them,' Ess says. 'It's what Bill would want. You know that. He'd give his jacket to a beggar on the street. He's the most generous man I know.'

'But what if he's not really dying? What if a miracle happens?' Part of me is waiting for him to open his eyes and look at me.

Essie sighs. Takes my other hand in hers.

'Darling, that's not going to happen. You know it's not.'

A nurse interrupts us. 'Your partner Liz is here,' she says to Essie. 'She's out in the waiting room. But it's strictly two visitors at a time, I'm afraid – even for family.'

Essie looks at me. 'Will you be okay if I go and see her for a minute?'

I nod. All I really want is Bill.

* * *

I have drifted towards sleep, holding Bill's hand, my head resting on his chest. When a quiet voice says my name, I startle.

'Angelica? I'm Julianne. Your sister mentioned that Bill is a registered organ donor. Do you feel ready to talk about that?'

Julianne explains that she is the organ donor coordinator for this unit, and that I can ask or tell her anything that's on my mind. Straight away, I feel that I can trust her.

'He is,' I say. 'We both are. But I can't bear the thought of him being ... carved up.'

Julianne is patient. Knowledgeable. Passing me a tissue, she asks whether I'd like more time to think it over, but also makes it clear that time is of the essence.

'I need my sister,' I whisper. 'Could you find her for me?'

The moment Julianne leaves the room, I dissolve. Tears drip off my chin.

'Oh, Bill, how can I do this to you? Your beautiful body, your soul. Isn't our soul bonded with every cell of our body? Why do I think that? What if they take your organs and your soul goes with them? What if it gets ripped into little pieces?'

Essie must have heard this last anguished question. Pulls her chair close to mine and takes my hand – the one that's not glued to Bill's.

'What are you talking about, Ange? *What* would get ripped up?'

'His soul, Ess. His beautiful soul. Oh my god, he could end up tortured, wandering the ether forever.'

Gently, she turns me to face her. 'What on earth gave you that idea?' she asks.

'The cell thing,' I say. 'You know – the soul is in every cell. Isn't it?'

She's looking at me as though I've gone mad. Maybe I have. Have I?

'Angel. Darling. First of all, no one knows. It's all theories. And to be honest, that one does sound pretty crazy to me. Where did you hear it?'

'I don't know! I don't know, alright? Maybe I made it up. It just popped into my mind and I can't get rid of it. What if I do the wrong thing?'

I rest my forehead against Essie's and wail. Let her hold me until my sobbing subsides.

'What do you think Bill would say?' she asks. 'He had pretty clear ideas about most things.'

And then I realise. This *is* what he wants, definitely. He was a hundred percent sure about registering as a donor, even when I had doubts.

'Yes. Yes, okay. Okay. We'll do it,' I say. My body straightens up, taking on Bill's resolve. 'I'd better let them know. Can you get Julianne for me, Ess? I'd like to tell her myself. You go and find Liz.'

Julianne rests a hand on my shoulder. 'Angelica, I promise you, as time goes by, you'll be glad you've done this. Every family I've worked with tells me that it brings them comfort, knowing their loved one has passed on the gift of life to others who previously had no hope. Thank you.'

And then she says the magic words: 'All the rules disappear now, Angelica. Visiting hours, number of visitors … It will take us around forty-eight hours to prepare everything; do assessments, notify recipients. We'll move Bill to a room at the quiet end of the ward so that you can spend the entire remaining time with him. Your family and friends can visit whenever they wish. If there's someone special you're waiting on, please let us know. If we can, we'll wait for them. Remember, you're in control. We'll do everything we can to make this time as precious and as rich for you as possible.'

She hands me her card, and tells me I can call or message her whenever I need to. Momentarily, I imagine what it must be like to do her job. She must be some kind of angel.

They are moving Bill to the quiet room and have asked me to leave for a short while. 'Someone will come and find you as soon as he's settled.'

In a daze, I walk towards the lift. Press the button. The doors slide open. There are people inside. I can't stand it – seeing others going about their business as though this is any normal day. But I step in anyway, and the doors slide shut behind me.

As I walk towards the cafeteria, I can hear Liz's raised voice. She and Essie are sitting at a small table just inside the entrance. 'I know it's horrific, Ess. But you have to go – the kids rely on you. The school won't run itself. Angel's strong. I'll stay with her until Sage arrives.'

Essie is crying. Liz's tough love isn't what my sister needs right now.

Ess sees me first. Puts her hand on Liz's arm. 'Here's Angel,' she says. There's a warning tone in her voice.

'Sweetie!' Liz stands. Pulls out a chair for me. 'I'll go and organise some more tea.'

When she returns, Essie is rubbing my back. I'm explaining about the quiet room. Telling her what Julianne said about visitors, timing, support.

'She told me I'm in control,' I whisper. 'But how can I be? Bill's dying and there's nothing I can do to bring him back.'

As we talk it becomes clear, even to Liz, that Essie cannot leave me. Liz says she will pick up Tashie, our little dog. She'll take her out to their home in the valley, settle her in, sort out something with the school and with her own boss. She'll organise fresh clothes for me and for Ess. And she'll come back.

She's galvanised now that she has tasks to complete. Stands.

Hugs me. Holds Essie in a warm embrace, murmuring something I can't hear. And then she's gone.

Bill's new room is eerily quiet apart from the faint hum of the ventilator. He looks exactly the same as when we left him – eyes closed, plastic tube between his lips, head bandaged; other tubes draining into vinyl bags beneath the bed, and wires everywhere leading to monitors that now have blank, silent screens.

'We're monitoring him remotely,' says the nurse. She's come with us to make sure we have everything we need. Comfortable chairs. Bottled water. Plastic cups. A buzzer to press if we need anything.

I am sitting on the edge of the armchair closest to Bill, holding his hand. Again. Ess sits back a little, leaving us space.

I'm numb now, heavy. There are so many things I want to say to my darling, but my tired, overloaded brain can't find the words. Tears trickle down my cheeks. Maybe that's my new normal.

There's a flurry of activity in the doorway and when I look up, Sage is there. Our baby sister. Essie and I have been together all our lives. Our parents named us Estrellita, the little star and Angelica, the little angel – firstborns, twins. Sage, the wise, practical one, arrived two years later.

'Angel! Oh my love!'

Sage wraps her arms around me awkwardly – I won't let go of Bill's hand.

For long minutes she clings to me. Ess stands behind her, stroking her hair.

As children, we'd been inseparable. Under Aunty Fran's benevolent supervision, we'd rioted through childhood as princesses, jungle explorers, intrepid adventurers and in our teenage years, as rock chicks and rainbow warriors for peace. It must have been tough on Sage sometimes – the special closeness between me and

Ess. Even then, she was sensible, reining us in when my dreams and Essie's boldness took us into risky territory.

These days, though, we're not close at all. I'm not even sure why she's here.

Sage loosens her hold on me. Essie has taken a seat on the far side of the bed and Sage slumps into the chair beside me.

'What happened? How could this happen? Bill was such an experienced rider …'

Ess tells her about the oil slick on the road. Sage shakes her head.

'You see?' Her voice is rising now. 'This is what I was always afraid of! I'm sorry Angel, but his stupid obsession with the bike! How many times did I tell him to grow up? To be responsible? How often did I talk to him about …'

Essie is on her feet in a flash.

'Out!'

She grabs Sage's arm and hauls her from the chair. Marches her out of the room.

I can hear their voices as they walk away.

'… well, it's the truth! … didn't mean to upset her …'

'… so insensitive … Mrs know-it-all pain in the butt … not the time or place …'

Sage being Sage, I think, vaguely. As my focus returns to Bill.

When I open my eyes, Julianne is sitting beside me. The ICU is brightly lit twenty-four seven – I have no idea whether it is day or night, or how much time has passed since my sisters left. I rub my eyes, feeling the creased skin on my cheek where it's been resting on Bill's shoulder.

'There's a visitor waiting in the family lounge, Angelica,' Julianne says, 'but I wanted to check with you before sending him in.'

It's Don, Bill's boss. Associate professor in the politics department at Sydney Uni. He's been to our place for barbecues a few times.

'Oh. How did he find out?' I ask.

'Essie's been making a few calls,' Julianne tells me. 'Just the people she feels are close to Bill. The ones who might like to see him before he goes.'

I look at her, bewildered. 'Goes where?'

'Before we take him to theatre for the organ donations, Angelica. We have several recipients organised now; we're just waiting on the paperwork and logistics for a couple more.'

She's kind. But it's her job to remind me that this is real. I have lost my bearings and am adrift.

'Oh god! I don't know what's the right thing to do,' I moan. Julianne tells me that Essie will be back in a few minutes. Asks whether Don can come in now, or whether I'd rather wait.

I think for a moment. 'No. It's okay. Bill would want to see him. But I have to stay too. That's alright, isn't it?'

Julianne nods. Reminds me that I'm in control. Even though I know I'm not. If I was, my husband would wake up and come home with me.

I remember Bill used to smile at Don's eccentricity. Fifty-something, his greying hair dishevelled, weather-beaten face a testament to the time he spends alone in the bush. He's wearing his trademark tweed jacket with the leather patches on the elbows, and olive green corduroy trousers.

'Angelica. My dear girl. What can I say? Such a tragedy.' He rests a hand on my shoulder. Shakes his head.

I motion to the chair opposite. 'Why don't you hold his hand,' I suggest. 'He'd like that.'

Don's words filter through to me, although he's speaking softly.

'You've left us in the lurch, you silly bugger. What the hell are we supposed to do without you?' Don wipes a fawn hankie across his eyes. Blows his nose. 'You've been like a son to me, Bill. Such a brash, bolshy lad when I took you on. A mentor to all the young bloods now. You were in line for senior lecturer. Did you know that?'

He leans back. Sighs. Looks across at me.

'We'll miss his terrible jokes,' he says. 'I never once knew him to get the punchline right, you know. That was funny in itself, I suppose.'

'His dancing's pretty awful too,' I say. Don nods. Smiles. Perhaps we are both recalling faculty parties.

Bill's chest rises and falls in time with the ventilator as Don and I face each other across the bed.

'Such a sharp wit though, when it came to teaching,' Don says. 'He'd have those students sitting up and taking notice, even if the lecture was about the bloody constitution. Maybe a few thought he was a smart-arse, but most of them thought the world of him.'

He leans in towards my lovely husband, both hands resting on Bill's arm now. 'Farewell, my dear boy. I'll see you in the big beyond.' Like an old man, Don heaves himself to his feet. 'I'll be seeing you soon, no doubt, my dear,' he says, kissing me on the cheek. 'If there's anything I can do … Anything at all …'

When I look up, he's leaving, shaking his head, his gaze still fixed on Bill's inert figure on the bed.

Essie is sitting beside me now. My rock. Liz will be back in a couple of hours, she tells me. Their friend, Clyde, is going to look after Tashie. 'I've read the riot act to Sage,' Ess says. 'But she and Mike would like to visit later.'

'I guess it's not fair to keep her away,' I say, 'so long as she leaves her shitty judgements at home. The same for Mike. Are they planning on bringing the children?'

'They reckon it would be too hard on the kids,' Ess says. 'And they'll only stay a short while. I think they both just want to see Bill one last time.'

I sob. The reality won't sink in. Even though I've signed all the forms. Even though Julianne keeps popping by to check on us and to bring me up to date on recipients and timing. Even though there is a steady stream of doctors and nurses coming and going, making sure Bill remains stable so that his organs will be healthy and viable.

'I'm busting to go to the loo,' I say, finally. 'You'll stay with Bill, won't you, Ess? And I'll message Sage. Okay?'

'Of course, my darling. He won't spend one second on his own. We'll make sure of that.'

As I'm walking back towards the ICU, someone calls my name. Steve. He and Sean are just behind me.

'You sure it's alright if we both come in to see him?' asks Sean. 'The nurse at the desk said the two-visitor rule doesn't apply now for Bill.'

They are shocked when I explain about the organ donation, but they pull themselves together and hug me, one of them walking either side of me.

'Jeez, Angel,' Steve says. 'We should have guessed he'd want that. Yeah. Good on him!'

Essie stands as we enter the room. Says hello to Bill's friends, who go and sit on the chairs on the other side of the bed.

'I'm going to duck out and make a few more calls,' says Ess. 'Check when Aunty Fran's flight is landing.' She kisses me on the cheek. I nod.

'You can talk to him,' I tell the guys. 'They reckon he can't hear us. But who knows? I've been talking to him all the time.' My voice cracks.

'Agh, Billy, mate ...' Sean is shaking his head. 'What the fuck, mate? Why'd you have to take the lead? It should've been me. I'm the crazy one, right? No strings, no attachments. No one would really miss me.' He leans back, swallowing hard.

Steve puts his arm around Sean's shoulders. 'You know what a stubborn shit he can be,' he says. 'Once he'd finished his coffee, he just wanted to get going. That's nobody's fault mate. Just rotten bad luck.'

They talk to Bill about bikes and about the old terrace house they shared during their uni days.

'I'll never forget the first day you turned up at the house, Billy,' says Steve. 'We'd advertised for a girl. Remember that, Sean?'

'Yeah, we had.'

'Yeah, and then we heard this kwacker pull up out the front. The wicked green machine. So that sealed it. As soon as you walked through the door, we knew you were the one. Three Kawasakis in the back courtyard – what were the chances?'

'You were such a bushy, mate. That bloody scruffy beard, long hair, steel-capped boots covered in mud. Took us a while to sort you out and get you into the Newtown vibe.'

We sit in silence for a while.

'Don't know what I'm gunna do without you, Billy,' murmurs Sean.

'Maybe we'll give up the riding, eh, mate?' says Steve. 'Or maybe we can set up an annual charity ride in your name? What do you reckon, Sean?'

They've run out of things to say. But I can see it's hard for them to leave.

'Well, Billy, me old mate, I guess this is it. Be seeing ya.' Sean stands. Pats Bill awkwardly on the shoulder.

'Don't you worry, Billy. We'll take good care of Angel. She's a damn good woman. And she's strong. She'll get through this. I'm not going to say goodbye, mate. I reckon we'll meet again on that highway in the sky.' Steve hauls himself out of the chair, his cheeks wet with tears.

They hug me, and then they're gone.

For a while, it's just me and Bill, breathing in and breathing out. Bill's chest gently rising and falling. My heart breaking. I think it will never mend. 'I wish I could go with you, my darling,' I whisper.

I am beyond tired. Dozing off, jerking awake. When did I last eat? It doesn't matter. My hands are wrapped around Bill's.

There are voices in the corridor, speaking softly. Essie's, I think, with Sage and Mike. They hesitate in the doorway, then Mike comes over and gives me a hug before they sit on the chairs opposite. Sage hasn't said a word.

'We've been praying for him, Angel,' says Mike. 'And for you.'

I sigh. Shake my head.

Sage meets my gaze. 'I'm sorry, Angel. You know I love you. It's just that ...'

A warning glance from Ess.

'Well, anyway, we just wanted to say goodbye to Bill.'

They don't stay long, and it's a relief when they leave.

It feels as though Essie and I lost touch with Sage when she met Mike. As though she had found a comfortable home for her personality in his church community, and her views narrowed once they married. What had once been wisdom and responsibility morphed into rigidly held beliefs.

Essie and I look at each other. There's nothing worth saying.

Julianne drops by to tell us they can proceed with the transplants as soon as we say it's okay. But she knows we're waiting for Aunty Fran.

'When I spoke to her, she'd just come through customs,' Ess tells her. 'She should be here within the next hour or so.'

Julianne assures us that's fine – they can wait a little longer.

Suddenly, I am gripped with terror. My entire being is screaming NO!

Yet Ess and I sit here, on these crappy vinyl chairs, as though everything is normal. I have just enough self-control left to understand that a meltdown wouldn't help anyone.

I stare at Bill's long, lanky body on the bed. At his beautiful damaged face. Desperately trying to imprint him on my brain.

We hear her coming before we see her – Aunty Fran, bustling down the corridor, breathing hard. Essie goes to meet her at the doorway.

'Oh, my sweet, sweet girl,' she murmurs as she gathers me into her bosomy embrace. 'I can't believe it.'

She releases me and subsides into the chair beside me.

'What on earth happened? Not Bill ... not our Bill ...'

Yet again, Essie explains that it was an accident. A sliding door moment with the worst of outcomes.

Most of their conversation goes over my head. All I can think about now is that it's almost time. I wish Aunty Fran hadn't rushed. That she could have given us another hour or so.

'I remember when you met,' she says, breaking into my reverie. 'It was as though it was meant to be, wasn't it?'

She rambles on about how we both adored *Priscilla* and *Muriel's Wedding*. Both drank double-shot lattes, loved road trips, camping, politics, art, dogs, the theatre.

'To be fair, Bill was more politics and Angel more art,' says Ess, smiling.

Memories drift across my mind: Bill with a microphone, charismatic, speaking at rallies; me at the front of the crowd, cheering him on. Bill leading the chants at marches and demonstrations. Essie's right – he was a political animal through and through.

'For a laidback guy, he was pretty feisty and determined, wasn't he?' says Ess.

'The boys were saying earlier that he could be stubborn,' I murmur. 'But really, he just knew what he wanted.'

'Well, that's the truth,' says Aunty Fran. 'I'll never forget your wedding. He said he couldn't think of anywhere more perfect to get married than in my garden, with the rhododendrons in full bloom.'

My memory drifts back to that sunlit afternoon in the Blue Mountains. Our vows. In sickness and in health ... till death do us part ...

Oh god! I can't bear this.

'Tashie's all settled in at Clyde's,' says Liz, who has just arrived back and is sitting beside Ess. She's changed out of her gardening clothes. Why do I even notice that? Stupid. She's brought stuff for me and Ess too. But getting changed isn't on my radar.

We are all here now – my family. The quiet hum of the ventilator keeps us company. Bill's chest rises and falls.

But I am a weeping mess of confusion and panic. I can't do this. I can't let my darling go. What was I thinking, signing those papers? Yet my mind knows he has already gone, even as my heart races and tears flow down my cheeks.

When Julianne arrives this time, I see compassion in her eyes.

'We're ready, Angelica,' she says. 'I know how hard this is for you; for all of you.' She looks at Fran and Essie and Liz. 'I'm glad you're here to support her.'

Bill's donated organs will give five people a new chance at life. She says she can tell me a little more about them later if I wish. But for now, I should know how grateful each of them is; how much our generosity means to them and their families.

I hear her saying something about the surgical team; that we can walk with the wardsmen and nurses as they wheel Bill to theatre.

'They'll be here in about five minutes. I'll leave you to say your private farewells.'

Five minutes! Noooo! I touch every part of Bill that I can. Hold him. Kiss him. Stroke his face, his hands, his arms. Time has stalled. Time is evaporating. I am numb, yet every cell in my body is vibrating with dread.

I am vaguely aware of Liz reaching under the bed for the pink plastic bags that contain Bill's helmet, boots, jacket, jeans. 'Better take these,' she mumbles, 'or they'll end up getting chucked out.'

And then they are here. They position themselves around Bill's bed and begin wheeling it from the room, some of them walking alongside, bringing the equipment that is attached to him.

We follow, a tragic procession walking through a maze of clinical corridors. Ess and Aunty Fran are either side of me, holding my hands, Liz close behind.

The team stops beside a set of wide double doors. A nurse touches my arm. 'It's time, Angelica. I'm sorry, but we have to take him in now.'

The doors swing open inwards. I can't look. But I can't look away. The doors swing closed. And my world ends.

3

April eighth, 2008. Twelve months since they wheeled Bill into the operating theatre. Today is the first anniversary of his death. As if I need reminding.

We lingered in the corridor outside. No one knew what to do. Julianne came, I think, and took us to a private room where we could sit and talk. And cry.

And then the rest of my life began. Impossible, that I should walk away and leave my husband for professionals to deal with. But what choice did I have? Sometime during the previous forty-eight hours, Julianne and Essie had organised undertakers who would look after Bill's body once the operation was complete. All the paperwork was done.

I was adrift. A widow at thirty-four.

And I am no closer now to finding myself than I was on that bright autumn morning.

'Is it okay if I drop you at Strathfield?' Essie asked Aunty Fran. 'Of course, sweetie,' she replied. Strange, the things I recall. Even stranger, the vast gaps and warps in my memories.

I remember we walked through the hospital carpark, the four of us, to Liz's battered old four-wheel drive. I remember Aunty Fran clung to me as she stood on the footpath outside the railway station. 'My darling, darling girl. I'm always here for you, whenever you need me. Come and stay with me in the mountains. Or I'll come down and stay at your place. Just tell me what I can do to help, and I'll be there.' I sobbed as she picked up her luggage and walked away.

We drove home.

Essie parked in front of the slender old Annandale terrace that Bill and I had made our own, the place where all our dreams had taken shape. As my foot lifted up onto the worn stone step, tears streamed from my eyes. I couldn't see the faded mosaic on the front porch, the etched wattle blossoms gracing the glass panel in the old wooden door.

I felt the firm grip of Essie holding me up while Liz took my bag, found the key and let us in. Bill's ghost was everywhere, sprawling on the sofa, tinkering with the television, straightening up to wrap his arms around me. Flashing that special smile.

They walked me through to the sunlit kitchen and lowered me onto an old pine chair. My favourite spot, where every morning I sat over muesli and fruit, and coffee made by Bill. Tashie's water bowl and old blanket lay untouched beside the back door – no wet nose to comfort me this morning. In the centre of the table, wilting roses drooped in the ceramic carafe I used to use as a vase. Deep velvety red roses, brought home by Bill that Friday evening after work.

I knew it was over then; that I could not keep breathing and feeling and living without him – my muse, my exquisite lover and my precious friend. A cold clarity filled the room, chilling the sunbeams to a standstill. I sat like a statue while grief flowed around me and pooled at my feet.

Although three hundred and sixty-five impossible nights have passed, in many ways the nature of my devastation hasn't changed. Yet in those first hours and days, there was so much to be done. Life carries you along on a glacier of practicalities and time passes despite your incapacity.

That cold shiny morning in my cosy kitchen, the circle of women held strong. Liz was playing mother. I recall slow-motion screen grabs of her picking up the kettle. Taking it over to the sink. Filling it full before flicking the switch and waiting for the water to boil. 'When all else fails, drink tea,' she said.

Sitting beside me, her fingers resting on my brittle hand, Essie started talking about the things we had to do – a social worker at the hospital had given her lists and names and brochures. Explained the etiquette of post-death trauma.

First, we needed to find Neil.

Essie told me she had given his name and date of birth to the police – they would use their networks to search for him. You'd think the brothers would have been close. But it was never like that. An eight-year age gap, and Neil so strange and reclusive. There were times, Bill told me, when he would have relished the company and support of his big brother, but Neil didn't want it that way. At fifteen, he'd hitch-hiked away from the family farm and never looked back. Wouldn't come home for the funerals of their parents. Didn't send comfort or money. Yet Bill never gave up – that's how he was. He'd hoped one day Neil would come around, sit with a beer or two, talk over old times and what had gone wrong. He wanted his brother to meet me. For us to get to know each other.

My phone rang and Essie answered, speaking quietly. Steve.

Would we like him to drop by? Was there anything he or Sean could do? She told him no, but said she would talk to him soon about the funeral. They're Bill's good mates but this was family business.

We needed to tell friends and colleagues. But our contact lists were all over the place – address books, Bill's phone and computer as well as mine. Since I couldn't move or think, Essie glided around the house collecting numbers and making calls. Yes, it's unbelievable, hideous, obscene. No, he didn't suffer, he was unconscious the whole time. An organ donor? Yes, generous to the end. Of course, I'll pass that on to Angel. Details in the paper. We'll see you Friday at the north chapel. She phoned Steve back, went through the list, asked him if he could think of anyone we might have missed. Asked if he could pass the message on to Sean and their other friends as well.

Still no news of Neil. The police had promised to let us know as soon as they found him, yet part of me hoped they wouldn't. But Bill would want him here. Wouldn't he?

Somehow it was done. Liz and Essie had everything arranged. Except for my survival. Which no one could begin to tackle then.

On the Friday of Bill's funeral crowds gathered on the neat lawns and pathways of the crematorium. People I didn't recognise were murmuring uneasily in groups and solitary travellers shifted from foot to foot. Was one of them Neil? I'd only ever seen childhood photos of him, so I wouldn't know. Don was there, of course. He and Bill's campus colleagues all wore black – who knows the right thing to do on these occasions? Dozens of stunned students, dressed in op-shop formal, huddled in clusters, heads down, pale-faced. Old friends from school, neighbours, a couple of teachers. My friends and family. Our friends and family. Sage and Mike, standing slightly apart from the rest of us. So many people and me, completely alone.

They carried his coffin from the shiny black hearse with reverence up smooth steps and down the carpeted aisle to rest on a shrouded bench beneath soft lighting. His friends shouldered the load. A random thought drifted by me … that this is compassion – to carry the burden of a young widow's grief on the day of her husband's funeral. Essie and I had chosen native timbers for his coffin and that morning we smothered the lid with hundreds of deep red roses. Later, I would take them home and sleep with their sobbing perfume.

It was a good funeral. We did it well. We played his beloved Eagles – 'It's Your World Now' – and people stood up and spoke about the wonderful man he had been. They told stories and called up memories, some of them funny, all of them inspiring love and desolation. Holding back tears, Essie explained how Bill's generosity had given new life and hope to five individuals who had been close to death. Don said that as a teacher and lecturer, Bill was one of the best, that the corridors of the politics department had grown dim without his irreverent presence. Steve spoke of Bill's love of speed, his loyalty and selflessness, his wicked sense of humour and his crappy jokes. Aunty Fran, bless her, said he was the best thing that had ever happened to me.

As 'Amazing Grace' dissolved me, we watched his coffin slide away beyond this realm. And it was done.

I found myself outside in the lunchtime sunshine, greeting people one by one. Comforting those who didn't know what to say, patting shoulders, brushing hands. The endless queue. And eventually, being gently but firmly moved along.

Bill would have loved his wake. Everyone was there, except for Neil. At our local on the corner, just at the end of our street, we drowned our sorrows that afternoon. Aunty Fran had put a tab on the bar, and the drinks flowed freely. Essie and Liz sat either side of me, guarding my sanity. Sage sat at a nearby table with Mike, both of them drinking lemon squash. Liz told me later that they only stayed for one drink before slipping quietly away. There was a moment when someone told a story about Bill getting drunk and dancing naked on a table. It made me laugh. To think of it now, I wince. How could I have laughed? But I did.

Soon afterwards, I bought a hessian bag from the charity store. I kept that bag on the dresser in my kitchen and put my crucial paperwork in it, so nothing would be lost. I put all our documents in there – Bill's death certificate, the house deeds, my chequebook and our passports. Birth certificates, his and mine. Our marriage certificate. I carried it everywhere with me, and at night I hung it on the bedroom door.

The bag was rough and raw when it was new, but over time it sagged and stretched and faded. Holes grew where strands had worn through from snagging. But I didn't care. I rarely left the house other than to walk the dog or go to work or shop for food, and when I did, the bag travelled with me.

On the morning of his thirty-ninth birthday I poured Bill's glittering ashes from their sterile box into my ceramic carafe and stoppered it with cork. I set it carefully on the kitchen dresser, gave it pride of place. Several times, the phone rang, but I let it go. Listened to messages later from Sean, Steve, Essie and Liz, Sage and Mike, Aunty Fran, Don, a couple of Bill's other colleagues. I didn't have the heart to call them back. That evening I drank red wine by the fire. Toasted my lanky, dark-haired, dark-eyed darling. I drank to everything we'd had and lost, and kicked at the empty bottle as I stumbled upstairs to my lonely bed.

In the morning there was another message from Steve. We

need to know what you want done with Bill's bike, Angel – something like that. Days later, I sent him an email. 'Take the bloody thing to the wreckers,' it said. Then I wished I hadn't been so harsh. He and Sean still rode every Sunday, as far as I knew. I couldn't bear to think about it.

In the endless stretch of weeks and months, life flowed on around me. Nights and seasons passed me by while I lay crying, and went to work, and came home, and ate dinner, and drank wine, and nursed hangovers, and made the bed, and washed the clothes, and shopped for food, and walked the dog. Too many bleary mornings, too many wine bottles in the recycling bin. I thought I should stop buying wine, yet I yearned for the oblivion it brought.

One evening, sometime in November, there was a knock at my front door. Tashie scampered up the hallway, barking furiously. Two young police officers introduced themselves and asked if they could have a word. Not another devastation, surely. Ice filled my veins.

They refused cups of tea and stood awkwardly by the kitchen table, updating me on the search for Neil. It appeared he had left the Kimberley mining settlement a couple of years before, saying he planned to travel overseas. Thailand, somebody recalled, or was it Vietnam? Immigration had no record of his leaving the country though, and the trail went cold. They were sorry, they said, but unless there were legal reasons for locating him, there was nothing more they could do.

I remember thinking they seemed glad to escape; moved swiftly towards their marked car as I stood at the front door with my little brown dog, watching them go. Too much grief in my house.

And that was the end of our search for Neil, or so I thought. I'd done the best I could and, in truth, I felt my body relax a little. What would I have done with him if he'd turned up? What could we have said to each other that would have made any difference? It was all far too late.

Essie and Liz wanted me to come and stay with them, and Aunty Fran had a bed permanently made up for me in my old room in her mountain cottage. But I had been set adrift by loss and grief, and knew I had to anchor on home ground, waiting for steadiness to return. I needed to focus on breathing through the minutes and hours and days and nights. To maintain a routine. To eat drink and sleep. To keep my heart pumping and my bowels moving.

There is nothing you can take for granted when life itself collapses and disappears.

At the magazine where I worked, they stayed as far away from me as desks and staff meetings would allow. Kindness faded into silence. Email became a normalising influence. We managed to meet deadlines, and get the jobs done. My pay went into the bank on the second Thursday of every month.

The weekends were much worse. No deadlines, no routine to adhere to. I stayed in bed on radiant days, stumbled out into the streets in unwashed clothes to walk Tashie, ate scantily from pizza boxes and takeaway containers. Too many nights I paced the hall, sobbing, drunk, calling out Bill's name.

To mark our tragic anniversary, I've begged Bill to send me a sign. Anything. If I had the courage, I'd go to him, but life's visceral forces hold me back.

I drag one foot after another into our garden on this chilly April morning. Tashie runs ahead, snuffles at something in the flower bed, then plonks her solid little body down beside me, huffing a sigh of contentment that we have come outside.

Tears squeeze from my closed eyes and dribble down my chin. Here they come again. You wouldn't think a human body could be such a tear factory. I am too weary to wipe them away and they drip onto my old matted jumper. Autumn has me wrapped in cosy wool and daggy track pants despite the watery sunshine.

The wooden slats of our garden bench remind me of how Bill came home one Sunday afternoon triumphantly lugging that long flatpack carton. Plonked it down in the garden and strode off to the shed to fetch his tools. In less than an hour he had constructed a rustic bench where we could sit with drinks and books and weekend papers. We christened it immediately, him with a beer and me sipping white wine. To us! we clinked, smiling, believing this was another sweet beginning in our lifetime of decades together.

The rough slats bite into my skinny bum, reminding me of why I need to eat. Weight has been sliding off me for a year and nothing fits. The softest of breezes caresses my face and I feel the warmth of the sun coaxing my lips into a small smile of pleasure, despite it all. This is why seeds grow, my mind says. Such is the force of life-giving light we find it irresistible, and life persists, even through the darkest hibernation. I think I feel a hand resting on mine, and dare not open my eyes to not see him.

'Bill, my darling,' I murmur. 'Please, darling! Please send me a sign.'

And I am astonished. Pure, fluted notes pipe into the stillness of my garden. A repeating rhythmic melody carries me towards bliss. A butcher bird? Here? My lids are gummed together and open bleary on the world. All I can see is the grey-green of our wattle tree, steadfastly guarding the shed as it has done for the past three years.

The magic of those crystal sliding notes sends shivers up my spine. My gaze is drawn upwards among the feathery leaves and shimmer-green branches to a solid black and white bird with a hooked heavy-duty beak and useful claws. It is looking at me sideways, its jaunty head set at an angle. The silence lengthens as we commune. And here it comes again, that sweet love song dissolving veils of corporality. Then I remember. There was a time, in the country, when Bill pointed out a pied butcher bird and told me about their exquisite song but couldn't find the words to do it justice. And now he has delivered it to me.

My heart floods with melancholy waves of joy. Heavy with shock and gladness my body lets go at last, packing on weight in an instant as the melody brings me back to earth and anchors me into life. Hope seeps through me and silently I pray that Bill really has heard me and sent a sign. I make a deal. If I'm right, the bird will be here again tomorrow at the same time, in this place where butcher birds have never sung before.

The leadenness of the past fifty-two weeks turns to gold, if only for a while. Tashie stirs but doesn't move, although her tail twitches in a way that says she's happy. My body doesn't shift, but it has changed. Perhaps we have turned a corner. If the messenger appears again tomorrow, then I'll know.

In my dreams last night, for the first time, I heard Bill's deep voice just as it used to be, calling out 'hello' as he breezed in through the front door every evening after work. 'I'm home, darling! Where are you?' he'd say.

Something in my body knows he's near, even though people tell me to let go, move on. Grieving time is over, someone said, recently. Clearly, they've never been in this fathomless state.

I'm wandering painful halls of recollection that yesterday were locked and barred, a passage eased by the blissful melody from a small bird's throat. Everything feels lighter this morning and I'm dressed and ready for the test. Optimistic. Buoyant even. Knowing Bill, he won't let me down. Next minute, I'm wracked with nerves, and wondering whether I'm going crazy.

I'm not going to feed it or coax it back in any way. I have to be sure. If it's been sent by Bill it will turn up all on its own. I wander out into the garden, coffee in hand, book tucked under my elbow, Tashie trotting at my side. Don't want to seem too keen. Again, a sliding thought whispers that I might be going crazy. I sit. The slats of the bench are warm and hard. Sunshine glints on heads of orange marigolds among the cabbages in the veggie patch.

Weariness washes through me and my eyes close. My ears will have to do the work this morning. The weight of my body threatens to sink a crater into the earth beneath the bench.

Who knows how much time has drifted by? Until the sweet notes surround me once again. Tears flood my face. The butcher bird has come. Bill heard my deal. My breathing steadies and time expands. Everything is possible, nothing known or clear or understood, but open to inspection and consideration. Again and again the melody flows, a single regular tune, fluted many times.

I sit, eyes closed, feeling warm air on my skin. As my breathing slows and my body softens I sense the tension beginning to give way. Muscles long unrecognised sting with pain. Lightness floods the space around me and inside, as the melody continues. There is little awareness of my body now. Even my seeking mind rouses only slowly with thoughts of Bill, enquiries, and the anguish of never-ending love. In this new world of softness and light I seek him differently, less from anger and despair than from curiosity, opening to what might emerge gently into this light.

The melody has quieted, but peace remains. A faint scent wafts into my consciousness. What is it? So familiar. Yet not anything to do with the garden. Leather, blended with leather dressing and Sunlight soap. Essence of Bill. I am adrift on waves of serenity, and comforted by love.

A rustling of leaves and scuffling brings me back. I am in our garden but everything seems bright, vivid, more alive. And the butcher bird is torturing a grub high up in the branches of our wattle tree, thrashing it from side to side against the soft green wood, intent on breakfast, some kind of celebration.

Looking down I realise Tashie is curled at my feet, deep in a dream, twitching. For the first time in a long while, thoughts of seeing Essie cross my mind without generating instant exhaustion. When I go inside, I'll call her.

4

'Hey, darling. Remember me?'

Essie squeals.

'Oh my god, you're back! I was getting ready to call the men in white coats, Angel. Come on out! Can you come now? I'll wait an hour or so and put the coffee on. Bring Tashie too – she must be just about going spare. Oh my god.'

Tears down the line. Both of us sobbing and laughing. It's Sunday and the whole world is new again. For the first time in a long time the sun is shining just for me.

Driving away from home feels adventurous today, instead of painful. As I turn into Coxs Road I feel spurts of life pulsing through my veins and see a parking spot right outside the bakery. Another little sign. I have a drive ahead of me. What will I need? This kind of planning is a revitalised sensation – it's been lost in the mists of time and grief that are lurking at my back. I buy water in a bottle, and a crusty sugar-smattered custard-filled pastry – our favourite kringle from the best cake shop in town. Climb back into the car.

I trace my way along those old familiar roads, until the bush takes over. We are heading north-west to the river and the valley and the ancient sandstone escarpments that hold the whole thing together. Sliding a disc into the player, I sing my heart out, crying in the chapel with The King.

Ess has been living out here with Liz for a few years now, driving into the city for culture fixes and friends and recently for me, on those rare occasions I could let her in. The school and the kids and her horses have become a world she doesn't want to leave, a forgotten valley community connected by the rugged hillsides and the river.

We career down the hairpins towards the water and I'm filled again with wonderment at those tough men and horse-drawn drays that cleared this road through dense bush – tall gums, cassia and leptospermum, wattle and grevillea and soft green-cream flannel flowers. People were different then, in their heads if not their bodies. No technological expediencies to blur their edges. Hard labour and the ringing of sledgehammers and axes slamming through rock and timber, forging a way to the life-giving waters of the mighty river down below.

Turning left around the final hairpin, I pull up at the tail of the ferry queue. I wonder whether Ess needs milk but it's too late to turn back to the shops. She'll have long-life in the cupboard anyway. Long life. Sorrow tugs on my heartstrings, dropping me abruptly into floods of grief. Go away! I want to feel peace. I want dry eyes and soft, smooth skin. Normality.

We crawl down the hill behind the other vehicles, but the red and white boom gate drops as we reach the head of the queue. Urgent clanking of chains and growling of motor as the laden ferry hauls up her drawbridge and follows her rust-stained cables across the swirling river. My hand reaches down, stroking Tashie's ears, tickling under her chin. And suddenly my face is wet with tears again. Bill loved this ritualistic journey to the valley.

The wide expanse of shimmering water eddies and flows as the ferry returns, its twin cables dripping and singing in the sharp breeze as the salt tears crust on my cheeks and the ferry glides towards us.

Suddenly, through the sighing of eucalypts and the lapping of tiny waves I hear a flute-like tune – the butcher bird. I wonder whether Essie will believe that Bill is still around?

Graunching of heavy metal on concrete stirs me to action. Turn the key. Start the engine. An ancient LandCruiser crawls off the ferry, down the ramp and up the dip, driver heaving the wheel to guide his vehicle onto the road, grinding through the gears as it trundles up the hill. A gleaming Beemer follows impatiently behind. And a little red Barina. Now it's time to load. The ruddy-faced ferry driver sweeps a grand gesture in our direction, hurrying us on and up to the front of the barge. Seeing my face, he tips two fingers in recognition, then turns away, embarrassed, knowing the story. In such a cradled community, there are no secrets.

From my vantage point at the front of the ferry I gaze out across this ageless river, comforted by its endless flow, the turquoise houseboat tethered to the far reedy bank, an old weatherboard cottage nestled on the scrubby foreshore, and the timbered hills rising behind them, right up to the sky. Liz has been working here of late collecting samples, preparing to plant, protecting and reviving this precious stretch of the world.

Metal wheels turn, pulling the ferry cables through, hauling the heavy vessel out into the current, its heading set by these weighty parallel wires as it toils back and forth. It's been this way for well over a century. No bridge can find its footings in this terrain, with its shifting riverbed and the sandstone base crumbling beneath a silted muddy bottom. Love it or hate it, the river measures life in rhythm with the cycles of the moon and the earth. There's no rushing here.

Yet we surge towards the concrete ramp, engine growling in

reverse, slowing the heavy barge, the driver lining her up expertly. It's low tide and the drawbridge grates on the edge of the wet concrete ramp, taking hold, steadying our docking while weighty chains are locked together. As the gates swing open, I am waved off, leading the slow procession into a different world, where Mother Nature insists on showing her hand.

How many times have Essie and Liz done this drive? The road demands my attention, meandering around the curves and humping shoulders of this tributary to the mighty Hawkesbury. It's well over a year since I've been here, but nothing seems to have changed. Stately eucalypts line the roadside, climbing steep rocky hillsides to the west, while to the east lush flat paddocks feed black Angus cattle and always, the river laps against the shore. An old wooden dinghy nudges the sandy bank, tugging on its frayed bit of rope. I remember it was there last time I drove by and wonder if anybody ever uses it these days. I think I saw an old man fishing in it once, with a little white-haired child in a floppy hat.

Through sheltered glades and down onto grassy flats the road winds and wanders, bringing sharp memories of wind in my face, my knees and thighs welded to Bill's leather-clad haunches as the bike leaned in and out of corners. Sharp pain shoots through my arms into my shoulder blades, dragging a sob from my belly and slowing the car. Fuck! Nowhere's safe from this grief. I don't want it any more. I look up and realise I've pulled into a gravel drive-way, hard up against a rickety wooden farm gate. So be it. This is where I get out and collect myself. Tashie stays in the car. Mad howling echoes off the sandstone valley walls and I gaze around, seeking its source, only to find its origin in me. Oh for god's sake! Pull yourself together. Striding, hurling fistfuls of pebbles, crazy woman growing grief cairns on the side of a lonely road. Until the rage subsides. I feel ashamed. And hope that no one's home in the house up on the hill.

Back in the car, I prepare for a civilised arrival at the school.

The holidays have just begun and Essie has the place to herself for a couple of weeks while Liz is on her annual pilgrimage to New Zealand, visiting her father's family.

Their sweet little cottage nestles into the hillside behind demountable classrooms and the smallest school hall in all creation. An old wooden schoolroom shaded by a wide verandah sits off to the left, with water tanks nearby, taking full advantage of the roof space on all the buildings.

As I slow down at the 40 kilometre sign and flick my indicator on, Tashie leaps into action, dashing back and forth across the back seat, tail wagging madly, yapping like a pup. I'm amazed she remembers. Gravel crunches beneath my tyres and I swing hard left through wide opened metal gates.

The Lady Hellinger is still in full bloom, butter yellow petals lighting up the darkness of her glossy green leaves. A rose bush planted, so the valley wisdom goes, by an early settler almost a hundred years ago. High up on the hill, a wallaroo hops into the shadow of the trees. Not a thing has changed. My heart aches.

There's a neat spot waiting for my car. Ess must have mowed it this morning. And sees me coming.

She's running, taking the steps two at a time, down from the cottage to haul open my door and wrap her arms around me. Oh, Ess. How I needed this. We extricate ourselves from the tangle of arms and steering wheel, pull my basket from the boot, clip on Tashie's lead. My little dog has wriggled herself almost inside out with joy and would take off up that hillside like a streak if we let her go. Not good for the wildlife. We'll put her in the yard.

Essie is leading me inside, fingers entwined in mine, talking nineteen to the dozen. She can't keep the smile off her face. How I love this woman!

Through small rituals of kettle boiling, mugs warmed, coffee scooped into the plunger, we settle around each other. The magnetism of our linked lives and hearts settles me into her kitchen. We've never been apart so long and some of my ache eases just by being near her. Aunty Fran once told us it was the most shockingly wonderful moment of Mum's life, realising there were two of us. Not identical, but so very much alike. Double trouble, people would say as they bent down to our stroller, offering a finger to be gripped, or patting a chubby knee.

I extricate the kringle from its sugary paper bag, slide it onto the rose-patterned plate and carry it out to the verandah. Sagging rattan armchairs remind me of countless evenings spent gazing out across the river, watching the sandstone cliffs glow crimson and violet and gold, reflecting the setting sun. Some nights, a crescent moon would be revealed, already climbing up above the ridge, transiting into the jet black sky, Venus close behind. A luminous love song.

Ess goes into the kitchen for a knife, small plates, a box of tissues, coffee mugs, the plunger and the milk, until the battered old table is laden with our feast. A tray would have been a good idea. We laugh. Chat about the river, how low the tide is today, the water level also dropping in the tanks – there's been no rain for weeks.

I ask Essie how she feels about Liz going to New Zealand without her – again.

'It still hurts,' she says. 'There's a part of Lizzie that she keeps locked away from me. She keeps saying there's so much shit she needs to work out, especially about her Dad, and she needs to spend solo time with her Maori *whanau* – the huge extended family.' Essie sighs. 'Maybe one day she'll be ready to let me in.'

'I hope so, Ess,' I say. 'I mean, look at what happened to Bill. None of us ever knows how long we've got, do we?'

We sip our coffees, silent in the face of mutual pain.

A pair of swallows swoops and dives across the front yard, swifting towards the schoolhouse, darting beneath its eaves. They've stayed late this year with the warming of the seasons, Ess explains. Usually, they disappear in March. Now, though, autumn is definitely settling in. Leaves crinkle on the old pecan tree across the paddock, the one that shades the neighbour's house in summer and fills with raucous white cockatoos every year at harvest time. In a few weeks, there will be hard white frost most mornings, a fire glowing constant behind smoky glass in the slow combustion stove.

'I called Sage a couple of days ago,' Ess says. 'Thought she might like to bring the kids out for a visit while Liz is away.'

'But she still said no, right?'

'Yep. Won't bring them into this house of sin.'

I shake my head. 'That bloody religion. She's left me a few messages, always says they're praying for me and for Bill's soul. I haven't called her back.'

'Yeah, apparently she prays for me too,' says Ess. 'No point talking about it really, is there?'

'No point at all. I've got enough going on without worrying about her narrow-minded judgements.'

I reposition my bum on the cushion, feeling the cane chair creak and shift. Everything is settling. The valley is working its magic. In the sublime late morning light, blades of grass shimmer. Yellow roses droop and sway in the gentle breeze, releasing exquisite perfume. And I hear the melodic notes of a butcher bird's call. Tell her, it's saying. Tell her Bill's here. Tell her …

Ess shifts in her chair beside me, sensing the quickening of my breath, the stirring of my mind. I must have straightened slightly. Tell her …

'Bill's here,' I say, surprising both of us.

I look across at Essie, lean forward, and launch into my story.

'I was in the garden at home the other day, sitting on our wooden bench, and I'd been begging Bill to send me a sign. It felt like some kind of trance overtook me. It was weird, Ess. I might have been crying, I can't remember. I cry all the time. Anyway, that birdsong cut the air and hit me in the heart. My eyes were closed. It came to me that this must be the butcher bird Bill always tried to describe when he talked about his years on the farm. You know – when he was eight or nine? After Neil left home, and he didn't have any friends and he roamed the paddocks and talked to the cows? The melody took me on some kind of journey, I don't understand … god knows how long I sat there. But when I came to, everything had changed. The light was different. And I didn't feel so desolate any more.

'You'll probably think I've gone crazy.' I eye her cautiously. 'But I really felt as though Bill had sent me a message.'

Ess isn't laughing, nor is she edging away, as people do when confronted by possible madness. She is being careful with me though.

'There's an old man in the valley,' she says, slowly. 'Clyde. The one who looked after Tashie. We're good friends. On the surface he looks like all the old-timers around here – a bloke with some land and a few horses, growing watermelons in summer and waiting for rain.

'But …' she hesitates, 'he talks sometimes about the veils between the realms, about how much we don't know and about mysteries. He'd probably agree you've had a visitation.'

Essie looks at me, waiting to see my reaction. The light in the valley is sharper now, edging our faces with shimmer. We always guard each other in moments like this, wary of incoming hurts or potential for damage.

'All I know is that it was real, Ess. I tested it. I made a deal, and the next morning, he came back. I smelled him. I smelled the leather of his bike jacket, the dressing he softened it with, the scent of his fresh-showered skin. I could almost feel him stroking my hair.'

For the first time, I have found a way to talk about my grief, to help Ess understand. It dawns on me that she probably does anyway. But couldn't get near enough to comfort or cushion me.

I smile, relieved. Start to laugh. Of course Essie gets me. It's a twin thing. She's laughing too.

And then it stops. Sober and spent, my body sags back into the chair. Ess has gone inside. I hear a match flare, water tunkling into the kettle, the faint hiss of gas.

Bill would be smiling if he were sitting here, I think. He'd tease me, reach over, entwine his fingers with mine. We'd talk about strange phenomena, things no one can properly understand. Mention films we'd seen, books each of us had read. It would be intelligent, casual conversation, befitting our status as young inner city professionals. By the time Ess brings out fresh coffee, I have tears sliding down my worn-out face. Again.

Knowing it can't go on like this forever is no remedy when you don't know how to stop. Books and experts, both of which I gave up on months ago, tell the grief-stricken it's okay. Give permission to the tears and the waves of despair. But I don't want to know the generics of my state. Struggling to live through grief takes every skerrick of my energy.

'That butcher bird's been hanging out here all summer.' Ess breaks my reverie, pouring without asking as she refills my mug. 'There've been mornings when Liz and I have watched him for ages. He sometimes sits just there, on the corner of the verandah rail, tenderising his breakfast.'

Our conversation meanders, touching on Aunty Fran's latest art exhibition, the work Liz has been doing down at the river. And we talk about Bill's superannuation payout, my shock and dismay at receiving this windfall when all I want is him.

5

'So what are you going to do, Angel?' The question nearly knocks me off my chair. I thought we were being gentle with each other. 'You're re-emerging, sweetheart. You've managed to get yourself out here. And the bird ...'

Tashie grabs our attention, rushing at the garden gate, then dashing along the fenceline. Cars have been passing every fifteen minutes, a dribble from the ferry. Sometimes one or two, or a cavalcade of five. This time, it's an old battered Land Rover, dull green disguised with dust. Slowing down. Indicator on.

Everything in me springs to attention. People. Someone I don't know.

Essie reaches out her hand, brushes my arm.

'It's okay. It's only Jane, dropping by to bring the eggs. She won't stay long.'

We both stand, and I disappear inside. Ess walks down the steps, arms out, greeting the woman who has navigated Tashie's welcome and is heading across the yard.

I can hear exchange of news, vibrant conversation. This woman is a force. Through the window I can see her – well past middle age, wild grey hair let loose, a tangle of untameable tight curls. She's wearing workman's trousers, faded green as well, one back pocket ripped half away and hanging down. A man's work shirt baggy on her wiry frame. She's not much taller than a ten-year-old, but has such presence.

In a woven basket lies a clutch of pale eggs, enough for Essie for the week. Jane puts her basket on the verandah table, stretches, looks around.

'Company, Ess?' She glances at the coffees and the dog, my car, our kringle crusts, the tissues. Now I feel rude, hiding in the house.

'My sister Angelica's come out for the day,' says Essie, an intimation in her tone. Of course – everybody knows. I want to hide, to stuff the pain inside a cocoon and disappear. But there's something else as well. An almost magnetic force dragging me towards companionship.

I open the old screen door, a hesitant smile lifting the corners of my mouth. The boards on the verandah are warm on my bare feet.

'Jane, my sister Angelica.' The woman leans forward, strong brown hands reaching out, taking one of mine.

'My dear, I've heard so much about you. Welcome to our little patch of heaven.'

We sit, Essie dragging over another chair.

'I have a bit of a dilemma, Estrellita.' She's down to earth. No awkwardness at meeting the widowed sister either. 'You know I've been getting organised for a long stay in Nepal? They need me at the orphanage. My short visits are less and less satisfactory. It seems inappropriate each time I leave, as though I'm a deserter.'

She tells me about her passion for a project that takes in children from devastated villages and helps rebuild their lives. She talks about community, hope, commitment.

'It's just that I struggle so to leave my cosy home,' she says. 'Twin passions really. I built it myself, Angelica. It's very hard to close it up and walk away. But I can't cope with letting it out to strangers. So there's the thing …'

As the sun slides further up into the sky, we sit and yarn, Essie and Jane filling each other in about local happenings, mentioning how badly we need rain.

'Well, must be off.' Jane's up now, stretching. 'We all move on, you know, Angelica. Impossible as it might seem to you at the moment, you are going to be happy again. It might take a day or a year or a decade, but the wheel will turn. You'll see.' And she puts her arms around me, embracing grief, brushing dry lips against my cheek. 'Get Essie to bring you out for a visit if you're here again in the next few weeks. I won't be leaving for a while yet.'

A chill shudders through me as the Land Rover rumbles down the track, turns north and drives off up the road. Did that old woman dare to confront the unspeakable? Essie has walked down to the gate to check for mail and I see her long dark hair floating in the breeze as she comes towards me, Tashie pulling on the lead.

Beyond them, light glints off the river, that ever-present witness lying silent between its sandy banks, pooling at low tide, hours behind the mother flow that pours in from the distant ocean.

The yard gate clinks shut. A flurry of wet breath and sloppy tongue rouses me. I haven't seen Tashie so happy for at least a year.

Essie's stretched out beside me again, head resting on the back of the chair, a far-off look in her eye. When I follow her gaze, there's nothing but the backlit blue of the sky topping those sandstone walls, folding the envelope, securing this world within worlds.

'It's back,' she murmurs. 'Every day this week. Usually a bit later in the day when the thermals are at their peak.' She's pointing far up into the high horizon, showing me the bent tree silhouetted, the crag of rock, the shadow of a cave. 'Just above that, circling, you can see it. You must be able to see it?'

But I can't and I can't. And then I do. And the breath escapes my body like a sigh. There are wedge-tailed eagles nesting in the remote reaches of that bushy national park escarpment. The black dot shapes itself in my imagination into compact body, wings held wide, wingtips adjusting to the lift and swirl of warm air rising off the rock. Circling and swooping, it carries me with it, levitating my spirits and taking my breath away.

'Don't go yet, Angel. Why don't you stay the night?' Essie, firstborn of twins. The boss.

I bring my heart back into my body, feel my pulse settle as I release connection with the eagle. On the verandah of this old cottage, in a place where time feels eternal and sluggish river tides mark out the revolutions of the earth, I am shucking off some of the leaden weights that have sunken into my organs. The dark cloak of grief has thinned in this golden light.

The stillness of warm air holds us gently. A fly buzzes, Tashie's ear twitches. A crow's mournful cawing drifts across the valley.

'So, my Angel, where did we get up to? What do you reckon you'll do once your contract is up?'

Shit! Can't she leave me alone?

I have been working as a graphic artist on a fashion magazine. It's easy. It's what I've always done. Some days they let me work from home. The company has changed hands, new management has been installed, a hurricane of change is swirling through the building. All existing contracts are up for review. Essie's right – I do have a decision to make. But not today. Everyone will be interviewed next week, offered options, given a month to work it out.

I am reluctant to select change. Anything that anchors me is precious, even this mundane job that asks so little of me while my real self lies shattered.

What other options do I have anyway? Anguish bursts in my belly. No other options. No sense of direction. An abyss at my back and the dark narrow tunnel up ahead.

'I don't fucking know, Ess! The last few hours, I've been feeling kind of okay. As though I could release the pause button and Bill's Kawasaki would come roaring up that road and turn into your driveway.

'And now it's all come crashing down on me again. I have no fucking clue what I'm going to do. Stop pushing me!'

'Whoa! Take it easy! It was just a question …'

We sit a while in silence. I want to leave. Get back home.

But she won't let it go – bossy bitch. 'Have you considered a change of scenery? You know we'd love to have you here for as long as you want to stay. And Aunty Fran's spare room's yours if you'd rather be up in the mountains.'

'I can't leave our house,' I whimper, a dull ache throbbing in my gut, leaning me forward in the chair. 'It would feel like I was deserting everything we built together. I just can't, Ess. I don't know if I ever can.'

'I didn't mean selling up and leaving, Angel. It was just an idea. If you're not ready, we'll let it drop.'

I'm leaning back now, trying to ease the pain. There is never any way of knowing what will set me off. If I don't understand this anguish, no wonder others can't. My best idea is to hide away. I knew that all along. It takes too much energy to anticipate all the risks. I shouldn't have come.

My vision lifts to the skyline above the trees and rocks. There is no black dot. No eagle now.

6

The next morning I drive home early, shower, dress, smarten myself up, and go straight into the office in the city. I'd phoned ahead and my manager is waiting. I hand in my notice, discuss the possibility of freelance work, collect my coffee mug and my diary, and leave. I sense they are relieved.

So this is the first day of the rest of my life. It feels like progress – making a decision, acting it out. I feel stronger, and determined to move forward. Where and to what I'm not sure. Perhaps I should make a list. For starters, I need to sort out my finances. And I'll have one more try at tracking down Neil – he should be told.

It's a divine day, late autumn, with winter twirling its chilly fingers around leaves, transforming their colour, plucking them free. I'm wearing the pink angora cardigan Bill bought for my thirtieth birthday, feeling him near, hoping for the butcher bird.

I have no real plans when I take my coffee out into the sun-washed courtyard, but I put the carafe of ashes, a notepad, a pen and the hessian bag of documents on the bench, waiting for a chat with Bill.

This is newborn territory. I hold my fragile infant self with care. Randomly, I recall that Aunty Fran is impressed with her financial adviser. Maybe that would be a step forward. Get his number. Go and talk to him. Put that on the list.

Self-help gurus recommend following your passion. But without Bill, my life is passionless. Tears threaten, yet I am determined not to cry. I focus on the feeling of cool air on my skin. What would Bill suggest? Rich colours flicker through my peripheral memory, bringing with them a faint whiff of linseed oil and turps. My painting gear's been sitting in the shed this past year, untouched. Brushes bundled in bottles, prepared canvases propped against the wall, large ones at the back. I used to love to paint.

Bill adored my abstracts and hung them proudly on the lounge room walls. They're still there. I haven't changed anything in the museum that was our home. Again I feel my mood slipping and reach out to catch it but I'm too late. Tears ooze between my aching lids and I wonder for the millionth time where they come from. I let the sobs rise, chest heave. My nose is running and my hand reaches automatically for tissues. Bitterness assails me, and for a moment I think I might vomit. The only thing I'm good at now is grieving. Years ago, we saw bitterness eat away at our neighbour like acid, reducing her to desiccated parchment in the weeks before she died. The vow I made then springs into my mind: not that route. Bill would be deeply disappointed if I let myself degenerate that way.

Sunlight kisses my cheek. For a moment, I think it's him. And then it hits me – I am actually fighting for my life. I'm stunned. Just the other day, and a hundred days before, all I wanted to do was die.

My coffee has gone cold, but I sip it anyway. Realise that going to the office day after dreary day has been holding me together, structuring and defining my days. Panic starts as an icy fizzing in my toes, and runnels through my knees and loins to join forces with my racing heart. Darkness threatens. I sit very still. Close my eyes. Focus on slowing my breathing. Who would help me if I fainted in the garden?

Colours pool and dissolve behind my eyelids as sunlight washes away another layer of grief. There's a spacey feeling of being utterly alone.

Tashie licks my hand – gentle, loving licks. When I open my eyes she's quizzing me, her head tilted to one side, body crouched ready for anything. Pats, play, a walk. She's full of life and my fingers trail through her coarse hair, digging in, scratching her back till that leg twitches reflexively, making me laugh. Maybe I can go on.

Back to the list. Today I'll phone Aunty Fran, organise to visit her and find out more about the money man. See whether she knows of a private detective I can brief about Neil. There's no butcher bird around and yet I sense Bill is nearby. Something's changed in the way I feel about him.

I gather up my stuff and walk inside. It's early afternoon and the wintry sun slants into the kitchen, caressing the pale buttercup walls. Today I can deal with dishes, eating, phone calls. Even my clothes are organised and respectable although I'm not planning on going out. Life's details have gathered me up and got me moving.

I'm always astonished at Aunty Fran's capacity for work and play. She's baked a cake, written down the names and numbers I asked for as well as websites, authors I should read, details of her upcoming exhibition. Over cups of tea we talk about the weather, the garden, Fran's art, her friends and local community.

Subtly, she shifts the focus to me, checking on how I'm really feeling. How well (or not) I'm coping with spending so much time on my own. She is pleased and impressed that I'm beginning to reconnect with the practicalities of life and living. And repeats her open invitation for me to come and visit. To stay as long as I like, even if she's away.

We talk about what I'll do if I manage to locate Neil. If we do find him, what then? Like me, she feels slightly uneasy, unsure what kind of man he has become and how he might react.

And then she talks to me about contacting Sage and trying to make peace with her. 'She's your baby sister, Angel. I know she's a pain in the arse, but family's family,' she says.

I feel anger and bitterness welling up. 'Why should I be the one to try and fix it?' I say, my voice rising. 'Why can't she call me? Apologise? She's always so high and mighty. Always right, as far as she's concerned.'

Aunty Fran sits back, shocked. 'Well, it's good to see feisty Angelica making a comeback,' she says at last. 'I'll stay out of it then, darling. You're both adults.'

We sit in silence for a while, letting the dust settle. Soaking up the sounds and scents of the garden and its surrounding bush.

When our conversation starts up again, she raises tender topics like the sorting of Bill's clothes, disposal of his ashes. Sits patiently with me through the tears. And finally agrees we can talk about it later.

Tashie has been chasing butterflies around the garden, exhausting herself. She sleeps the entire way home in the car. I think again about Sage and her girls, and push the pain away. I really don't need that shit right now.

The next day, I set up appointments with the financial adviser and the bank. I leave messages for a couple of sleuths. Later, I slump on a kitchen chair and cradle Bill's ashes. Faded rose petal perfume merges with the faint smell of leather; essence of Bill. I relish the warmth of his old sweater loose on my frame.

Winter has arrived in full force, chilling my bones. The smell of rain is in the air but the deluge doesn't come. I bring out my knitting, the TV program, some DVDs. Our gas fire substitutes well enough for the real thing and with the curtains closed at night I can imagine both of us sipping a good red, discussing the day. Often now, I feel Bill near me and reach out to take his hand. And when the tears trickle they no longer etch my skin.

My skinny body is taking on shape again. Sometimes, I even eat three meals a day. But when I laugh, I berate myself for showing signs of inappropriate happiness. And when I cry, I wish away the tears, exhausted beyond despair.

7

I am sitting cross-legged, one of twenty people at a Zen meditation information day. We're an unlikely assortment of folk ranging in age, I'm guessing, from sixteen to seventy. The teacher has explained the basics. Our goal is to silence the mind. That shouldn't be too hard. My mind's cottonwool most of the time.

A sublime note peels into the space, signalling silence, the closing of eyes and the settling of buttocks on hard round black cushions. Zazen. We've been instructed to count each breath, aiming for ten. Then repeat. Easy. Breathe in, one. Breathe out, one. Breathe in, two. Itchy nose. Oh. What did he say? Smile at distractions – don't attach to emotions like annoyance and frustration, just go back to the beginning and start again. Okay. Breathe in, one. Breathe out, one. This time I get to three before the thoughts drift in. I'm thinking how much that chime reminds me of the butcher bird's melody and how I haven't heard it for quite some time. Oh. Back to one.

* * *

At home, I am floating through days, drifting on whimsy, making up reasons for filling the time. At night, I sit by the fire and knit. Write emails. Watch movies. Sip red wine. Talk on the phone.

Essie and Liz call every few days, or I call them. News from the valley calms me, grounds me in nature. Sometimes we squabble – usually about what I plan to do with my life – but we stick to the rule of making up before the call ends.

They persuade me to be the bigger person; to take Aunty Fran's advice and phone Sage. It's a superficial conversation that leaves me unsettled and angry and hurt – no hint of apology from Sage for the nasty scene she caused at Bill's bedside. I won't be calling her again any time soon – I refuse to invite more pain into my shattered heart.

The nights are still hard. I'm finding excuses not to go to bed, sitting up way too late. I don't want to lie alone in our big bed, filling such a slim space between the sheets. Emptiness accompanies me night after night and tears seep into my pillow.

It was a leaflet in Luca's cafe that caught my attention and persuaded me to seek solace in silence at the Zen class, but I'm finding it a difficult practice. Harsh. Remote. Maybe it's not for me. I like the breathing in and breathing out. I like those fleeting moments of serenity. (The teacher calls it emptiness.) The other meditators seem pleasant, but they don't chat. Perhaps I'm barely visible, deflecting tentative approaches. After a few weeks, I decide to explore other styles of meditation. I know I'm drifting, but the anchor is not on its chain.

This morning I opened my window to a sweet heady perfume that almost made me swoon. For a moment, there was room for nothing else. Evocations of myriad pleasures poured into the room. I could almost feel the scent of jasmine brushing my skin and infiltrating my lungs.

First hint of spring. Where did those winter months go? I've done a few design jobs for agencies and enjoyed them. No pressure. Good money. And a way of filling time. My finances are sorted, at least for a while. I haven't been up to the mountains to stay with Aunty Fran, but it's clear the family thinks I'm showing signs of life. When Essie and Liz call me now, they sound less anxious.

In my old dressing-gown I wander downstairs to put the kettle on, intending to take my tea out into the garden. When I open the back door, Tashie runs out to wee, an instant bounding of joy bursting into the soft dawn light, dashing round and round the small yard as though she's been freshly charged. Her delight in being alive leaves me breathless.

The mossy cobbled bricks are cool and damp beneath my feet. The tea in my rose mug sketches spirals of mist in the crisp air. I shiver. Go back inside and pick up a pale pink pashmina off the sofa. Winter's fingers cling to me still, belying jasmine's promise.

There's dew on the bench and I wander into the laundry to pick up an old newspaper, lay it down, carefully sit, both hands wrapped around my mug. Peace suffuses my limbs, relaxes me against the back of the bench. On the raw dark sticks of the pruned rose bush, something shimmers. Looking closely, I see there are minute swellings, embryonic hints of new leaf buds. Furled life, preparing to burst into the world.

The last of my tea has grown cold and I tip it onto bare earth. Make a mental note to get out and do some gardening in the next few days. And wonder, for the thousandth time, what will become of me. Meditation promises stillness of mind in which answers might present themselves. I close my eyes. I'll give it another try.

Counting each breath of this cool scented air sweetens my blood with essence of damp earth, fresh green foliage, star-blossomed jasmine. Dawn chorus of city birds twitters all around me. So much life, busy feeding and greeting. And I hear, for the first time in weeks, the aching melody of the butcher bird's call. Bill. Wetness in my eyes. This time, no sobbing, but uneven breath, juddering me out of my reverie.

The idea of painting is with me again. I can almost smell the oils, and the turps. Vivid colours flood my imagination, settling into images of Bill. Sometimes, to my horror, I can't recall the details of his face. But this morning he is here. An image from our wedding forms before me. That one where I'm looking up at him and we're laughing, cutting the cake. Elopement was our plan, but the girls insisted on a small group in Aunty Fran's garden. I see the delight in Bill's eyes, feel his hand under mine on the cake knife, the weight of his arm pressing down. Other images tumble over this one. Bill on the bike, in the shower, laying pavers, dressed for work, reading the paper.

I'm startled by the rustling of Tashie in dry bark in the corner of our yard, shocked to feel a smile on my face.

I will paint him. Set up a shrine in the shed. Why has it taken me so long to think of this?

Dawn has vanished, overtaken by the day. I hear cars passing in the street, voices calling goodbye and hello. There is a lightness in my breathing as I stand up to go inside, Tashie padding ahead, wanting breakfast. Today is different.

Dressed in old jeans and one of Bill's faded shirts, I'm busy collecting albums, photo files, printed images from the computer. There's a purpose to my work that I haven't felt in many months.

Out in the shed, dust cakes thick on bottles and boxes, lumps of wood. This was Bill's domain, although he always enjoyed me being here with him. Neat rows of wall racks display jars with rusty lids, screwed onto beams of timber. The jar screws off the lid. This seems so clever and whimsical today. Suspended from the wall, these old jam jars catalogue nails in graded sizes, screws with

Phillips heads and straights, tacks, grommets, rawl plugs red and grey. Tools hang on stencilled outlines on the wall.

I've brought a heavy carton out with me, with all my painting gear. I am equally organised, in my own peculiar way. I shuffle the carton onto the cabinet in the corner. Set about cleaning up and claiming space. Bill was tidy, but time and neglect have covered everything in dust. It's hard to know where to start. I step outside, keen to feel a breeze and the warmth of the sun. And there's the bird. In the wattle tree, high up on a branch, warbling its throat out.

8

When the phone rings, I have to extricate myself from balls of wool and tumbles of knotted yarn. Painting Bill has opened other windows in my imagination, spilling out a burst of weaving and knotting and collage. Vivid purples and magentas intertwine with lime greens and sapphire, gemstone brilliance draped around the room. I have converted our study into a magical cave and am obsessed with creation.

The phone is down the hallway in the kitchen and I run, stumbling on the rug, to catch it before the final ring.

'Angelica? Angelica Jameson?'

Gruff male voice, not someone I know.

'Who's this?'

'Don't recognise your own brother-in-law, eh? Been a while, I guess.'

Shit! A chill shivers down my spine.

'Neil? Neil! Oh. Hello. Where are you? We've been trying to find you.'

'Yeah, well … time flies when you're having fun. Bill home?

Thought I might drop round for a beer, if yer can put up with me for an hour or so.'

Even his voice sounds alien; nothing like Bill's. He could be anyone. I don't want him here. But can't bring myself to break the news over the phone.

'Umm ... how about we meet at the pub later this afternoon? Six, say? You know, the Golden Lion, on the corner up from our place?'

'Like that is it? Alright then, I'll see yers there at six. Seeya.'

And he's gone.

My hand grips the back of a chair. Neil. Bill's stories of boyhood spats and punch-ups come back to me as I slide onto the old pine chair. But Bill never explained the reason behind their final falling out. Neil was always different, he said. Moody, like their mother.

At least he's fucking alive, I think. Tendrils of bitterness wind through my thoughts. Wrong brother gone too soon.

I call Essie to see whether she and Liz can join us at the pub. It would be good just to hear her voice right now.

'Lawson Valley Public School. Can I help you?'

Thank god I've caught her just before the end of lunch.

'Hello, sweetheart!' she says. 'What're you up to? Is it hot down there? I've got the fans on and we've all got wet flannels on the back of our necks. Bloody hot for this time of year.'

'It's Neil, Ess. Neil's turned up. I picked up the phone, thinking it would be you, and it was him.'

'Holy shit! Where is he? What does he want? Are you okay?'

Suddenly, I know I'm not.

'I'm pretty shaken up ...'

'But he hasn't come to the house? Oh god – and he doesn't know about Bill?'

'That's it, Ess. I couldn't bear to tell him over the phone and he's a stranger – I don't want him coming here. I've organised to meet him at the pub.'

'Not on your own, Angel. No way. We have no idea what kind of man he is.'

'I told him six o'clock this afternoon, and I'm hoping you and Liz can make it. Do you think Liz could finish up early?'

'Sweetheart, we'll be there. In fact, why don't we come to your place and we can all walk up to the pub together?'

'I love you, Essie! What would I do without you?'

'Love you too, Angel girl. Gotta run. It's lesson time. See you a bit before five.'

It must be after one o'clock already. There's nothing in the house I feel like eating. I change my paint-spattered jeans for a lopsided skirt and my singlet for a floppy top, grab my purse and the hessian bag. Hunger and the need to get moving outweigh my uneasiness. Tashie knows the signs. Beats me to the front door, grinning and yelping, leaping at her lead that hangs on the hall-stand. She just about wriggles out of her skin getting through the front gate and her wet black nose quivers as she greets every passer-by like a long-lost friend.

Luca's cafe at the local shops has been there as long as we newcomers can remember. The old folks say Luca's father, another Luca, started it back in the fifties, bringing aromas and tastes of Italy to this white-bread suburb. We reckon it's the best coffee south of the harbour bridge.

Andrea greets me from behind the counter.

'*Ciao bella*, you're late today. Are you eating with your latte? Anything for Tashie? I'll get her some water.'

We settle at our favourite outside spot, Tashie flopping happily near my feet. On my table there are jasmine stars in a small green glass vase. Their perfume wafts and blends with coffee in the air, and the scent of warm morning-baked bread.

Sitting in the post-noon shade, I ponder loneliness. The friends I had from work have faded away. I struggle to remember their names most of the time. Even Bree and Cassie, my closest circle beyond Ess and Liz, have stopped leaving messages. I never returned their calls.

Suddenly, again, I'm sick of myself and of widowhood. Sick of grief and grieving. When Mum and Dad died we were all too young to understand the loss. Grief was softer then. Aunty Fran filled our hearts and lives with such love and playfulness that memories morphed, sadness welled up and faded swiftly. That was the fickle hand of fate as well, most people said. Wrong place at the wrong time. They were catching the train to work. Eighty-three people died, among them our Mum and Dad – Maddie and Bob. Investigations showed the tracks were dangerous, that maintenance had been neglected.

Bill's parents didn't pass easily either. June suffered her private anguish, hanging her life on a tree, leaving Arthur to drown in his sorrow and Bill to run the farm although he was barely eighteen. The second son, an afterthought, not weighty enough to hold his mother on the planet nor able to save his stricken father from despair. We talked about it a lot – mental illness, depression, broken-heartedness. Why Neil seemed to have inherited those genes and Bill walked free. We mulled over sudden and early death, never imagining it would revisit us so soon.

A shadow falls across me. Andrea, weight on one foot, has her order pad and pencil at the ready.

'You're too skinny, *cara*. Let me feed you some of Luca's ravioli pesto. Pumpkin and ricotta. What do you say? Yes?'

Andy's been a force of nature over the past year or so, cajoling me into eating, tempting me with sweet treats every time I order coffee.

'Only if I can have a double shot latte first,' I say, as she bends to ruffle Tashie's fur.

When she slides the creamy mugful in front of me, I reach out, take an automatic sip.

'Not reading today, my Angel?'

'Hmmm … something on my mind, Andy.'

For once she looks perplexed and I see that she's afraid to stir up sadness.

'Well, *cara*, whatever it is, a full belly will help.'

After I've eaten, I spoon the last of my ravioli into Tashie's bowl and she licks at the aromatic pesto until the metal gleams. Andy was right – Luca's cooking is delicious.

'See you tomorrow *cara*?' Andrea says, as she hands me my change. Her little hooks – she's keeping an eye on me.

We walk to the park, Tashie pulling at the lead.

'There you go, girl! Run!'

I slide her Frisbee out of the hessian bag and she dashes back from her mad circuit, props in front of me, pleads with me to slice the hot pink disk into the air again.

It's almost four by the time we wander home, Tashie to flop contentedly under the kitchen table, me to shower and get ready. I'm still getting dressed when I hear Liz's voice.

'Angel? Only us, sweetie. We've let ourselves in.'

When I walk into the kitchen, Essie's lifting a lush bunch of home-grown silverbeet from a flat, wide basket.

'Fridge? Or freezer?' She presents the dark green leaves as though they were roses.

'Oh … thank you! Fridge is fine.'

'I feel like a stiff scotch but maybe we'd better stick to tea for now,' says Liz. 'Want to have my wits about me when we meet up with the prodigal.'

She flips the switch on the kettle and pulls three mugs down from the dresser, reaches for the teabag canister.

'So, Angel … Did he say where he's been? Any idea what he's been up to?'

'Not a thing, Ess. All he said was that he wanted to catch up with Bill … have a beer …'

I can feel my heart hammering, threatening to rise up and choke me.

'Sweetie … sit down.' Liz nudges me onto a chair. 'Here, open your mouth. Rescue Remedy. Deep breaths. That's it.'

Her strong fingers massage my shoulders. When I open my eyes I see Ess sitting opposite, leaning towards me, a frown bothering her lovely eyes.

'We really don't know anything about him,' she says. 'Maybe we should keep an open mind?'

'Yeah. No point talking about it now. Let's see what he's got to say for himself.' Liz sits down beside me and sips her tea.

Ess pushes the heavy old pub door open and we step inside, our eyes taking a while to adjust from the late afternoon brightness. Soft lights gleam on rows of glasses behind the bar where three old-timers are propped, yarning quietly. Nev, the barman, nods hello. There's no one else in the room.

'What'll it be, ladies?'

I'm ready for that stiff scotch now and we order three doubles. Liz wants a beer chaser with hers.

'How've you been, Angelica? Haven't seen you for a while.' Nev won't pry, but I can see compassion in his eyes.

'Getting there thanks Nev. How about you? You're looking pretty fit.'

'Yeah, can't complain. Good to see you girls anyway.'

'Hey Neville,' says Liz, 'anybody out the back?'

'Yeah, actually, there is. Some blow-in. Turned up on his own about an hour ago. Why? You girls looking for a bit of action?'

Regret flits across his face the minute the words are out and he turns away, embarrassed.

Liz raises an eyebrow. Must be Neil? We pick up our drinks and walk down the wooden steps that lead to the beer garden.

In the far corner of the courtyard sits a middle-aged man with a long scruffy beard. Greying hair, thin on top, in need of a cut. He has Bill's eyes. An old blue heeler lies quietly at his feet. A cigarette rests on an ashtray, curling smoke into the evening air, and a half-finished beer sweats beside his left hand on the wooden bench table.

'Angelica?' he says, shunting the chair backwards and rising to his feet. His gaze darts from one to the other of us and settles on me.

'Neil?'

He's not what I expected although I don't know what that was. Not as tall as Bill. Stockier. His old leather jacket comfortable across broad shoulders.

'Pull up a pew, then, all of yers. Yer right fer drinks? Smoke?' He shakes a Marlboro packet in our direction, spilling a couple of cigarettes halfway out. The blue dog stirs but doesn't get up.

'No thanks, I don't smoke,' I say, sitting opposite him. 'Neil, this is my sister, Essie, and her partner, Liz.' I hold my hands together under the table to stop them shaking.

A smart comment dies on his lips and he looks away. Picks up his glass and drains it.

'So ... where's me little brother then? Still slavin' away in the ivory tower?'

We'd rehearsed this bit. I sit quietly and let Essie do the talking.

'Actually, Neil, Angel's been trying for ages to get in touch with you ...'

He looks up. 'Bastard's too fucking lily-livered to front me, is he?'

'Neil. Please. Shut up and listen.' Ess is standing now. It's what she does when she wants to stay strong and contained.

'Bill's dead, Neil. He died in April last year. We've had the police looking for you. Then a private detective. God knows where the hell you've been ...'

If we expected a reaction, it wasn't this. His fists crash onto the wooden bench and a howl of pain rips the air.

'What the fuck! You fucking little ... Waddya mean, he's fucking dead? Jesus, me little bro ... aahhhh ... fucking hell!'

The blue dog's on its feet, nuzzling its master's elbow while the big man drops his head into his hands and sobs.

'Everything alright here, ladies?' It's Neville, speaking quietly into our tableau.

'Thanks, Nev. It's okay.' Liz glances up at him, then turns her attention back to Neil.

The blue dog's whining, pawing at his master's knee. My brother-in-law's dark eyes are red-rimmed and bleary when he lifts his head and fixes his gaze on me.

'You poor bugger. What the fuck happened?'

He pulls a neatly folded handkerchief from an inside pocket and blows his nose, wipes spittle from the corners of his mouth, checks his beard. Refolds the hankie and puts it away.

'He had a motorbike accident,' I say.

He drops his head again, shaking it from side to side. Teardrops darken the wooden tabletop. Whatever he is and wherever he's been, he loved Bill, that much is clear. Suddenly, I want to ask this man about his brother. Reach for connections into the past. But my own grief silences me.

A young barmaid reaches between Liz and Ess and lights a candle in its holder in the centre of the table. Moments later she appears again, puts a double scotch in front of each of us. Fades away.

In the hour or so we sit there, Neil unscrolls his story, telling the public bits, leaving vast gaps unexplained. We don't ask. Whiffs of danger waft from him, hiding among cameos of red-dirt mining towns, bush camps, prawn trawlers, enclaves of men who didn't welcome cops or sheilas or anyone who wasn't one of them.

I hide the details of my life from him as well, mention the idea of moving although I know I'll never leave our home.

He says he's leaving town tomorrow. Scribbles a phone number on a cardboard coaster.

'Yer won't be needing me again most likely, but just in case. This'll find me, in a pinch.' It's a Queensland number. A cattle station, he explains.

He wants to know where Bill is buried, shakes his head at the news of ashes in a jar. Stares aghast when I mention the organ donations.

'We'd written our wills, Neil. We were planning on starting a family. He said his organs would be no good to him if he was dead; that they should go to people who needed them. And he absolutely didn't want to be buried ...'

My memories shift to that sunlit morning. We were laughing, tossing around ideas, doing the responsible thing. It all seemed so abstract.

The last of the light has faded from the sky. More people have settled at tables in the beer garden and the soft sounds of conversation and laughter and clinking ice nudge at our sombre mood. We are oddities in this candlelit courtyard.

There's nothing more that any of us are prepared to share.

Neil struggles to his feet, pushes back the wooden chair. The blue dog stands, looks up at its master expectantly.

'Best be off then, eh? Hope yer'll be alright, Angelica. Looks like yer in good hands anyway.' He nods at Essie and Liz.

I want to stand up and hug him but none of us moves.

'Take care, Neil,' is all I say. Liz and Essie murmur goodbye.

We watch as he ambles up the steps into the pub, notice the faded insignia covering the back of his jacket. I realise I am breathing again. Look slowly from my sister to her soulmate, their faces soft in the candle's glow. Sigh.

'Well. That's that, then,' says Liz.

Over salt and pepper squid and burgers and chips we talk about him. We've switched from whiskey to red wine and I feel the floatiness of alcohol and relief easing my thoughts. He was more or less what we expected, but not, somehow. Was there a resonance of Bill? We heard a throaty roar, a bike starting up, minutes after he left the pub. Probably Neil.

There is so much I don't know. So much he could tell me about Bill and their childhood on the farm. Perhaps I'll call that number. Not now. In a few months maybe.

I tell Ess and Liz about my projects, the slithery silk and rough twine, the vivid colours. My paintings of Bill. They talk about school, kids on horses, new growth on the riverbank, a few days of welcome rain. My eighteen months of reclusive living feels like a fading nightmare now. Gloom and grief still lurk in the corners of my heart, but sadness has overtaken them most days, slipping along with sunshine and moments of joy.

Essie is talking about that woman, Jane, who brought the eggs. I remember her wild grey hair, her energy for everything, her battered four-wheel drive. From what she said last autumn, I imagine she must be well entrenched in a Himalayan orphanage by now, but apparently her plans have been derailed. Ess is going to visit her, wondering if I would care to come along. Jane has some ceramics I might like to see before she packs them off to a gallery where pricey stickers will put them out of my league. Alright then. I'll go. We make arrangements for Thursday of next week. It's a good excuse for a country drive.

* * *

The girls walk me home, hug me goodnight. As they head off on their long drive back to the valley, I think about the images of Bill emerging out in the shed. Parts of him I never considered precious have taken on prominence – his hands, the faint scar at the side of his left eye. Larger than life or death, canvases line the benches, each one different from the next.

Night's weary blanket drapes around me once again and I wander upstairs. The darkness brings its own brand of grief, nights passing infinitely slowly, dredging up hideous desire. I lie in our queen-sized bed wearing a nightgown to sedate the aching in my womb and my vagina and my heart. It doesn't work. Skin aches for the silkiness of skin, of hardening erection, tenderness, passion. My hands wander over my thin body, searching for completion, finding only the roundness of my lonely breasts and the isolation of my clitoris, frenzying to climax. Yet I am sterile as a cold stone in a metal vault. How could death have neutered me? When my body was preparing to grow new life? Even Neil, that gnarled stranger, felt sorry for me. The tears come again, soaking into my pillow, plastering strands of hair to my face.

In the morning, it will be different. My mind tells me that, but my body doesn't understand.

9

On the morning of our visit to Jane's, Tashie has thrown up on the back step. Her nose is dry and hot to touch, her body listless. Panic assails me. The vet's number is on my fridge door. 'Bring her down,' they say. They can see her straight away.

I wrap her limp heavy body in a towel, carry her carefully to the car, lie her on the seat beside me. Lucy is waiting for us, surgery door open, bright lights blazing. But Tashie's head barely lifts, tail hardly twitches.

Gentle professionalism takes her from my arms, lies her on the cold metal table. Watching Lucy work rivets my attention, all my hope and dread suspended in the air.

I can't lose Tashie too.

Silent probing, temperature taken, hands running over coarse soft hair, detailed inspection of paws. Ah. There it is. Tashie flinches, brave, no growling or snapping, responding to Lucy's discovery with gratitude, a febrile lick. There is a shard of glass piercing her front paw pad, buried deep, the dark flesh puffy and tender. Lucy looks across at me and smiles. 'She'll be right as rain in no time.'

'Oh thank god! Thank you, thank you!' Smile glimmering through my tears.

I'll have to leave her for a minor operation. Let her stay overnight so that Lucy can be sure she is responding to the antibiotics, and not licking her bandaged paw. I'm embarrassed at my intense reactions, and Lucy turns away, giving us time. Tashie's in my arms, warm against my chest. I can feel her breath, her steady heartbeat. She will be alright. Her lazy dry tongue licks salt drips from my chin.

I have to go. Before grief cracks me open completely.

When I put my key into the front door lock, the house feels empty. Unbearable. I grab a coat, my boots, the basket. Water, apples, a banana for the road. I want to show Essie a painting I've done of Bill, the only one I'm happy with so far. Dash out to the shed, ignoring Tashie's chewed grubby toy. Wrap an old sheet loosely around the oily canvas. Carry it back to the kitchen to put with the other things.

I shower. Wash away the dread. Dress in sensible country clothes. Pretend I am solid.

I am in the car at last, heading west-north-west, Eagles playing 'It's Your World Now', booming life back into my brittle bones. Missing Tashie. Letting life haul me forward.

Once the suburbs drop away I am driving through bush, the bitumen curving and winding on ahead. I put my window down and let the scent of eucalyptus fill the car. Far out on the western horizon, across rolling green valleys and dark stands of timber, mountains shimmer in a violet haze. My breathing settles. I am on the road again.

On the drive from the ferry I don't see another soul. I am later than planned but it doesn't matter. Jane is packing, preparing finally to depart. Ess is on holidays. As I round a corner, peacocks scream from a paddock to my left, scaring the wits out of me until I spy the blue-green-purple flash of feathers on display.

When I slow down on the bend before the school, something catches my attention on the river. There's a little houseboat tethered to the shore. It wasn't there before. I wonder whether people occupy it regularly. Imagine waking every morning to the rising mist, the tangy fresh scent, the magic of the river.

Essie's waiting on the verandah, dressed in jeans and riding boots and pale pink blouse, brown jacket draped across the chair, a cardboard box propped on the table beside her. I love this woman, mirror image of my soul. If she is beautiful, perhaps I might be too. A possibility I had abandoned.

As I pull up on the flat patch of lawn she closes her front door, collects her things and walks down the steps, smiling. 'Good morning, gorgeous. How's our girl? You must be missing her?'

I tell her about the dread I felt when I thought I might lose Tashie. About the flood of relief when Lucy assured me it was a minor issue that could be easily fixed. If Ess sees that I've been crying, she doesn't mention it and I'm grateful for her sensitivity.

We head off down the gravel driveway in her station wagon.

I've never been out as far as Jane's place, beyond the end of the bitumen. The river sweeps close in against the road, carving steep banks, running deep, with dark shadows swirling around the trunks of long-dead trees. Jane's property is beyond the village where the old families settled more than a century ago, growing vegetables and fruit to feed the colony that clung to alien harbour shores. Back then, the river was a mighty force, lifestream to raw-boned men and women struggling to access this country's abundance of food and shelter.

I hear a butcher bird's melodic fluting and take it as a welcome.

* * *

Late morning light sits golden on sandstone ridges, heat shimmering already, with summer yet to burn its way into the year. It is late September, and there has been little rain since May. Essie tells me that conversations at the pub are focused on the topic of water, the price of filling a 20,000 litre tank. Riverflat paddocks ploughed for watermelon seeds lie fallow, awaiting the rain. It hasn't been this dry since 1967. Trayback utes and battered old farm trucks grumble along the road most days, loaded with bales of hay – feed for cows and horses. It's not good, this early in the season. The bushfire brigade runs exercises more serious than social, preparing for the worst, clearing trails, checking access, doing back-burns, testing hose connections.

Ess points to a track coming up on our right, winding in past a mailbox made of aged timber and clay, a rustic masterpiece standing by the propped-open gate. 'Jane's place is just in here,' she says.

A kookaburra on a eucalyptus branch checks our arrival. Flies buzz on a soft furry mess by the shoulder of the road. A lone crow mourns in the distance. Everything else is still, hazy. Waiting.

Essie has been filling me in on Jane's plans, explaining how the funding for her Nepalese project struck a hitch, required all Jane's business and diplomatic experience to set it right. How she despaired, for a while, of ever making it back there. How passionate she is for this project, for the children whose lives can be tenuous as breath.

Spreading paperbarks arch above us along the pale gravel track, guiding our way. The ridge rises high up to the west, its sandstone rocks smudged dirty yellow among dull green foliage, tall gums etching wavy lines against the sky. We are entering another world where time meanders and humans are incidental, where nature holds the future in her gentle, firm embrace.

The house, when I see it, could have grown there too, emerging from the earth, edges blurred against a curving backdrop of dusty green. Cosy. That's how Jane described it, and I can see why. Curving mudbrick walls entertain small odd-shaped windows on the southern end while around the corner to the right, vivid soft green leaves entwine and tumble across a slatted pergola, shading worn pavers and slumped old rattan chairs. The living dull green roof creeps like unkempt eyebrows over wide eaves. I imagine goblins dwell here but see Jane, tea towel in hand, wiping dirty smudges from her face as she comes around the side of the cottage, waving a welcome.

'I've been mulching the garden beds before I go,' she says, dropping the tea towel over the back of a chair and reaching out her hand. 'Welcome to Walden, Angelica.'

I hear history in the name. And slip further into a pool of other worlds, protected realms, private space. Essie hauls her cardboard box off the back seat, slides it onto the massive table under the pergola. Offerings for Nepal. Jane's organisation sends container-loads of goods much needed for the school and clinic over there.

'Would you like a guided tour?' Jane says, slipping her boots off and leading us indoors. 'My husband Richard and I built this cottage ourselves, years ago. We made every brick with soil from this land. We used to joke that our home was made of equal parts sweat and love, spiced up with a few choice words.'

To our left is a wall that curves away like the line flowing through the middle of a yin-yang symbol, but interrupted towards the rear by a doorway, curtain-draped. 'That's my bedroom,' Jane says. 'Coolest part of the house in summer. Warm in winter too.'

The living room opens out to the north, flowing through lovely old French doors onto the patio beneath the vine-clad pergola. An exquisite woven rug feels silky on the soles of my feet and pale greenish light filters onto a fat armchair that faces its matching sofa like an old friend. Central to everything, as though its chimney might hold up the roof, a curved brick fireplace squats close to the floor, black fire tools propped neatly beside it. It has been swept clean, although its floor is smudged sooty and grey from years of use.

'Both of us loved light and fire,' Jane explains. 'Richard needed fire at the heart of everything. He was an Aries, you know.'

In a few steps we have moved behind the fireplace into the kitchen, where a cream enamelled wood stove backs up to the fire's brick chimney. Even though the day is warm, I feel heat emanating through the stove's heavy door and a kettle simmers on the hob. The aroma that's been teasing me since we got out of the car is very strong. Jane is baking a cake, I realise, in the midst of packing to leave.

'The bathroom's through that door there,' she says, pointing to our left. 'And that's it. Walden. Everything I need. Of course, my studio's an absolutely necessary adjunct. I spend half my life over there when the spirit takes me. And out in the pergola in autumn and spring.'

She reaches down to the levered handle on the stove, easing it up, opening the solid door, releasing essence of orange into the air. 'I'm not likely to be eating orange and poppyseed cake again for quite a while. It's a little treat, for all of us. And a welcome for you, Angelica.'

I'm touched by her warm generosity, the orderly rhythm of her life at a time when most people would be frazzled and edgy.

'We'll eat outside. Can't stay indoors on a day like this.' She has slipped the cake tin onto a wire rack and covered it with a clean soft cloth. 'This can sweat for a while before I make the tea. Or would you prefer coffee, my dears?'

Though I've missed my morning coffee, it seems like a tea party and we make plans for a pot of Lady Grey. Delicate cups and saucers stack on a tray on top of three unmatched plates. There is milk in a blue and white jug. We walk single file towards the pergola carrying the makings of our feast. Jane insists Ess and I take the rattan chairs while she settles herself on a hewn wooden bench on the far side of the table, looking back inside her house.

Essie's been here before, many times. They are old friends, she and Jane, although she's never really told me the story. All I know is that Jane has lived here for years, off and on, and that leaving will not be easy for her. The depth of her commitment to those children must be immense, I realise now, feeling this world within worlds wrapped around us. It strikes me that the city might never have existed. That all other possibilities are illusion and only this is real.

Jane tips the aromatic cake deftly from its tin onto the cloth, flips it back onto a wire rack, lets it sit. Steam drifts from beneath the rack as the cake cools. When it's ready, Jane will make the tea, she says. This feels like ceremony. A quiet convention of women, the natural order of things.

Essie asks how everything is going, wants to know that Jane's plans are running well. Does she need help with anything? I am a friendly observer as they check through lists, confirm dates, talk about the weather.

'I think the cake should be right now,' says Jane. 'Could you cut it for us, please, Estrellita? I'll bring the teapot out.'

My eyes light on Essie's and we smile, relishing this fairy tea party in the bush. I wonder what happened to Richard, but don't want to ask.

Jane's teapot is a riot of hand-painted roses, deep maroon on fine china. Now that she's back, the ceremony can begin. We make a toast to her future, to service and adventure, possible achievements, the unknown. She will be gone for at least two years, she tells us, has confirmed that with the Nepalese authorities. I envy the passion that will pull her away from such comfort into that hard-working foreign region.

Ess wants to know what will happen to Walden while Jane's

gone. What will happen to this living, breathing house if it sits empty.

For a while, Jane is silent.

When she leans towards me, there is such sadness in her eyes. We are meeting on a plateau of grief. I understand now that Richard can never come back, that this house is much more than a home. Memories dwell here for Jane, melded into the sod roof and every mud brick.

'Would you stay here, my dear?' she asks.

I can't breathe. I too have a precious home, the house that Bill and Angel bought. A place full of love and joy and pain and grief. The refuge I cannot bear to leave.

In the soft brown of her gaze my perspective shifts. I can't recollect my reasons for hanging on, for staying at home forever. Oh yes. It comes to me. I can't leave Bill. Hot tears ooze from the corners of my eyes, blurring my vision and breaking the spell. Confusion bursts like a searing bubble in my chest. The green world spins. I feel faint.

When I open my eyes Essie's face is close to mine, her hands rubbing my fingers, voice calling my name. 'It's alright, Angel. We're here with you. Rest now. Jane's fetching a cold cloth and some water. Rest, sweetheart, it's alright.'

I'm lying on an old daybed under the pergola. The whole world is pale backlit green, redolent with the scent of gum leaves and orange and bergamot, the river and the earth. Everything is vivid, gently bright, wondrous. Essie's long brown hair drifts like a halo around her lovely face, her blue eyes are pierced with concern. And something else. That looks like hope.

'That was such a shock, Angel. Are you up to talking? Or would you like to rest?'

My mind is in a dream where Bill's voice resonates, bumping

against my thoughts and feelings. I feel as though I've gone mad, sought treatment and emerged sane.

Jane is kneeling beside me, cool damp flannel folded on a tray alongside a glass of water. 'Let me put this on your forehead, my dear. I'm terribly sorry. It was never my intention to cause you distress.'

I sigh. And smile. 'Perhaps you've just saved my life,' I murmur. 'There's nowhere else on this planet I would rather be.'

I feel the ripples of astonishment from Essie. Soft-wired to my heart, yet she had no idea I had made up my mind. Neither did I. Jane seems at a loss. Nobody says a word. The idea has shaken us all and we need time to settle, to let this outrageous suggestion take form.

I realise I need to pee, urgently. Ask Essie to take my hand and lead me to the toilet, not trusting these rebirthed legs to be steady or strong. Jane's bathroom is a well of contentment with its deep claw-footed bath set to gaze out on the hill where tall gums reach for the sky. Streams of distress empty into the toilet bowl, flowing from my body like remnants of a previous life.

When I emerge into the kitchen Essie and Jane are standing by the stove. They have brought in all our plates and cups, the leftover cake. Jane bends and opens a small door at the bottom of the stove, pulls a chunk of split log from the niche in the bricked wall, drops it onto glowing ashes, watches as the fire licks again.

'Even though I have gas, I like to keep the stove going once it's been lit for the day. Until we're in the worst heat of summer. More efficient.'

Everything about her is efficient, I think, smiling at them. There are arrangements to make, discussions to have, instructions and lists. A deep introduction to the mysteries of living remote from the rush. But I am running on empty and we all know this is not a good time for those things. Jane still has much to do, in any case. Another date is set. And then we're leaving. Warm embrace, Jane's hand resting long moments in the centre of my back, soothing and strong.

'This is a generous place, Angelica. It will hold you as it has held me – you've made a wise decision. I'm very grateful to you, my dear. And so is Walden.'

10

What have I done?

Aunty Fran will be all in favour – she'll probably want to come and stay once she's seen how beautiful Walden is.

But what will Sage think? If I tell her, I'll no doubt get a lecture about how isolated the place is, that it's dangerous for me to live on my own all the way out here in some tumbledown shack in the middle of nowhere. That's that, then – I won't be telling her anytime soon.

Suddenly, there is so much to be organised. What will I do with our house, with all our belongings? And I can't begin to envisage strangers living in our home. Reality punches hard, gutting me as I move cushions, straighten magazines, put a book back on the shelves.

My baby self is crawling across the floor, hauling her body onto the sofa, dry sobbing, gulping short, panicked breaths. Don't pass out. No one will hear me fall. I breathe, and count, short painful breaths. Do it again. Breathe in. Count. Breathe out. Count.

Steady. Back to one. Exhaustion overwhelms me. This is too hard. Too much. Too soon.

I must have slept. Or perhaps I did faint. Tashie is licking my feet, concern creasing the soft fur between her eyes. When I push myself upwards and sit, the room wavers. Straight edges take a while to steady into line. I breathe in, deeply. The panic has evaporated, and I feel stirrings of confidence and hope.

Now Tashie needs me to play. She's picked up her rag doll from the corner of the room and is bumping it against my knee. Throw the doll. Throw the doll. Rump quivering, tail wagging despite her bandaged paw, she makes me laugh.

Lists are good. On the kitchen table I have laid out the notepad and pens, different colours for separate tasks. This place. Jane. Agents, removalists, cleaners. I'm unsure where my burst of energy has come from but I'm ready to use it. I still don't feel happy about renting out our home but I can't leave it empty. And selling is not an option.

I phone Jane. Check what she wants me to bring when I visit next week. Her voice steadies me, gives instructions, asks small favours, makes this circus real.

'Obviously, Essie and Liz will help you with the packing and moving,' she says. 'But there must be others, Angelica?'

'Not really,' I reply. 'I've lost touch with everyone I used to know.'

But once we've hung up, it occurs to me: Steve, Sean, Don. For months after Bill died, each of them offered to be here for me. But I pushed them away. And now it feels awkward, almost as though they, too, have become ghosts. I add their names to the list – I'll think about it later. There is a support network that I had forgotten about.

In the shed I have no idea where to begin. All Bill's treasures have to travel with me, surely? But I can't pack properly until I know what space there is at Jane's. She mentioned a studio. That's a plus.

The days flit erratically, disappearing into uneasy nights. I spend time in our garden pulling weeds, trimming edges, spreading mulch. Avoiding the list. I take hours one day weeding the cracks between the old brick pavers, down on my hands and knees on a calico sack, immersed in minutiae.

When the day arrives for my trip to the valley, I wake as excited as a Christmas child. I am taking Tashie with me this time. Boxes of basics like batteries, flour, rice and wine. Foundations of a fresh start. My basket bearing cheese and pate and good bread for our lunch.

I stop at the servo to top up the fuel, check tyres, oil level, coolant. Practical things I will have to be good at when I'm living out there. None of this seems real but driving the long, winding road keys me in. Within a matter of weeks, this drive will be the journey home.

When we stop at the ferry, Tashie is grinning, knowing this place, the adventures that wait on the other side. This time the river is a surly, greasy grey. Heavy clouds are roiling in from the west, promising rain. At last. A good omen? We're not at the front of the ferry today, but tucked in beside the driver's cabin with a Telstra van blocking our view. There is a strong smell of mud. The tide is out.

When we drive past the school, there are children playing and screaming on the grassy slope that runs down to the road. Recess. Essie will be inside, making magic for the class before lunch. I toot the horn. A few of the children wave, not recognising the car but ready to make friends anyway. Country kids, with only a whiff of city to link them to this busy century.

Tashie is frantic, dashing back and forth on the rear seat,

yipping to tell me I've gone the wrong way. 'It's okay, little one, we're going to visit our new home.'

The road turns to dirt about a kilometre before the village. They've been hustling the council for years to continue the bitumen at least that far. To rescue this small community from the grains of fine, pale dust that seep into clothes and cupboards, hair and creases of skin. To make the way passable when the rain comes, slushing gravelly mud under vehicles and churning out potholes big enough to drown a rabbit in.

Driving through the village I wave to a woman outside the general store, slowing down as we crunch by, not raising too much dust. I have a strong sense that she knows who I am and why I might be here. No secrets in the valley. I feel exposed, outed in a way I have never enjoyed. Bill and I were a self-sufficient unit. Alone, I am a solitary wanderer with hermit leanings. I wonder how I will live with gatekeepers as alert and present as the woman at the store.

As I make the right turn into Jane's entry lane I notice she does have a sign, 'Walden,' painted in fading colours on a piece of wood wired to the gate. I must have missed it last time, taking in everything else. There are numbers on the gatepost too: 2536.

Ess has told me that Richard and Jane arrived in the valley many years ago from England, seeking refuge. From what, no one seems to remember, if they ever knew.

They built the cottage with their own hands and straining backs, calling in tradesmen occasionally for wiring and plumbing – the few things they couldn't do themselves. It took them several seasons, the story goes, during which the people in the valley observed the sporadic arrival of trucks delivering loads of clay, straw bales, old timber doors and tiny wood-framed windows, plates of glass, rolls of turf, solar panels, the stove. Few locals were invited to the cottage that grew up out of the earth. But most people liked this couple who would drop by the store once in a while for basics like milk and tea and butter.

Ess told me Richard and Jane lived like that at Walden for a decade or more, Jane producing earthenware bowls and coffee mugs that she would take into the village from time to time to sell in the gallery. Richard's lean form rarely propped up the bar at Ted's pub, but he made a name for himself as a carpenter with fine skills and a good eye. Honest, too.

Then Richard died. A heart attack, or a stroke. Jane never talks about the details, even to friends. What Essie knows is that this dignified old woman has lived on her own ever since, travelling overseas from time to time, building another life among children who live close to the sky. Coming home to her riverside retreat. Elusive. Strong. Contained. A loyal but distant friend.

I am driving along the tree-lined laneway now, shifting states already, feeling my body relax. Tashie has gone quiet, sitting at attention on the seat beside me, ears pricked, nose twitching.

Jane is in the garden, near the sheds. I realise there is so much here that I didn't see before. She hears the car and straightens, picks up a basket full of leafy greens, walks towards us.

'Angelica, my dear. You've made it. I did wonder whether you might change your mind. Walden isn't for everyone, you know.'

She is prescient. Has picked up on my doubts and trepidation. We have met only twice yet I am walking into her world, at her invitation, seeking asylum by a river in a haven of glowing green, this place where time seems to dissolve.

I have brought Tashie's lead and a long rope so that we can tie her up to the pergola. Her nose has gone into overdrive and she has little time for civilities with Jane. Every hair on her body is taking in fresh sensations, her nose filtering unfamiliar smells. Jane brings a bowl full of water, sets it down, speaks kindly to my little brown dog. Then turns to me.

'I think coffee might be in order this morning, Angelica. Does that suit you? We're going to need all our energy to work our way through my list.' I nod gratefully, and we take my few things from the car into the cool of the cottage, store pate and cheese in the fridge.

'That's the first thing you need to know about,' comments Jane. 'Gas fridge. Our solar system won't support electric – they suck energy at an enormous rate. When we go outside later, I'll show you where the gas tanks are.'

I've never heard of gas fridges. My trepidation spikes. Am I up to this? I notice that the bricked niche beside the stove is filled with neatly split small chunks of timber. Kindling and folded newspaper in a huge shallow basket to the side. Further arcane mysteries.

The pergola has burst into cascades of violet-blue dripping through pale green. The fragrance that greeted me at the car is almost too much to bear as we carry our coffees outside, arranging our small feast on the massive slab table.

Jane has a spiral-bound notebook, grubby pages flipped over to reveal her list. 'Angelica – essential' she has noted at the top of the page, underlined. Her writing is graceful, looped large, flowing strong. I focus on drinking my coffee. Pull out my own notebook and pen and put them on the table. I'll need to pay attention, which isn't easy in this serene place where distant water murmurs over sand and tiny insects zing. Tashie pants, flat out on her belly on the pavers.

Momentarily, my focus drifts. I see two women drinking coffee in the shade of a wisteria-covered pergola at the back of a mudbrick cottage deep in the bush. One is older, with wild grey hair and a wiry body, tanned to leather. The other is young, damaged. Beautiful but sad. Her wavy auburn hair falls well below her shoulders, her blue eyes glisten.

When I look up, Jane is sipping her coffee, pen in hand, ready to go through the list. We talk about firewood, mail delivery, garbage, battery room, generator, diesel tank, water tanks, and the water pump down by the river. How to tend the living roof. What to do when the phone line fails. Important names and numbers. One by one, items solidify, sketching in the details of the life I am about to live.

'There's a real-life guardian angel, of course,' Jane smiles. 'You might think you're out here on your own. But help is never far away.'

She tells me about Clyde, the man with horses who grows watermelons on the river flat. Ess and Liz's friend. Clyde lives a little further out, around that tricky bend, up on the hill. His number is by the phone. Or if I raise the rainbow flag on that makeshift flagpole over there, he'll see it and he'll turn up.

'I'll introduce you before I leave,' Jane tells me. 'He's the kind of man you feel safe with. Great at fixing things, and knows the valley like the back of his hand. He'll fill you in about the other locals too.'

Jane wants to take me on a tour of the land, show me her studio and the sheds. The battery room beside her laundry. A track that leads down to the river. Tiny wooden shed where the water pump hides. I realise quickly that my city joggers are not going to survive in this terrain, that sturdy boots should be high on one of my lists.

She explains how she and Richard decided on an earthen floor when they were building the house. Made the mud floor tiles in a different set of moulds, flatter, squarer than the bricks they created for the walls. Explains the special care required for this ancient kind of flooring.

She is leaving in mid-December, another few weeks. Our time for making plans is running out. We need to be all practicalities now, down to business. We have mentioned the idea of a lease, some formal arrangement. Her solicitor has drawn up a document that I will take home and read.

Over lunch, we talk about the work she does in Nepal. Our

conversation roams through themes of being useful, helping others, finding a purpose in life that is beyond personal gratification. Jane seems to vibrate with an energy not her own, animated like a girl in the early throes of a passionate affair.

She wants to know who will be living in my house when I'm out here. 'I don't know, Jane. Don't know how to start looking for someone who will cherish our home ...'

'Have you considered offering it to students? Your house is convenient to the university, isn't it?'

The thought makes me shudder. Parties, spilt drinks, burns in the carpet, loud music to irritate the neighbours.

'I'd rather have a quiet spinster, I think.' She laughs. 'I know I should put it in the hands of an agent, but it would have to be someone I can trust completely. I'll ask around.'

We brush crusty crumbs onto the grass. Gather up plates, the butter dish, our mugs. Long shadows stretch towards the sheds. Daylight drops away early here, the moment the sun slides behind the tree-lined ridge. Another novelty, this visible turning of the earth.

I want to be home before dark and Jane has many jobs to attend to. She tells me the house is like a child, always in need of care and loving attention. I wonder again what I have taken on.

11

Tashie is quiet on the drive back to the ferry, curled up on the floor behind my seat, not stirring even when we fly past Essie's place. My mind is a whirling dervish of lists, jobs to be done, arrangements, fluttering excitements. Next time we come to the valley, we will be staying. Jane will do a formal handover, reveal the last of the arcane secrets of living at Walden.

The street lights are blinking on as we turn into our street. Ever since Bill died it's been a nightmare coming home after dark. Putting the key in the lock of a door that opens into loneliness and rooms full of tears. I leave the hallway light on all the time to create illusory safe passage. Just as well, today. I can make it through to the kitchen without running. Pretend I am a normal woman returning home from a day in the country with friends.

The roses I picked last night have released their deep swoony perfume. Colourful lists on notepads lie exactly where they were when we left this morning. No one has been in. We are safe. I wonder whether I will ever get used to living alone.

I let Tashie out into the garden where moonlight and floodlight sketch familiar shapes and shadows against the fence, into the corners by Bill's shed. Our shed. I am exhausted. I call Tashie to come back inside, feed her, check her water bowl, make sure the blankets on her bed are a comfy nest. Make toast for me, spread on the butter and Vegemite.

In the morning, I avoid my lists by going for a walk. Tashie leaps and dashes on the lead, thrilled to be heading up to Luca's, eager for friendly pats and a possible treat. I will miss all this. I will miss Andrea, the coffee, sitting in pooled sunlight at a tiny table on an inner city footpath.

'Hey, stranger, haven't seen you for a week or more.' Andrea grins, heading for the espresso machine, latte glass in hand. 'What have you been up to?'

I tell her about the move, surprising us both with a burst of excitement as I do my best to describe Jane and Walden and a world of strange beauty by a slow-flowing river, no more than a couple of hours away. She's never heard of the place. Not many people have. But she thinks it sounds like an amazing adventure.

'Oh, Angel! That means your house is going to be empty? I suppose you've already organised tenants?'

'The truth is, Andy, I have no idea what I'm going to do about the house. My heart is halfway to the valley but I can't seem to wrench the rest of me away.' My body sighs, sagging back into the chair. 'There's so much of Bill and me etched into the walls, I can't imagine anybody else living there.'

She stops, looks at me, one hand on her hip, dishcloth in the other, ready to wipe tables. 'Is that so?' There's a gleam in her eye. 'You know, my cousin and his wife have just arrived from Italy. They have a tiny baby, Lucia. At the moment they're staying here with us, but they're looking for a place where they can settle. What do you think?'

Something somersaults in my chest. I can't breathe. This is real.

'Tell me more about them,' I hedge.

'Well, Angelo is pretty much like his name. Such a lovely man. And Sabina is the cousin-in-law from heaven. We feel blessed having them with us, even for a while.'

They sound too good to be true. My anxiety is melting away, yet I am wary. 'When can I meet them?' I ask, hoping she will say tomorrow, next year, never.

'Give me your number and I'll ask them to call you when they get back,' Andrea offers. 'They're in the city sorting out the details of Angelo's new job. Some high-flying corporate position.'

I have brought Jane's lease documents with me to read in the sun. But it's too hot, almost summer. We move to a table in the shade. Settling down to peruse pages of legalese, I come to the sections in plain English that spell out the arrangement Jane would like to make. I'm confused. We haven't discussed terms and conditions, but there are several here, in the large print. Waiving of rent in lieu of payment for all running costs including diesel, gas, pump and battery maintenance – there's a list. Open-ended tenure for a period no less than six months, continuing indefinitely. Then this: 'In the event of my death, ownership of the property known as Walden is to pass unencumbered and in full to my tenant, Angelica Jameson ...'

But I barely know the woman. The page blurs and my hands fly to cover my face as I lean back in the chair. What does she mean, 'pass unencumbered'? Images of Walden flash up on my inner screen – the sweet curve of the western wall, wisteria dripping from the pergola, a worn track leading down to the river. I weep. Again. Today, this is more than I can handle. Too much generosity, too much kindness.

Andrea sees me sobbing and silently slides a box of tissues onto the table. Rests her cool hand on my shoulder. 'Do you want to talk about it?' she asks, softly.

I nod. 'Have you got time to sit for a minute?'

'Of course, *bella*, of course I have time for you. What is it? Something to do with Bill?'

She sits, hands folded around mine, deep brown eyes filled with concern and curiosity. She is as bewildered as I am when I tell her of Jane's extraordinary gifting to me. 'I've only met her a few times,' I sigh. 'Why me? Why would she entrust me with the home she built and loves? Only if she should die, of course, but still ...'

We sit for a while tossing around possible reasons, trying to explain the inexplicable. I will have to call her. Get to the bottom of this.

Andrea assures me she will pass my number on to Angelo the minute he returns. Waves away my money when I go to the counter to pay. 'You're like family now,' she smiles, anticipating a done deal. 'It feels perfect for everyone, Angel. Maybe it's just meant to be.' She hands me a small package. 'For Tashie, when you get home.' No doubt it's pastrami. I smile.

When I phone Jane she has just come in from the garden and seems to have been waiting for my call. Listens patiently as I try to stay calm and polite.

'You know, Angelica,' her voice is coming from very far away, 'you know, my dear, that we cannot hold onto anything forever. In fact, you know this much better than most people of your age.'

I have slipped into a kind of hypnotic state, sitting on the edge of my chair, leaning on the kitchen table.

Jane is still speaking. 'When Richard and I built Walden, it was our intention to live closely with the natural world, to deepen our relationships with forces unseen. We wanted to learn more about ourselves and many other things, and we did. Do you understand?'

I feel transfused with glimpses of illumination, have a sense of her reasoning and her determination, her generosity. Yet struggle with acceptance.

'Surely there must be someone closer to you?'

Jane explains that she and Richard were unable to have children. That when she met me, she had a feeling ...

We talk it round and round until I agree to consider signing. After all, she could live for a hundred years. It is probably hypothetical. We laugh, leave it on a lighter note. Turn to discussions of hay bales for large-scale mulching, a new filter for the water tank, the rising price of diesel. I will see her again next week and we will settle the paperwork then.

Tashie is out in the garden, sniffing hard at something in the corner, digging furiously. I see she has found a long-forgotten bone. She is easy to please.

As I turn to walk inside, I am arrested by the melody again. That butcher bird is sitting in our tree. Immediately I spot it, throat pulsing, small body quivering with serious intent. As though it has a message that it must get through to me. Repeating its perfect tune.

This time I walk towards it, softly, in bare feet, my eyes fixed on its location, ears full of its pure, sweet song. 'What is it?' I murmur. 'What do you want me to know?' The melody pipes on and on, imparting only joy.

Perhaps that is enough? The lesson for today? Joy and gratitude swarm with confusion in my overwhelmed mind.

1 2

When the move comes, it is harder and easier than I expected. I have spent the past weeks sorting and storing, setting to one side those treasures that are part of my everyday life, the ones that will travel with me. Sturdy cardboard cartons lean flat-packed against walls, waiting to be folded and taped into shape.

Angelo and Sabina have been to visit several times. They are delightful, just as Andrea described. Vivid holograms of the family Bill and I might have become. Loving each other and life, their baby Lucia, and our house. No doubt there is more to their family dynamic than they are showing me, but they seem to be my best option. My only option right now. The second visit, they bring a tape measure, make notes. Later, we drink coffee in the garden and eat the pastries Andy sent.

I have decided to take only the things my heart cannot bear to leave behind – Bill's tools, my paints and canvases, photos, our books and CDs. A few other precious things. Tashie's bowls, her bed, blankets and toys. Everything else will stay. It suits us all. Jane had no intention of emptying out her house, anticipating my fresh beginnings nestled within the framework of her daily life. Angelo's company is paying for their relocation, will pay the rent. We agree on market value, and the lease is signed. Six months, with an option to extend. They are in Australia for a three-year stint, but I want to keep my options open.

On moving day, a couple of weeks before Christmas, I wake to the sound of raindrops pit-patting my bedroom window. It hasn't rained for forty-three days. Now this. My ancient bones languish in the bed where Bill and I last made love. Where his fingers and lips and silken skin adored me. Why did I think I could leave? What madness was that?

An agony of memories lulls me in and out of waking, leadening my body under the covers. Perhaps I will stay in our bed forever, weeping.

When next I open my eyes there are slants of watery sunlight across the summer doona. A quantum light-shift. Now I will get up. I feel Bill's presence in the room, sitting on the edge of the bed. The scent of his warm body mingled with bike leathers drifts around me. Perhaps he will be with me wherever I go. I hope this is true. His ashes are carefully packed.

Steve has borrowed a truck and he and Sean are due to arrive at 8.30 am. Don is on standby in case we need him, but the guys say they'll be fine. It's a day for old jeans and t-shirt, my new bush boots. It's a day to tie my hair up and wear a cap. By the time they arrive I have everything ready – boxes stacked in the lounge room, Tashie fed. In the past few days I have cleaned and scrubbed and vacuumed, polished windows, had someone come and clean out the gutters. Now the bed has been stripped and my bedding is in a bag in the boot of my car.

Angelo and Sabina have a set of keys, my numbers (although the mobile won't work in the valley), an introduction to their new neighbour. They will move in on the weekend, when Angelo has time.

While Bill's mates haul the packaged remnants of my life to the truck, I walk outside. Stand in our shed where fluorescent light shines cold and brazen upon stencilled outlines on the wall, the naked work benches, an old wooden stool. The spotless floor rejects me, the space echoes emptiness.

Dizzy with shock, I stagger into the yard. Sit on our bench. Which will come with me. I sit on it one more time in the garden Bill and I dug and planted. Sit with my feet on the bricks he laid. I am slipping through time warps of grief and recollected joy.

Ess wanted to take the day off work, to come and help me. I told her I would be fine. But I'm not. Now I want to call her, beg her to rush to my side. But it's too late. I am making this departure on my own, accompanied by Bill's sturdy friends and a cute brown dog.

It feels as though Bill is here too, proud of me, urging me on. I must be making this up, yet I imagine my cells vibrating to the rhythm of his soul. But am jolted back to solidity by the clang of metal doors closing at the rear of the truck.

And the horrible realisation that the men have forgotten our garden bench.

They carry it out to the truck while I boil the kettle, make ritual with coffee grounds and warmed milk. Two sugars in each of their mugs, none in mine.

It is already warm in the kitchen and the dawn rain has moved on, leaving a steamy day. I have closed the bathroom door on Tashie who is beside herself with disruption and excitement. I'm afraid she might run into the street with the men.

We sit one last time in my yellow kitchen, drinking aromatic coffee, eating shortbread biscuits, discussing the plan. They will follow me out of the city all the way to the river. We have timed the journey to arrive there at high tide, so the truck can drive easily onto the ferry ramp.

I ask the men to wait outside while I say goodbye to my home, to lifetimes of faded memories and tears. I have already put Bill's ashes and the hessian bag full of documents on the front seat of my car, with a water bottle, an apple, some treats for Tashie. My bag swings from my shoulder, car keys are clutched in my hand.

I walk upstairs and touch every wall, check every window lock, brush vagrant memories into the chambers of my heart. Our bed is bathed in light, naked, stripped bare. No longer wanting me near it. I turn away. Walk back down the stairs.

Tashie is on her lead, eager to be on our way. I have closed every cupboard. Every power point is switched off. There is nothing left to do. Tears are coursing down my cheeks. One last time, I pull the front door shut behind me, turn to say farewell, walk down the worn front steps and close the gate.

As we convoy through the suburbs I am crying, chest heaving, the reds and greens and ambers of traffic lights blurred. Stop. Go. Think about it. The truck tails me, and Tashie sits panting on the floor behind my seat.

Now we are cruising on the long stretch of bush-lined road, the mountains to the west hazed with eucalyptus blue. I am happy and excited. Or grief-stricken and bereft. It's hard to tell. There is a familiar odour in the car, a whiff of leather. My crazy yearning wants it to be Bill. When I glance left, he's sitting here beside me, very calm. We have a conversation, an everyday normal chat about the heat, the length of this drive, Jane's generosity, my state of mind. He tells me he is proud of me, that I am doing exceptionally well and that he is fine. He tells me that he loves me and he always will. I tell him that I'll always love him too.

Glancing at the road, I see we've travelled a long way. I check my rear-view mirror, relieved that the truck is still there behind me. When I look across again, the passenger seat is empty and the faint scent has gone. I touch the seat but there is no body warmth, no evidence that anyone was there. And yet I know with certainty that Bill has given me his blessing. The air inside my car feels lighter.

* * *

Our procession across the river is saluted by a raised hand and a grin from the ferry driver. Once he has chained the gate and got the ferry moving, the man wanders over and leans on my car roof above the open window. 'So, we've finally got you, have we, love?' He laughs, glancing behind me at the truck. 'You better watch out. Once this valley gets into your blood you might be stuck here forever. I've lived out here for thirty years and you couldn't move me on if you paid me.'

He knows I'll be looking after Jane's place, knows that she's heading overseas. Thinks it will be nice for me to be living closer to my sister and it's amazing how much we look alike. This man knows more about my life than my few remaining friends do.

Steve has eased the truck off the ferry, taking his time, not wanting to jostle my precious things. He pulls up beside me in the gravel rest area, waiting for directions. 'How are you going, Angel? Everything okay?' His kind face looks concerned. 'I thought you'd changed your mind for a while back there, you were driving so slowly.'

But it's fine. From here, we will drive the twenty kilometres out to Essie's, pick her up and keep on going. Jane is expecting us for lunch. I can see that the men are awe-struck, checking out the high sandstone ridges, the timeless bush, the river's expanse.

Essie has organised food for us all – a welcome feast, and a farewell to Jane. We load everything into the back seat of my car with stern words of warning to Tashie. But she's happy to be sitting on Essie's lap, nose aquiver, tail twitching, checking out fresh scents and scenery.

A couple of old codgers look up and wave as we drive through the village. They don't seem surprised. Jane has left the gate wide open but we stop anyway. Sean and Steve want to check the lane, make sure the truck won't get damaged by any of the overhanging trees.

When we arrive in the clearing, Jane is there, standing in front of the house. I have never seen her dressed like this before, in a long skirt and city boots, silk singlet elegant on her slim frame. Like me, she is ready for transition.

'Welcome to your new home, my dear!' She opens her arms wide, holds me, brushes warm lips to my face.

Essie makes the introductions while I take Tashie for a walk, anxious to settle her in. I will tie her up to the pergola so she can be near us at lunchtime. Jane gives directions to the men. She has cleared out the small shed by the back door next to the battery room. They can put my cartons there. The cottage is compact and there is little space inside for anything extraneous.

On the long table under the wisteria Essie is laying out our feast. Liz has baked cobs of wholemeal bread and there is cold roast pork, pickles, homemade jam. Thick slabs of yellow cheese are layered on a plate. Bowls and dishes of pate and chicken and fresh salad greens. Sean and Steve ease into their seats, ravenous but polite, as Jane sets down jugs of iced lemon water.

'Before we eat, I'd like to give thanks for the forces of goodness that have brought all this into being,' Jane says, surprising our hands that were reaching for knives and bread and cheese. 'I'm eternally grateful to Richard, for finding this little piece of heaven. To the community, for allowing us to settle.' She speaks of sandstone and gum trees, wildlife, the river, the seasons, good soil, abundance and gratitude. Then invites us to eat.

For a while there is the healthy silence of hungry people appreciating excellent food. When Steve speaks, it is to ask Jane about the valley – how many people live out here, how they earn a living. Conversation livens into details about the school, how the children ride their horses or catch a meandering bus that takes an hour to bring them from upriver every day. Sean wants to know about Jane's orphanage.

By the time we have packed up leftovers for Sean and Steve to take home, and carried stacks of plates and glasses inside, the sun is blazing a trail towards the western hill. The men want to get the truck back before dark. There is hugging all round, a promise to keep in touch.

Then they are gone, and a stillness settles on us. Three women on a hot, hazy afternoon, two on the brink of adventure, the other holding everything steady. The heady scent of wisteria drapes around us, mingling with the faint whiff of gumleaves and something I have come to know as river.

Jane will stay one more night, settling me in, showing me the intricacies of stove lighting, when and why to flick the generator switch, how to pour diesel, the best way to clean an earthen floor. She insists that I move straight into the bedroom, that she will sleep on the couch. She has already made up my bed with fresh, clean sheets.

To catch her flight she will be up before dawn, waiting outside for Clyde to take her to the airport. Without warning the screen shatters on my vision of this dream, my breath comes in short, painful gasps. Vistas of long hot lonely nights and heat-addled days roll towards me.

Essie sees me slipping. 'Let's go for a walk, Angel. Come on. Get your cap, we're going down to the river.'

She pulls me firmly by the hand. Tashie yelps and leaps, but this is no time for walking the dog. Chest-high fronds of softly seeded grass brush us as we walk single file along the track. In the whispering heat of late afternoon the river laps against its banks. Essie pushes through heavy green foliage, holding back branches so that I can pass, all the time moving closer to the water, to the shimmering ebb and flow of this valley's ever-changing heart.

Breaking through into a light-flooded clearing I realise she has been here before, knows about the almost-white sand, the mound with its short soft grass, this secret place where sisters can sit and be initiated into the river's arcane ways. She pulls me down beside her, keeping hold of my hand, urgent, silent, fierce.

'There's no way to go except forward, Angel,' she murmurs. 'Look at the river, how it moves, always moves. Does it question its purpose? Think about giving up or turning back?' Then she points to the forested hillside reaching up to the vivid blue sky, the ancient smudged sandstone that long ago lined the ocean floor. 'Sometimes the change is so slow that even the gods seem unaware.'

I don't know my sister in this mood. For the first time she seems older, world-weary and distant.

'Do you think it's easy,' she says, 'being known in society as a dyke? The butt of pub jokes and snide looks from sleazy men?'

The rules are broken, lying brittle on the sand at our feet. Fine bands of anguish are stretching and snapping in my chest, razoring my breath. I look away, ashamed.

'And,' she continues, 'my baby sister tells me to my face that I'm a sinner; that I'm going to hell when I die. She won't even let me be alone with her children for fear I'll harm them in some way. And of course she'll never visit me and Lizzie in our "house of wickedness", as she calls it.'

My hand reaches over, touches her arm.

'I'm so sorry, Ess. I've been a long way away, haven't I?'

'You've been mourning your beloved, sweetheart,' she says, turning my face to hers. 'It might never fade completely, the yearning, but your life can't stay in freeze-frame forever. Life's not like that. No matter how tough it gets, we have to go on.'

Something has cracked open between us, letting in a fragile new intimacy. The river flows like a wide satin ribbon past our feet making its way to the sea – surging and ebbing, memorialising perpetuity. By the time we finish talking the sun is a garnet orb nudging the ridge behind us. It's time we went back.

Rich scents of paprika, herbs and fragrant rice greet us as we stroll towards the house. Everything is bathed in a red-gold glow. I haven't seen the cottage from this angle, the way it hugs down onto the earth like a sleepy child at the end of an adventure-filled day.

We will feast inside tonight, in a room lit by candles, with warm air wafting through screens. One more ritual meal. Jane tells us she has heard from her colleague in Nepal and that the people are excited at her imminent arrival.

Starting in the kitchen she walks me one more time through the skills and secrets of my new home. She has left detailed notes in a red book on the table beside the phone. If I get into strife, I am to call on Clyde. He was busy the last time I came, so we didn't meet. Maybe he will drop by on his way home tomorrow. I feel Jane's comfortable trust in her old friend. After dinner and the dishes, we head for an early night. Ess is leaving, Jane arranging sheets and plumping a pillow on the couch.

I walk with my sister out into the starry night where galaxies glimmer and frogs and crickets chirrup in the cooling air.

'I'll be back tomorrow,' Essie says as she hugs me close, kisses my hair. 'I love you, Angel. It's a gift, having you this close.'

As her tail-lights vanish into the darkened lane I look up, and turn. On the eastern ridge, clear as a stencil, a fine crescent moon gleams beside the brightest star.

Jane has come out and is standing beside me. The rhythmic flow of life pulses in the balmy insect chorus, becoming our breathing, merging us with the earth.

When we turn to go inside, Jane takes my hand, folds it between hers. Searches my soul with her eyes. Then nods. 'You belong here too,' she says quietly. 'It's your place, just as it has been Richard's and mine.'

13

The stars have all but faded from the velvet sky as I wave goodbye to Jane. There has been the briefest of greetings with Clyde – a tall man, weathered like the rocks, white hair a survivor's emblem. Loading Jane's cases into the back of his ute, securing them for the journey to the airport, shaking my hand. Jane and I said our farewells inside, over steaming cups of tea and honeyed muffins. She will call me from Kathmandu. We will keep in touch. I have not had a mother for a long time. We leave many things unspoken.

Tyres crunch on gravel long after the lane has swallowed the red glow of their tail-lights. In the stillness of predawn I stand alone, surrounded by a thousand versions of green. A dark shadow quivers near the tree line. Wallaroo. Getting in early for a feed.

To my surprise, I slept the sleep of little children last night. Jane's big bed folded me in, lulled me almost instantly into sleep. I dreamed of ancient forested mountains where a deep, still pool offered healing waters to all who might make the journey, where animals who came to drink quivered with vitality, where the trees grew immense and tall, reaching strong leafy arms into the heavens. In the dream I submerged myself in the cool, fresh water of that pool, sinking down and down with my eyes wide open and my hair floating out, breathing in water with ease, walking eventually on a soft pool-bed of silt where crystals rolled beneath my feet, massaging gently. When the healing was done, I drifted up towards the light that glowed translucent green. I lifted my languid body onto a mossy bank and there I slept, waking in the darkness to the faint chink of cups meeting saucers, in the comfortable softness of Jane's big old wooden bed.

The sound of Clyde's departing ute has faded as I turn to walk back inside to feed Tashie. High up above the eastern ridge, beyond the river, pale clear sky takes on a gilded-silver glow. Cool air quivers with the pipings of tiny birds, chorusing first light. The scent of river and gumleaves emerges brand new from the departing night. Past the narrow track where Ess and I walked yesterday, the long grass of the river flat paddock glistens with fast-drying vestiges of dew. There are five wallaroos feeding now, the dark-furred male bigger than his harem of grey-brown females. They have seen me long before I noticed them, turning inquisitive faces in my direction, sensing for danger, aware of the change.

Jane and I have talked a lot about how to keep my little dog happy and the birds and wildlife safe. Jane showed me a well-fenced yard and the stable where she used to keep her horse, asked if that would keep Tashie secure at night, or when I go out and can't take her with me. She is such a darling pup, happy to follow me into this unfamiliar world. Keeping her alive has surely kept me sane on those tear-sodden mornings when I could have stayed in bed, but for the need to feed the dog.

It turns into a morning of crinkled newspaper, flattened cartons, bewildered woman walking round and round. By the time I have opened every box and looked inside, the place is strewn. I have nowhere to put my precious things until I tidy up. Last time I did this, there was Bill, taking care of the countless little jobs, setting up house with his bride. We had bought the terrace instead of getting married, then decided to get married anyway. We thought we had it all.

I shake my head, lift a hand to smack my face. 'Not that way, not on day one,' I caution, speaking out aloud into the still, cool room. I will take Tashie for a walk, check the mail. And then what?

Blazing sun seers my skull the minute I walk beyond wisteria shade. Jane and Essie both warned me about the heat, the way those sandstone escarpments set up a toaster effect. Already the birds have disappeared to cooler hide-outs and Tashie is panting flat out on the pavers. When Jane told me that the house was solar passive I didn't understand, but I am beginning to get it – inside, it is pleasantly cool.

There are three hats hanging on a wooden rack along the wall outside the back door. Which one is mine? I choose the straw hat with the wide brim.

The laneway is an avenue of bliss, leafy branches of paperbarks blocking out the sun. It's only a few hundred metres but seems longer on foot, and the track is rough. Once every year, the council sends a grader to deal with potholes, smooth out the gravel, top it up. Jane has left a number for the bloke if I need any work done in between.

They must have closed the gate behind them – to keep me feeling safe, or just out of habit? – and I fiddle with the chain to get it open. It is Friday, one of three days the postie makes deliveries, but the quaint box is empty. There has been very little mail for me in recent months, apart from bills, and most of those will transfer now to Angelo and Sabina. Loneliness looms at me again, moving through the canopy of trees like a shadowy monster just beyond my reach. We have been here on the roadside for several minutes and not a car or truck has driven by. Perhaps the world has ended.

Tashie is restless, and I juggle once again with the gate. By the time it is secured I am close to tears, backhanding sniffles as we turn down the gravel lane for home. Now I have to decide on some kind of outdoor shelter for Tashie. Organise something to eat.

Next time I stop, it is stifling. Best to go away for a while over Christmas, the valley locals say. But I am in hiding, don't want to celebrate Christmas, don't want to go anywhere.

I have set up Tashie's kennel in the stable where she will be safe and comfortable when I'm not here, and an outside bed for her under the pergola. If the air ruffles up off the river, it might bring a hint of cool. There's a ceramic bowl full of water against the wall in the shade, but the heat is relentless. This summer, Tashie will spend a lot of time inside the house with me.

In the evening, with the sun asleep behind the ridge, the faintest hint of breeze ripples through, lifting wilted leaves and tinkling chimes, whispering hope. All my treasures have found homes and my painting gear is by the door beside a neat stack of canvases on frames. Jane has cleared out a massive space in her studio and urged me to paint. She has asked me to send prints of my paintings for her to hang at the Nepalese school.

Essie drops by, bringing fresh bread, a basket of eggs, some more milk. Tonight, the rural fire service has a training session – she and Liz both have to attend. Should they check on me on their way home? But I tell her I'll be fine. It's uneasy, this brand new arrangement, especially after our heart-to-heart down by the river. In all our years together, it has never been like this – walking gingerly around each other, reaching out, pulling back. My brave face is probably unconvincing but it's what we need, and I wave once again when she drives away.

In the stillness of this starry night cicada thrumming swamps the sultry air, filling all my senses until I have to go inside and shut the doors. There are salad makings in the fridge, and Essie's eggs. I talk aloud to myself, working out the best way of cooking an omelette on an old gas stove, and go searching for the small frying pan. All the cupboard doors are shut tight in an effort to keep out mice and rats.

Tashie will sort out the rodents, I muse, cracking eggshells on the edge of a bowl, reaching for the whisk. My little dog has passed out on the floor, soaking up coolness through her belly, twitching in her sleep.

When she barks and rushes to the door I am instantly on guard, waiting for reality to knock. Do they knock in the country, I wonder, my breath coming fast.

'It's alright, Angelica. Just me.' I think I recognise Clyde's voice. 'Thought I'd drop by to see how you're settling in and let you know Jane got away without any problems.' He is making it easy for me, waiting patiently outside in the heat until I open the door.

I am glad to hear a friendly voice, and call out to him to come in. Ask if he would like to stay for dinner. I don't know why I feel at ease with this man I've never properly met. Or perhaps I am afraid of being alone here at night.

But Clyde is going to the training session too, wonders if I'd like to join him. It's tempting, but the thought of coming home here in the dead of night is way beyond me and I make an excuse about unpacking, being tired, going early to bed. He doesn't believe me, but he leaves.

The minute he walks out the door, I am full of regret. There is nothing here tonight for me to do after eating, washing dishes, wiping the kitchen bench. Jane said she didn't bother getting the television set up. If ever I feel the need, there are forms to fill out, technicians to ring, satellite hook-ups to arrange.

But for now, I am walking the dog, wandering aimlessly towards the river, drawn by the magnet of the moon. Tugging on her lead, Tashie has her nose to the ground, snuffling the thrilling scent of night-time quarry. We turn back, and I understand the value of the chicken wire fencing hooked into the ground around her grassy yard, keeping furry creatures safely out. She is happy to let me chain her up. In her world, everything is fine – she has food, shelter, fresh water, her own bed and me. 'No reason for you to stay,' she seems to be saying as she wanders into her now-familiar home, turns three nesting circles and settles down for the night.

A great weariness assails me when I think of going walking on my own. Dark ridges frame the sky to the east and west, channelling the Milky Way across the river, sending shadows through the trees and up the hill. Time to get inside.

Bill and I used to sit in our garden on hot summer nights, drinking margaritas by moonlight and talking about the children we would have. There would be a girl like me and Essie but she'd have red hair, from Bill's side of the family. Our big blue eyes, of course, and his olive skin. What a beauty she would be. And the boy, mad about machines, like his dad, and sensitive like me; a tall lanky boy with freckles on his nose and grubby hands.

Why am I thinking these things? There's a hot ball of acid churning in my gut, heavy as molten lead, sullen with slow-burning rage. In the earth-walled bathroom, when I go to brush my teeth, I see crazed patterns in the tiles, images of bloodstains in the bath, bone fragments on the floor. The harpy in the mirror screeches in pain, glimpsing grotesque shadows in the room. Here's my husband, my bloody damn-dead husband, trying to make love to me. Running brittle fingers down my arm, rattling in my ear. A scalding ball of bitterness erupts into the toilet bowl; sulphurous, putrid, searing my nostrils and burning the back of my throat.

In a shrieking fury I tear outside, desperate to do damage. Howls echo through the valley, seeping into stone, washing into eddies on the river, coming back at me. Deep anguish pours from my throat, keening to the stars, into endless inky sky. 'Why did you leave me, you bastard? Why? What made you so selfish, so stupid? Riding that stupid fucking bike!'

Unbelievable. I have echoed Sage's hateful words.

Leaves shred through my fingers as I hurl myself past trees, slam along the laneway, raging my pain. He is such a bastard, such a stupid, selfish, arrogant prick. Where are our babies now? Eh? Those babies you said you wanted, arsehole?

When the rage subsides, I don't know where I am. There are trees looming all around and I can no longer see the moon. Dust cakes my legs, I have blood on my hands. And a dead fucking husband turned to ash. I am staggering in circles, tearing at my hair, nails stabbing into fleshy palms. And I want to die.

And I sobbingly don't want to die because deep down inside the pain, a part of me senses that there is so much life to live. That one day, I might even want to swim and run and love and laugh and play and feel alive again.

When the sharp sting of the shower shreds my grief away, I can see my bones through the translucent skin on hips and collarbones and shoulders. Maybe I will die. I am mortified with guilt – useless, hopeless and weak. Utterly exhausted by it all.

In the darkest roiling hours before the dawn, mad plans trail through my mind. If I get up now and walk into the river, walk in deep with stones in my pockets and Bill's carafe of ashes in my arms, I will sleep. I will sleep forever, never troubling anyone again, or being in the way. Clyde will come and find the dog and set up searches. And I'll be gone. I'll be with Bill.

Round and round these stories swirl until I am weak with desolation, helpless in a foreign bed. Bill's lovely body lies beside me now, stroking, so forgiving, so not there. Vague waves of recrimination lap between us because it's true, what Sage said – he did ride that bike against my better judgement. Yet it did bring him untrammelled joy. I cannot even cry.

14

In the soft dawn of a new day, it feels impossible for me to live here. But I have made a commitment to Jane – no less than six months. Tashie saves me again, yapping wildly from the yard. Wearing shorts and a singlet and my boots, I grab her lead from the hook on the wall and dash across the pale grass to get her. And off we go, heading down the lane, cavorting in the early morning mildness before the heat sets in. By the time we get back to the house both of us are panting and ready to eat. Muesli for me, a bone and some biscuits for Tash.

I sit beside her under the violet-blue canopy of the pergola with my coffee, watching for that moment when the ball of gold bursts over the eastern ridge. What the fuck am I going to do?

There is no sense of Christmas in the air, other than the heat and the cicadas and the damp shimmer on my skin. And the flies. They drive me back inside, into our cave-like home. Tashie trots in behind me, flopping onto the cool earthen tiles. Maybe I should lie there with her. I can't muster the energy to paint or even draw, and all my art things are in boxes in the shed.

I am unaccustomed to the stillness and the green, to this

absence of accoutrements and cafes. The sounds of silence crowd around me. I lift the carafe of ashes from the mantelpiece, carry it into my bedroom, set it down. I will have to dispose of them soon, these silted remnants. Wandering around the living room, I explore Jane's eclectic collections. The tall shelves on the wall by the front door hold big books on art and ceramics, natural history, photography, the wild places of the earth. They're not what I'm after, although I don't know what that might be. In the bedroom, on a low set of shelves, rows of paperbacks line the wall. Randomly I pull out colourful spines, find one that suits me, settle down to read. This is a good spot for keeping cool, on the wide window seat looking onto the steep, forested hill.

I have dozed off and didn't hear the car. Essie is kissing my forehead, whispering my name. Water is running in the kitchen, filling the kettle. Liz must be here too. Something happening. Wonderful!

'Wow, Angel, you look all settled in!' says Liz, as Ess and I wander out into the kitchen. Tashie is licking feet and dashing back and forth towards the door – walk me, walk me – tail wagging nineteen to the dozen. She makes us laugh. Already it is thirty-eight degrees outside, so we settle at the dining table with our mugs of tea and Liz's wholemeal scones, spread with home-made plum jam on top of slabs of butter from the fridge.

It's different with Jane away, more informal. Dainty teacups remain on their shelf, napkins in the drawer. The girls are full of news about the fire season, the fire that burned down a house just the other week. Not that it was a bushfire, but still. The poor woman lost everything. It was probably started by an electrical fault.

I feel myself relaxing as the conversation ebbs and flows around me, massaging my aching heart, salving the wounds from my nocturnal rampage. I want to tell them about it, but I feel ashamed.

In the end it is Lizzie who says, 'You look a wee bit rough around the edges, Angel. Bad night?'

She points to my bruises and scratches, and the tangled mess of my hair.

The ball of molten fury gurgles and churns a warning. Don't start. You might scald them with your rage. But it spews out anyway. 'I'm so angry with Bill!' Sobs, gulping for air. 'I could kill him!' No one laughs. 'I can't believe he would do something so selfish, go riding on that fucking bike when we had all our dreams and plans. So many times I told him it was too dangerous but he wouldn't listen. It's too much ...'

Rocking rocking rocking on the chair, body convulsing, racked with grief and rage. Then they are holding me, one on either side, firm hands on my shoulders, voices strong.

'Keep it coming, sweetheart, get it out.' Essie's voice.

And out it pours, streams of vitriolic anger and regret messing on the table and dripping to the floor while they support my shaking frame. Until it's done, for now.

They lead me to the sofa, lie me down, massage my hands and my feet. It's okay. Somehow they don't hate my bitterness. It's hot outside but in the house it's cool. My body shudders and they cover it with a mohair rug. Someone goes to boil the kettle, someone sits with me. I am fading in and out. Someone's holding a glass of cool water to my lips, asking me to drink. I do it. Then the tea, sweet and hot, little sips. Someone holds the cup.

Later they tell me they have been waiting for this, waiting for the rage to burst through. They tell me it's a normal stage of grief and they've been worried that I had seemed so calm and in control. Amazing what you can hide, even from the people closest to you.

'Let's get you in the shower,' Lizzie says. 'Clean clothes, and then we're going out.' Tender and bruised, I am in their hands. It turns out there's a market in the village, for Christmas Eve. Is it Christmas Eve already? I had no idea.

The thought of meeting people is too much but we go, and it's good. No one seems curious about my febrile state. Maybe it's the heat. This is a perfect day for hiding in the old pub with its solid sandstone walls and cool, dim corners. We drink lemon lime and bitters to match my mood. Liz and Ess keep touching on the wound, dabbing it, checking its condition. 'It's okay, Angel, you have to get it out,' Lizzie says again.

'He would understand your anger.' This from Ess.

They reminisce about Bill, the real Bill, the one with warts and all, the one we love. They talk about his habit of wearing old-man singlets all year round, his gorgeous smile, how clever he was with computers and his corny taste in music and jokes. They talk about a man.

I mention again my sense that he's around. I talk about the bird. The comfort of having his ashes in my room. And what I should do with his clothes.

'When you're ready we'll help you sort through them,' Essie says. 'There are people in the valley who could use them. Or the op shop in Middleton, if you'd rather do that. Not see them walking around.'

Liz circles back to my experience with the bird. 'I've heard of things like this back home in New Zealand,' she says. 'If you feel him near you, there's a good chance that he is.'

The conversation drifts to what they have planned for tomorrow – Christmas Day.

Clyde is coming to their place for lunch, bringing a friend. And on Boxing Day we'll make a duty trek to Sage and Mike's, taking presents for the girls. Ess tells me that Sage phoned her with a list of suitable gifts. 'No books,' she'd said. 'We like to monitor the reading material our children are exposed to.' The look on Essie's face says it all. And reminds me that Sage doesn't yet know about my move. I haven't had the energy to broach it with her – I'm sure she'll find reasons to disapprove.

I haven't bought a single Christmas present, not gone shopping for anything but food, and not a lot of that. But Ess and Liz have put my name with theirs on all the gift tags. No matter how I thank them, it doesn't seem enough. 'You'd do the same for us if one of us was dead,' Liz says, straight-faced. We giggle, attracting attention from the few men and women who are gathered at the bar.

This is my life now. Andrea and the cafe are light years away, another galaxy. Ess and Liz are talking about their plans for the holidays, ideas for improving their garden, Lizzie's next trip to New Zealand to visit her folks. Ess might even have been allowed to go with her this time but has decided to stay, to be near me. I feel the burden I've become, feel it in my body, in my slumped shoulders, my bony haunches.

'You should go, Ess. I'm a big girl – I'll be fine.'

We laugh again, my tears glistening through hysteria at the ludicrous nature of this claim.

'I still have family stuff to sort anyway,' Liz says, laying her hand on mine. 'My grandmother's not getting any younger. And there's so much shit with my father. You wouldn't want to know.'

Ess reaches over and brushes damp strands of hair from my face. 'You have stuff to sort out too, sweetie. Like Bill's ashes. Especially that.'

'I've been thinking of setting him free into the river.' The words are out before the thought has fully formed. Perhaps if I can let him go, I might find a way to survive.

'Would you do it in the night-time or the day?' I hear Liz ask. 'We could check the moon's phases and the tides. Work it out like that.'

Ess pulls out her new diary and starts writing a pencilled list. First, I should choose the date and time. Maybe a full moon would be good, before Liz goes to New Zealand? There might be other things I'd like to send into the river's flow – a photo of me or our wedding, a few of his favourite things.

I'm shocked at how straightforward they are about this, and yet it feels right. My mind and heart are screaming NO, but I hear myself promising to give them a date and time.

Tashie is tied up to a post out the front of the pub and we hear her yapping. It's time to go. Awkwardness again. The girls want me to come and stay, to help them with tomorrow's lunch preparations. But I need to get home. Need to anchor, to hide away. It is intolerable, this feeling of displacement. In the end we compromise – they will take me home to Walden now and come back for me later in the day. Take me to their place for dinner and to stay the night.

I insist that they drop me at the gate – Tashie needs the walk. And I need to revisit the laneway in daylight. All that's left when they drive away is dusty green and stillness, sandstone ridges and oppressive heat filling the valley like an unpleasant guest who refuses to leave. Pale puffs of dust rise as we walk, settling on our feet, coating my legs. No wonder I was such a mess last night, I think. Then Bill is walking with us, unconcerned, lightness in his step. Unfazed by my tirades, it seems. When I reach for his hand my fingers trace thin air and the anger surges again. It's too much. I have to let him go.

By the time Essie arrives to pick us up I am prepared – Tashie's lead, her toys and her favourite blanket are in a bag, I have clothes and toiletries for the next twenty-four hours, and the kitchen is tidy and clean. On the bench is a note about January fourth – the next full moon. We'll do the ceremony then. Before the turning of the year can weaken my resolve.

After the dust of the drive, their cottage is a picture – verandah strung with coloured fairy lights, twin tubs of poinsettia bright beside the front screen door. Delicious aromas waft from inside – Liz has been busy in the kitchen. Full-throated cackling rips through the hazy stillness as a trio of kookaburras spot us from the trees, surprising me into laughter. Maybe it is going to be a good night after all.

15

Christmas morning dawns sultry and still, but the girls are up early, adding little touches to the room, rearranging dishes in the over-full fridge. There will be five of us, with Clyde and his friend. Six, if you count Tashie.

It's hot by the time we have breakfast, the temperature climbing relentlessly with the sun as it heats the valley toaster. Ess has set out a platter with slices of rockmelon, peaches, sweet yellow mango, luscious plums, red-black cherries, pecan nuts and almonds. We sit on the shady back verandah to eat, finalising the day's plans while Liz gets the kettle barbecue organised for roasting chickens and vegetables. Two organic chooks, potatoes, pumpkin, kumara, swedes, beetroot – a feast.

I gaze up at the morning hillside to the trees that climb this western ridge. The crepe myrtle is bursting with buds, promising a dusty pink display to celebrate New Year.

'What time are the others coming?' I ask, uneasy at the thought of meeting a stranger. 'They're invited for eleven,' Liz says. 'Don't worry. We still have plenty of time for coffee.'

Ess has gone inside and walks out now carrying a small stash of beautifully wrapped gifts. 'Happy Christmas, my loves!' she beams. I feel embarrassed but they laugh and bustle me, insisting on joyous sharing. Essie watches Liz open a tiny package wrapped in hot pink tissue – an intricate silver ring, inlaid with turquoise and amber. 'To keep me with you while you're away,' says Ess.

Liz has given Ess a necklace, a smooth amethyst teardrop on a silver chain. 'Your birthstone, sweetheart,' she says, and smiles.

For me, there is a short singlet-style silk nightie, cream patterned with pastel pink and violet petals, faint pale green leaves, a gorgeous wisp of a thing. And Tashie gets a meaty bone that will keep her happy for the next few hours.

They make it okay, me giving nothing in return. We try on our presents, laughing at my slip bunched up over skimpy top and shorts, gasping at the beauty of jewellery against skin. Lazing with our coffees, we drift through an hour before wandering back inside for showers and salad making, the ritual of setting the table with poinsettia napkins, red candles, best cutlery, and paper bonbons beside each place. Sentimental legacies from Aunty Fran who is currently somewhere in Portugal with friends. Cut crystal bowls hold sugary sweets, plump raisins, lightly salted nuts. And the ceiling fan pushes drowsy air around the room.

A crunch of tyres on gravel heralds the guests' arrival. Clyde is elegantly scrubbed and dressed, his white hair neatly brushed, a well-presented Christmas guest. And beside him strides a tall, lean young guy, long black hair held back in a leather band, skin the colour of polished mahogany. 'Estrellita, Elizabeth, Angelica, this is Hayden. I met him near the ferry a few days ago and offered him some work.' Clyde makes easy introductions as Ess holds the screen door open, ushering them in. I want to run and curl up in my bedroom. But force myself to stay and smile, be pleasant.

Clyde has brought a massive watermelon, harvested this

morning from his field, and Hayden is holding out two chilled bottles of riesling. Liz carves the chickens, and we help ourselves to vegetables and salads from bowls in the centre of the table.

The conversation roams around subjects like lack of rain, the endless heat, how sluggish the river flows, whether this evening will bring a storm. Hayden seems a little shy, but we get him talking by asking about his home – Canada – which explains the intriguing accent. By the time we're onto dessert – a spectacular pavlova – he's told us that he's twenty, that he flew into Brisbane and is working his way around Australia, staying mainly with WWOOF hosts, earning his keep and learning about organic farming. He'd hitched a ride with someone who dropped him in Lawsons Landing. 'It's lucky I spotted you,' comments Clyde. 'Not many places interested in organics here in the valley. And I can always use an extra pair of hands.' They seem very comfortable with each other for men who've just met, and I realise I know nothing about Clyde's personal life.

Day moves into evening and still we sit, sated with Christmas spirit, languid with goodwill. 'Well, we ought to be going,' says Clyde. 'Time to feed the horses.' There are hugs all around, even with Hayden, who almost feels like a long-lost member of the family. Nice boy. Clyde mentions doing this again sometime soon at his place, maybe for New Year. Then they're gone.

Ess and Liz insist Tashie and I stay another night and I don't have the strength to debate. They refuse to notice my lack of grace, sweeping me along in their chat, and the clatter of dishes and pans.

On Boxing Day we drive to the suburbs and fill our hearts with the joy of innocence as Sage's little ones play ball with Tashie, then ooh and aah over carefully chosen auntie gifts. We eat too much again. Aunty Fran calls from the Costa Vicentina, sending love down the line. I pick my moment to tell Sage and Mike about my move to Jane's place, hoping that Sage will keep her thoughts to herself so as not to spoil the celebrations. She frowns. Asks me to write down my new address and phone number. Says she will call me to discuss this 'unexpected decision'. I breathe a sigh of relief – drama averted, for now. Eventually, the girls drive us home and drop us at the gate.

16

Days roll like heat-balls into warm clear evenings, bathing me in sweat and dust whenever I venture outside, cradling me in a Walden haze of daytime greens and starry nights. Sometimes in the very early morning I walk on my own down the track to the river and sit on our mound, wide awake and dreamy, watching ripples move through mirror-clear water and dragonflies skim.

Time turns its wheel of light and dark, rising and falling like the tide that marks its limits on the river's banks. Each dawn, the sky begins to lighten and the promised ball of gold leaps up above the ridge, transiting the valley on its unwavering path and dropping like a stone at evening into the trees and rocks that edge the other side.

The charm of this place is casting spells on me. Some days I sleep in my big bed for hours on end, rising only to tend to Tashie, and feed myself or drink or pee. The nights carry me outside to roam the paddocks and the leaf-shadowed lane, the track to the river, the gravel road. Sometimes Bill comes with me, silently holding my hand, or telling me stories of pure realms where all doubt and concern dissolves away, where he sees clearly how I am faring, watches over me. When I reply, I am talking into darkness, seeking light. Tears come rarely now, have given way to long rants and raucous laughter, dirty accusations, mean slanting attacks designed to hurt. Or songs of love that slip and slide into saccharine lunacy. No one hears except Bill and me, the trees and the earth and the creatures of the night.

Thoughts of Bill's brother nudge my heart at times like this. Perhaps we should meet again? I could tell him more stories about Bill's happiness, his success, the way his colleagues and students adored him. And Neil could explain the mystery of the brothers' falling out. Tell me whether it even had anything to do with Bill. One morning I slide the stained pub coaster out from the back of my address book. Pick up the phone. Put it down. Breathe deep breaths, then pick it up and ring.

'Yeah g'day.'

'Neil?'

'Nah, ain't seen Neil in a while luv. Dunno where he's got to neither.'

There's no offer of message taking but I leave my name anyway. Say I might call again sometime.

'Yeah, no worries luv. No harm trying, I s'pose.'

When the phone rings minutes later, my heart leaps. But it's Clyde. Maybe there is a caretaking roster? Someone calls me every day on some pretext or other. He is organising a get-together with Ess and Liz and some other locals at the pub for tonight – New Year's Eve. He wants to pick me up at nine. Will I be here? No, I'll be dining with the Queen, I want to say, nasty demon sliding up my throat. But I surprise myself by saying it will be fine, and that I'll be waiting at the gate.

It is relentlessly hot. I have taken to walking around in singlet and shorts and ponytail all day, knowing no one will come. I'll have to think about clothes. There's a sundress I bought on holidays in Bali with Bill. It will do, although the fabric hangs loose on my skinny body. It's a pretty thing – bright peacock blues and hot pinks. New look for a new year. My heart's not in it.

I am getting better at managing the latch on the gate, am smiling with this small success when the ute appears around the bend, pulling over slowly to keep the dust at bay. It's a bit of a squeeze with three but Clyde and Hayden slide along the bench seat to allow me space.

In the village someone has strung coloured lights along the front of the pub and the general store – party time in the valley. It reminds me of being a child, when simple things made us happy and no one wanted much. So far so good.

By the time midnight cruises in I am well tanked on champagne, dancing in the roadway with Ess and Liz and a dozen others, all of us grubby from the dust, singing and hugging and crying, letting in hope and spurning despair. It's a charade that passes as fun. My minders have had a night off – if they notice I've been avoiding men, they don't comment. As the clock ticks over into January, everyone is equal for an hour.

Among the young ones, only Hayden has been quiet, sitting at a bench on the pub verandah, glass of iced water in hand, resting easy, soaking up the party atmosphere. Once in a while Clyde goes to sit with him before wandering off with another of the men for a yarn. Some of the women teasingly try to drag him up to dance. But he prefers to sit. Unusual young man, far away from home.

In the early hours of a brand new year, people drink Irish coffees and dream out extravagant plans for happiness and success. There's a lot of talk about rain, if only … Someone wants a new job in the city, talks of leaving, enrolling in film school. Another plans to travel overseas. My sister and her darling hope they'll have enough money saved to buy their own place this year.

Say something, my demon urges. Say anything. Make a plan.

The grey mist of blurry months and years refuses to take on shape and colour, will not heed my alcohol-fuelled command. 'I think I'll get back into my painting,' I muse. 'Oh, and I have to put some time into the garden.'

And release my husband's ashes from their jar.

17

In the morning there's a foul taste in my mouth and the sundress is stained and dirty. Happy New Year. Guilt shifts uneasy in my gut when I recall my promise to tend Jane's precious garden. Most evenings I have given it a bit of water, keeping vegetables alive, also nurturing weeds. Later today, if it cools a little, I will get out there and keep faith with my New Year's resolution. Something to look forward to at the end of another endless day.

While I'm there I will walk down to the river and clear weeds and fallen branches from the grassy mound. Prepare our ceremonial site. In three days' time the girls and I will gather to set Bill free. My stomach lurches and my heart stands still.

My food supplies are running low as well. Soon, I will have to go shopping. My life is reduced to this – domestic drear and madwoman's melodrama. What was it Bill used to say? I don't recall. I can't see his face this morning, can barely remember his smell. Time for coffee, good and strong, before I plummet off the edge. And Tashie needs to eat.

The wisteria has slipped most of its blossoms in favour of lush bright green leaves, bathing my morning haven in pale iridescent light. Alright, then, I announce to the humid air, I'll follow up on both my resolutions.

The sketchpads are over in the studio with my painting gear. It used to be a hay barn, Jane told me, this rustic timber structure looking out through spindly she-oaks to the river. Richard filled it in with rough-hewn walls and big windows, gave it deep eaves to moderate the sun. Jane's pottery wheels are tucked into one corner, covered with tarpaulins to keep them safe from the ravages of time and nesting birds. Tashie wanders around, nosing into corners, snuffling at scents I cannot smell. It's so easy to make her happy. Most of the space is mine, open and empty apart from the small stack of cartons in the middle of the concrete floor and my blank canvases on a long bench running along the southern wall. I could do something with this.

Forgotten treasures reveal themselves as I unwrap item after item from its newspaper sheath. Glass jars, crinkled tubes of paint, brushes, even a small travelling easel. The colour-caked boards I used to use as palettes. And a stack of sketchpads, right at the bottom of a carton, with two battered boxes of soft lead pencils, a flat tin of coloured ones and some fine black pens. I turn the pages of the sketchpads, dipping into memories of inner city parks, of Bill's shadow on a lawn, Tashie as a cute new puppy, the butcher bird. That bird. I haven't heard it for weeks. Or perhaps I've not been listening.

Hours have passed by the time we wander through the heat-brittled grass back to the coolness of home. Under my arm I have tucked two sketchpads and my hands are full of pencil tins and boxes. At last I have a plan. It's an unfamiliar feeling, this lightness in my step, the life stirring in my veins. My fingers are itching to grip the pencils. There is no time to eat. I sit at the kitchen table and open one of the pads to a clean, empty page. My hand begins to move. Before I know it, ten pages are filled with sweeping lines and soft shading, life revealing itself in fine detail and smudged innuendo. Walden cottage, like a benevolent being risen out of the earth. The sweeping curve of the river as it turns in to caress the reedy banks that meet my track. And people. People I haven't been able to see for ages. There's Maddie, our Mum, a soft, barely formed woman who didn't grow old. Bob, our larrikin Dad, wearing his navy suit, being the man, a responsible working class father. They have been photographic memories who prop on my mantelpiece, mythical apparitions I never really knew. Now they're coming back to life.

It's only the fading light that makes me look up, brings me back to the table and the wooden chair. The sun has dropped over the ridge. Already. I need a shower but first I will keep my promise to Jane and the garden. Walden is blessed by the river, so far upstream that it's fresh. I pump its generous flow into the back tank for use on the gardens. Just as well. In the big rainwater tank that serves the house the level has dropped below half, no matter how careful I am. Jane showed me how to tap the side and hear by feeling where the emptiness begins. It's another artform.

I should check the level in the garden tank too, in case I need to pump. Tashie is full of life, jolted out of snoozing when I walk into the bedroom to fetch a long-sleeved shirt and jeans. Anti-mozzie gear. The air might be cooler, but it's insect feeding time. Citronella rubbed into all the bare places creates an oily haze. Boots by the back door. Tashie's lead. We're ready. What a rigma-role for cultivating food.

There are many things I know very little about. Living here feels like a full-time job, the longer I stay. Sturdy wooden framing supports a wire mesh enclosure to keep the birds and other crea-tures from raiding the crop. Someone – Richard? – has created an ingenious entry gate. And a seepage system for irrigating the roots of plants, not wasting a drop. All I have to do is turn the taps and wait a while. And remember to go back, to turn them off.

It's dinner time for the wallaroos as well, our little family of five. They love the riverflat paddock where grass grows long and sweet in the sandy soil. I see them watching me, wary, ready to spring away if I move too suddenly or come too close. Especially with the dog. Better to wander up the lane.

Out of habit, I check the mailbox, although there is rarely anything there. Today is different though – there's a letter. An ordinary envelope, bulky, addressed in unfamiliar handwriting to my Annandale address. Angelo and Sabina have forwarded it on. I shudder. No more surprises, please. Not when I am just beginning to trust life again.

I carry it back to the house, pour a glass of wine and sit on the couch. For a few minutes, the letter stares at me from the coffee table, a ticking timebomb.

There is no return address on the back of the envelope – that was the first thing I checked. I slip my finger under the flap, pull out several pages of lined writing pad paper stapled together. Go straight to the bottom of the last page: Neil.

Maybe he did get my phone message? If not, why write? Am I ready for this?

I put the pages back on the coffee table. Sip my wine. Pick up the letter again and begin to read.

Dear Angelica,

I hope this letter finds you feeling better than when I saw you in the pub.

I'm writing because I'm not much good at saying what I want to say over the phone. But I feel I owe you a few explanations and an apology.

Sorry I walked out on you and the other ladies that day. I was knocked sideways by the news. Didn't know what to say.

I just want to let you know that I do have a heart in here somewhere. And for the record, I did love my little bro. I never showed it, to him or anyone else, but I felt it. And I still do. I miss him. Not as much as you do, I reckon, but more out of regret.

I've got a lot of regrets, but the way I treated Billy when he was a little tacker is the biggest one of my miserable life. Probably he told you that I treated him like shit most of the time, and that's true. But he never knew why, and even though he never will now, I want to set the record straight with you at least.

Our Dad was a nasty bastard. Hard as nails. Rough on our Mum and always handy with the strap whenever me or Billy got in his way. But our Mum, she was a different story. Up until the time Billy was born, she was kind and loving, always trying to do her best by me. Usually it was making cakes or knitting me a jumper, stuff like that. But after Billy arrived, she changed. These days, they'd probably call it depression. But I was only a little bloke myself, only eight years old as Billy probably told you. I couldn't understand why she suddenly stayed in bed a lot, only looking after the baby and getting dinner on the table every night so that Dad wouldn't go off at her. But that was about all. She never had time for me any more. No more cakes or jumpers or even cuddles. And because it all changed the minute Billy came along, I blamed him.

Dad found me blubbing out the back of the house one day and gave me a hiding. Yelled at me to toughen up. Be a man. Big boys don't cry, he said. And that was it. I never shed another tear until that night I saw you girls.

I started acting more like Dad. Knocking Billy around, breaking his toys, taking him down the back paddock and leaving him there. Horrible stuff. Cruel. I could say I was trying to toughen him up, but it wasn't that. I blamed him for taking Mum away from me. So as soon as I turned fifteen, I was out of there. Never looked back. Every so often, I sent Mum a postcard so she'd know where I was. Know I was still alive. I guess I hoped she'd write back and beg me to come home or visit. But she never did.

Eventually, I got a postcard back, but it was from Billy. It told me Mum was dead. That she'd hanged herself. By the time it reached me, the funeral was long gone. No way I was going home to see the old man, and I figured Billy wouldn't want a bar of me either.

A few years later, Billy sent me another postcard to tell me Dad was dead too. Drank himself to death, basically. But that one took months to track me down, so I didn't even bother writing back. And that was that.

When I ended up down south last year, I reckoned it was about time I had a go at sorting shit out with Billy, so I looked him up in the phone book. That's how I found your number.

Well, you know the rest of it. Story of my life. Always too little, too late.

Anyway, Angelica, I'm sorry. Sorry about everything. Sorry I'm not around to help you out. But knowing me, I'd just be a liability. Better all round if I keep out of your way.

I hope the enclosed comes in handy.

And if you feel like writing to me at that PO Box number I gave you, it would be good to hear how you're getting on. I'd understand if you don't want to though, so I'll leave the ball in your court.

Best regards,
Your useless brother-in-law,
Neil

I sit, stunned, the letter still in my hand. Tears are dripping off my chin but I take no notice. If only Bill had known. And poor Neil, carrying that guilt and shame around with him for so many years. No wonder he's a drifter, I think, fingering the staple in the corner of the letter.

Why is there a staple anyway? I gulp some wine. Turn the letter over. And there, attached to the back, is a narrow slip of paper that I hadn't noticed. A money order from a post office I've never heard of. Five hundred dollars, made out to my name. I'm sobbing now, grief flowing for Neil as well as Bill. The whole damn mess of their terrible childhoods.

Of course I'll write back. Neil deserves that much. I will thank him. Tell him about my move. Should I give him my address? Risk having him arrive at my door when I'm all alone out here? I read his letter again, finger the money order. I know in my heart I have nothing to fear from this lost man – the only part of Bill I have left.

1 8

I am captivated by my art, by the sweet shadings and harsh black lines that fill page after page, sending me out to the shops more swiftly than any need for food. It's a full-day excursion, finding somewhere that sells art materials, as well as a supermarket and places where I can buy new boots and clothes and a more service-able hat. Travelling out of the valley spins me out of my dreamy orbit into fast traffic and jarring noises. It's a relief to be back on the ferry, heading home.

In the morning I am up before the sun, ready to draw. I have set Bill's sad carafe on the mantelpiece again, edging his remains towards the door.

And I have rediscovered the watercolour pencils, exquisite shades of gold and violet and emerald green, and every colour of a rainbow, in close-up. Experiment with blending washes and hard lines, the fine-tipped pens.

Morning blurs into early afternoon. I have fed the dog, drunk coffee, eaten food. Worked pages slew all over the table, some stacked according to subject, others yet to be consigned. I feel as though I am waking up, working towards a goal or an achievement without knowing what it might be. Walden materialises over and over again – aerial views, imagined flowers rioting on the roof. Walden underground, its foundations like fat-toed feet deep in loamy earth, reaching for the river's hidden flow. Walden on a magic carpet ride, surveying worlds beyond the ridges.

And Bill. Bill naked, lying languid or flexing muscles as a joke. Bill on the fucking bike, his bones shattered and organs hanging out. Bill with glowing white angel's wings, longer than his body, luxuriant with feathers and softest down. Bill as a handful of glinting ash.

Maybe it's this focus on Bill that brings back the bird? I dash outside. That strong, pure melody is running shivers the length of my spine. I don't want to frighten it away. Then again, I have noticed in the past it seems quite bold. There it is! Right there on the pergola crossbeam, head tilted to one side, willing me to look and find. This time, I hear Bill's voice clearly, as though he were right beside me.

'Angel, Ange. Keep drawing, start painting again. When you focus like that you make it easy for me to dissolve the veils.'

I reach out and rest my hand on the back of a chair, keeping a grip on reality.

'Darling, Bill, I don't know how to do it. If I try harder, can I see you? Feel you?'

There's a sighing in the silence of shifting air, a shimmer. And then he's gone. I feel corporality lock back in. The bird sings its perfect tune again, never taking its eye off me, daring me to disbelieve. Or hope.

Tashie is whining and yipping behind the screen door, desperate to come outside. What did she see, or hear? I need a drink. No. No drinking in the afternoon, not alone. Not that slippery path. Shower's a better idea. I realise I have barely eaten anything all day. Okay. Get practical.

Once I am clean and dressed I'll do a load of washing, organise a healthy meal, tend the garden. I should start pulling out weeds. There are hay bales stacked inside the mesh for spreading as mulch. Jobs to do. Life's not all wine and coloured pencils. Or loving ghosts.

I am talking out loud to myself, touching the earthen walls, checking what's real. But I know it was him. Turning the moment around and around in my mind, I recall the faint whiff of Bill's leathers and Sunlight soap and male. There must be books that shed light on experiences like this?

Now the sun has slipped over the ridge I can do my garden thing, take Tashie with me, let her run in her yard while I set up for tomorrow's major onslaught. I have a new plan – to get my hands in the dirt, rein in the leafy chaos, pull these gardens back into shape. If I rise really early, before the heat sets in, I can achieve a lot. But first, there is a ceremony to get through.

Stagnating heat merges with evening drone as cicadas herald the night and a huge pearly moon rises over the eastern ridge. Essie and Liz are here. We have all gathered mementoes to send with Bill into the stream, and we put them with the carafe into a sturdy basket by the door.

'I feel like he'll be walking with us,' I confess, and both of them smile.

'It's natural to think like that.' Liz. Keeping me calm.

We close the door carefully on Tashie, leaving her in the house. And begin our procession towards the river's edge. Without laying plans, we have dropped silently into single file well before we arrive at the track. Twigs shift beneath our feet and a silver gleam lights the way, our walking and breathing aligned with the pulse of nature's serenade.

I am carrying the basket of remnants, cradled in both arms. A final embrace. And stop at the grassy mound. On the far side of the river an owl mourns at the dark. I put the basket on the ground and straighten up, determined to speak.

'Bill, darling, I sense you're here. That this ash is no more you than the clothes you used to wear.' Tears roll down my cheeks and I feel arms slip around my waist and shoulders as Ess and Liz prop me up. 'We all have to move on,' I continue, 'and this timing feels right. I love you and let you go.'

There are sweet words from Liz and Essie too, and the melody of 'Amazing Grace' quivers into the gleaming night. We reach down to the basket and lift items one by one to release. Until, at last, the carafe. From which the cork comes easily. And the job is done.

As the fine particles of ash merge with the water that flows past our feet I hear Bill's voice, strong and clear. 'I love you, Angel, I always will. Part of me will always be with you.' Surely Ess and Liz hear it too? Although they don't mention it.

We have brought with us a bottle of red, one of Bill's favourite vintages, and sit by the sighing water to share it with him. 'L'chaim!' Essie says, raising her glass. 'To life – in this world and the next!'

19

Something's wrong with the pump. Every time I try to start it there's a growl and a splutter, then it dies. Dammit. I stuck to my morning work plans and the garden is being transformed. Neat rows of baby lettuces, riots of marigolds, masses of tiny tomatoes, tender basil nearby, the herb patch orderly again. Food every-where. I checked Jane's books to make sure I only pulled out weeds. I've left the chickweed and the milk thistle and wonder whether Jane ever cooked them.

I will have to call Clyde about the pump. The water will be low in the back tank if I don't get it going it in the next few days. No rain forecast. I give thanks again for the river running at our boundary. Wander inside for a shower.

When I phone Clyde there's no answer. He's probably out feeding the horses. From what I've heard, they get fed before he eats, morning and night. He's handfeeding a lot these days, with so little pasture left. I've left a message for him.

Maybe I should bake a cake. More and more, I understand Jane's library is a treasure. She has mini-catalogued it in the red book, and I spend an hour browsing well-thumbed food-stained pages. Basic Butter Cake – can be adapted by separating the mixture into three lots, then adding cocoa, vanilla essence and red food colouring. Swirl the mixtures in layers in the tin, and presto – marble cake. Ice with rich dark chocolate icing. Yum! Her Christmas pudding – prepare at least three months ahead. I make a mental note. But it's the carrot cake that grabs me. I have brought bunches of sweet baby carrots up from the garden and cannot resist. I can pass it off as healthy food as well.

The phone rings just as I put the cake tin in the oven. An accent that could be American, deep voice, surprisingly slow. Then I realise it's Hayden, who tells me Clyde has gone into town for a couple of days to sort out some business. He's supervising the watermelon harvest, he says, but could come over tomorrow evening and look at the pump for me, if I can wait that long.

I am struck by the kindness of strangers. And feel awkward that I didn't recognise his voice. Hayden doesn't seem old enough to be running the show, but Clyde must trust him. He turns down my offer of dinner, says he'll be over about eight. Are my torches working? What tools do I have? Practical talk, then he's gone and the silence surrounds me again.

The night air is filling with tantalising aromas of baking cake. Time to take it out of the oven. And to sort my sketches, dreaming storylines as I stack them into themes. Images of Bill and Maddie and Bob shift and reconfigure, forming from lines and shapes and shadows, coming together in visions of canvases that might chronicle my life. No tears, just inspiration and vague stirrings recalling other times and gentle touch. Tomorrow, I'll paint.

In the night I dream of Bill – a strange, disturbing Bill who taunts me from the riverbed, slinks around corners, slides from my reaching hands. I wake in the dark, sticky and grubby in tangled sheets, uneven breath coming fast, my heart thumping. I don't want him like that. Bill was never like that. Was he? He was kind and considerate and good. Who is this demon apparition driving away sleep? The tears are back. Perhaps I haven't released him at all. I want to jump up, get dressed, yank myself from the mire of misery. But my body rolls and groans on the bed, thrashing and pounding, keening, weeping. In the hot damp mess of the night I grieve the loss of his touch, slide the palms of my hands down my sides, contour my hips, reaching for solace. Fingertips – are they mine or his? – caress my face, gently thumbing tears away, tracing cheekbones, stroking swollen eyes. My body is stretching, arching, feet planted, knees stretched wide. Waves of contorted anguish flow through me, tweaking my nipples, firming my breasts, throbbing deep into my womb. A roar shatters the sky, hurling me spent and sobbing into the darkness.

I must have fallen back into a deep and murky sleep beyond the realm of dreams. There is bright daylight by the time my eyes blur open. I have missed the dawn, my favourite time of every day.

I wander out to the kitchen. Take Tashie out for a wee. The cake looks cold and rubbery on its wire rack, and my mouth tastes sour. Thank goodness there is water in the house tank. I talk myself into a stinging shower, make coffee, feed the dog. She is anxious, soft paw patting at my knee, wanting to know I'm alright. Gorgeous girl.

It's too hot to work in the studio, but the imperative to paint clutches at my belly, driving me out of the house, propelling me towards the sweatbox over by the river track. I'll collect what I need, bring it back.

In less than an hour the space inside the cottage is transformed, three canvases propped on chairs and an easel, makeshift arrangements to serve my urgent need. I have two palettes going – one daubed with oozing globules of dirty reds, harsh browns and black, the other a cottage garden riot of pastels and shades of pink. In a frenzy of creation I douse myself in rage, emerging eventually in some kind of reconfigured trance to bathe in the still, soft forms of a bowl of roses taking shape on a small canvas I have separated from the other two. Bill has asked me to paint, and paint I will.

I am shocked when the light begins to fade, weary at the prospect of becoming a civilised woman who can talk about pumps and water tanks, a person who can be polite.

The brushes need cleaning and the room's a collage of abstract signs of madness. I need to recompose myself, and make frosting for the salvaged cake.

By the time Hayden knocks at the door a minor miracle has taken place. The rose bowl canvas, delicate work in progress, is leaning against the chimney bricks, and all evidence of dark eruptions is hidden away. The cake rests on one of Jane's gilt-edged floral plates, covered by an old-fashioned net dome to keep flies away. I am a fresh illusion in cotton shirt and pants with washed hair and a sane smile.

He's keen to get going, make the most of the failing light. 'Tell me again what it's been doing?' he says, as we walk to the low wooden shelter that houses the pump. I do my non-technical best – yes, I've checked the fuel feed. I think I primed it the right way. No, I doubt any dust or water could have got in. As a near-full moon floats up over the ridge, my job is to hold the torch and fetch tools.

His quiet, methodical approach is reassuring. I wonder how a guy this young has learned these things, seems to know his way so well around farming and machines. In my drifting mind Canada is a vast expanse atop the continental map of the Americas, a mysterious conjurer of deep green forests and snow-smothered peaks, Mounties in quaint red jackets, non-European people who speak French.

'That should do it,' he says, straightening up, wiping grease from his hands. He flicks the switch and we hear the reassuring sound of the motor. Thank god for that!

'Anything else needs looking at while I'm here?'

Kindness of strangers again. 'I haven't been here long enough to discover what might need fixing,' I say. 'Anyway, you must be exhausted. You've already done more than enough. I'm really grateful.'

Silvered shadows slip and shift through the trees as we walk back to the house. I might never get used to its living roof, the way it snugs into the earth. Hayden's not seen anything like it either, talks quietly about how he loves being here in the valley and about his grandfather's place back home in Canada.

He is happy to come in for cake and tea, content to sit for a few minutes at the end of the day.

I am not too surprised when he speaks of First Nation blood, of a grandfather steeped in traditional wisdom and the old ways. There's something in the angle of his jaw, and the long black hair tied neatly back at the nape of his neck.

He is travelling for a few years, now that his grandfather has passed away. Walking and working out the pain, he says. Keeping close to the earth, trying to put into practice the things his grandpa taught him as a child. It's fascinating, his views on family and the land. He eats slowly, with respect, but after a while almost half the cake is gone. In some ways he still seems like a boy.

'Well, time to say goodbye,' he says eventually, stretching as he stands. 'Clyde's back early tomorrow morning. I'll be moving on soon and I want to spend some time with him before I go.'

'You mean really goodbye?' I am taken by surprise. I thought he would be staying another week or two.

'I've promised some people I'll help out with their stone fruit harvest. I need to get on the road again.'

There's a restlessness behind the ease and I wonder what might be driving him, keeping him from staying still too long.

Silvery moonlight paints night magic on the ground when we step outside. 'Wow! Will you look at that!' he exclaims, and again I see the little boy. 'Have you ever been down to the river when the moon's full?' As if he knew.

The track is illuminated almost as though by dawn, insects cricking and chirruping in the undergrowth. He walks straight to the spot where Ess and Liz and I recently sat, takes off his boots and shirt, drops his jeans. 'You coming in?' He's laughing, a big kid let loose, wading out into the river, feeling with his feet for rocks and snags before he vanishes in a sheen of moonlit ripples. God, it looks like fun!

I've thought about swimming here but didn't know if it was safe. What the hell. I am down to my underwear before I can think any more, feeling the warm water lapping at my calves, washing at my knees. And then I'm in.

It's sublime, the shock of immersion, sweet clear sense of effortless grace. Moonlight burnishes our world and I am free, swooping down to clutch fistfuls of sand, bursting the surface with diamonds, hair plastered to my head and down my back. Hayden has swum way up past the bend and it's a while before I catch sight of him, long arms stroking rhythmically through the water, making barely any sound. He pulls up beside me, laughing, flicking hair and water droplets, his eyes shining.

'Hey, Angelica, race you to the tree!'

And we're off, twin dolphins frolicking, each of us wanting to be first, for the sheer joy of it.

That tree is a gnarled old willow, drooping its delicate fringe almost to the water's edge, showing me a shady place for future days. We rest for a moment, then we're off again, ducking and diving, splashing and playing like kids. Our hands touch when we dive, thrilling, electric, bringing us up close together, face to face. He is beautiful. And completely unaware. Frankness in his gaze, dark eyes gleaming with delight. And admiration.

'Your mom gave you the right name, Angelica,' he says softly, as he reaches to move strands of hair from my face. 'You look like an angel. Or maybe a water nymph ...'

Suddenly I am shy, self-conscious. Yet bold. 'And you could be the spirit of the river,' I murmur, brushing droplets from his cheek.

There's no other way now but intimate, nothing to do but adore. No world but this perfect moment. It's languid and gentle, slow quickening to bliss, sliding of bodies, entwining of limbs. This boy knows about love.

By the time we stagger back to the bank, we have shared worlds of tears, loved every tender place in each other's hearts and souls, bodies the medium for easing layers of loneliness and grief. My mind says I should feel guilty, that I am betraying Bill, but how could this be wrong? This sweetness that feels so pure.

He stands me in front of him, running his hands down my arms and the length of my body, down to my feet. 'Let's get you dry, gorgeous Angel.'

Balmy air brushes damp skin, drying us in minutes, leaving us hours for talking and tenderness as the moon glides across the valley.

Up above the dark shadow of the eastern ridge there is a faint lightening in the sky. In a short while, the birds will start their greeting chorus. This moment will fade to its end.

We have no idea where our underclothes are, and dress each other slowly in jeans and shirts, pulling on boots to make the long walk back into our other lives. Hayden has to go, wants to be there to help Clyde feed the horses. I have stories to tell myself, mysteries to fathom, dishes to wash and a dog to feed.

We know he is leaving and promise there will be no tears. Speak of planning one more meeting before he goes. I am standing taller and stronger as I wave his ute away, listen to the first stir-rings of birdsong, turn and walk inside.

20

It is going to be another stinking hot day and I want to paint. Everything I need is in the house. A kind of waking dream carries me through my early morning chores, suspending me between delicious reminiscence and sickening guilt. How could I have gone so easily into the arms of another man? I didn't stop to consider that Bill might be around, to think of ash mingled with sand and river water. I feel euphoric and filthy, wanton. If only I could talk to someone. But I am too ashamed to tell Ess. Afraid Aunty Fran would think less of me if I told her. And Sage is out of the question.

Yet time has a way of passing, no matter how you feel. I've worked that out at last – that nothing stays the same. I have started new canvases now, one of Bill in his angel suit, the other of Hayden. I am trying to paint some sense into the turmoil of my mind and heart and body. What would Bill say? What did he say? Surely he told me I could contact him via the paintings? Something like that? I've put on a soothing CD that is driving me mad – syrupy streamings of violins and harp. Maybe good hard rock and roll would suit me better on a day like this. Or the radio. Any other voice would be welcome in my head right now.

Clyde phones late in the afternoon. He wants us all to meet for dinner at the pub, to say farewell to Hayden. Who is leaving in the morning. I hear myself agreeing to the plan, telling him I'll meet them there, that I have things to do in the village. The prospect of squeezing into Clyde's ute with Hayden is more than I can contemplate. I have no idea how I will comport myself this evening.

Clothes drop to the bedroom floor, pile up on the bed. I have nothing to wear. Yesterday, it didn't matter. Tonight, it's impossible to choose. I sense Hayden doesn't care, that he sees straight into my soul, but I feel like a girl on a date. About to have my heart broken again. Or is it not like that? He was talking by the river about other ways of seeing and feeling, about the wisdom his grandfather taught. When I focus on that way of understanding, calm seeps through. We don't own anything, he told me. The joy of holding is in letting go. We are all connected. There were strange words he used for that – I can't recall. He said that we could always contact each other simply by thinking. And he told me I could do it that way with Bill, too. No shame. No ownership. No regrets.

This way of thinking is spinning my mind. Where is the morality in it all? What does commitment mean? Or love?

I choose a simple dress that hangs loose and soft from shoe-string straps. Pale creamy yellow, like the blossoms on Essie's Lady Hellinger rose. Faces of Bill follow me around the house, gazing out of photo montages, larger than life on the canvas that has him with wings. What does he think? How does he feel? I am so angry with him for deserting me, yet aching to have him here. So weary of the whole damn thing.

It turns out to be easy, at the pub. Everyone is mellow and melted at this end of a sweltering day. Essie has been working in

141

her garden early each morning, getting up before dawn. She is missing Liz, wishes that she could have gone to New Zealand with her. *C'est la vie*, she says. It won't be for long – Liz will be home in less than a week. And hopefully, this time, she will finally be ready to talk to Ess about her past.

Over dinner, Clyde tells us about the crop, offering to drop a couple of watermelons off on his way into the city in the morning. He's not sure how he's going to get everything done.

I hear my own voice offering to drive Hayden to the station and wonder if everybody knows. Do we have signs on our foreheads? If we do, no one seems to care.

Hayden is easy and gracious as always, not drinking, I notice. In fact, I've not seen him drink anything but water or tea, not even on Christmas Day. Why is that? So many small intimacies we will never share, this young man and I, this one who has shown me his soul.

I will pick him up at Clyde's gate in the morning and drive him into the city to catch a train. Everyone is happy with the plan. Ess asks if I can grab a few things for her on the way home, save her a shopping trip. I will buy groceries for Clyde as well. Valley time, valley ways. I have almost forgotten any other style.

The edge of the sun is lighting the top of the ridge as I pull in beside Clyde's gate. I slept deep and soundly last night, too tired for monsters or torment. Hayden has only a backpack and a soft shoulder satchel. Travelling light. Full of light. And shade. He makes our greeting easy, leaning over to touch my cheek, to kiss me softly. 'This was a perfect plan, Angel. Thank you for being my taxi driver.'

We have fun, singing and laughing as we drive, bewitched by the river as it comes alive with morning light. As we pull up behind a couple of commuters in the ferry queue, I realise I have not been out of the valley for a week or more, and ripples of excitement surprise me when I think of the city buzz. Maybe I'll drop in on Andrea once Hayden is on the train.

On the drive into town we relish every moment, our moods shifting between flirtatiously light-hearted and sad. Hayden is on his way to inner journeys that leave no space for commitment or long-term plans. I too have roads to walk that no one else can map, a trail behind me I still don't fully fathom. We are gentle and strong with each other's hearts, respectful. He uses that word a lot.

Central Railway Station's sandstone colonnades frame his lean figure as he turns for that final wave, eyes alight with uncomplicated love, and dreamy with anticipation of what might be up ahead. We have shared more in a couple of days than many touch on in lifetimes. I watch the sleek black of his hair disappear into the crowd, a young guy striding free and clear into his future.

The car knows its way to Luca's cafe, as though it went there only yesterday. Andy is thrilled to see me, arms wide open for hugs, a hundred questions spilling out.

'Angel! Look at you! All tanned and glowing! I haven't seen you like this for ...'

She stands back, sizing me up and down, beaming, heading for the espresso machine. 'We have the best Portuguese tarts. Luca himself made them just this morning. Sit down and tell me everything.'

It is a spool back in time and the news pours out. I paint vivid word pictures of the cottage that grows from the earth, its astonishing roof, the river, the moon and the heat, the time spent with Ess. The landscape gives me plenty to talk about, smoothing over raw and painful places and recent joy. Andy is captivated, insists on making me a hearty breakfast when she hears how early I left the valley. She tells me Angelo and Sabina love my house, still feel it's a blessing that we met. And then I'm on the road again.

At the last supermarket before the suburbs turn to bush I work through everybody's lists, stocking up on basics and treats, filling two Eskies with the perishable stuff. Filling my mind with busy.

I have time and space enough on the drive home to search invisible realms for Hayden, to try and contact Bill. To give confusion room to thrash about before I rein it in. None of this makes sense when I put it into thoughts but I feel every intimacy in my body. I have become more solid in the past few days, more substantial. The parts of me that have been missing are coming back, adding flesh to bony structures, streaming through my blood. Before I know it, the car is sweeping down the hairpins towards the ferry. I have driven the long road without noticing, lost in soul journeying, seeking meaning.

I do a circuit, delivering groceries to Ess, stopping to chat. Yes, Hayden got away just fine. Traffic was okay. City hasn't changed. She'll see for herself in a few days' time when she goes to fetch Lizzie from the airport.

Tashie jumps into the car, tongue hanging out, happy from her visit, and we head up the road to Clyde's.

He is out in the hill paddock when we get there, heaving bales of lucerne hay onto the back of the ute. The hillside is pale and dry, witness to the long drought, silently pleading for rain. We talk about Hayden. Clyde liked the young guy, saw something in him that you don't see much these days, some kind of inner strength and depth. Maybe you'd call it integrity, he says. He mentions that he has a forwarding address for Hayden in Canada, if I ever want to get in touch.

21

I have to contact Bill. Didn't he say painting will help make it easy? Yet I have painted my brushes bare and not heard a whisper from him. Maybe he's angry with me?

In the window of the general store I have seen a small notice advertising meditation days. Or is it weekend retreats? Maybe I should try that again? I am in the car, Tashie grinning by my side, raising dust plumes in the lane. I've taken to leaving the gate open of late. What the hell? Who's going to intrude, all the way out here? Slowly, I am becoming a local, beginning to trust.

There are a few people sitting at tables on the store's verandah. It's still early, and the day is yet to gather to its stifling extremes. A couple wave, the woman calls out g'day. Invites me to join them for a cuppa. Why not? It's been a very small circle in the valley – just Ess and Liz and Clyde. Time to show friendly intentions. And I won't look so odd, just checking the notice-board and disappearing. It turns out to be Janet, the woman who owns the store, who comes back to sit with me once she's made a pot of tea. Strong and black, steaming, made the way it should be, she says, with the water right on the boil. We sort out the ritual of milk – just a splash – and sugar – not for me, thanks – while the slow interrogation begins. They know a lot about me. That I am Essie's twin, that Bill was killed in some kind of terrible accident. They even know where I used to live. The grapevine is flourishing, despite or perhaps because of the drought.

'Somebody told me you're an artist,' says Janet. 'Is that right?'

I am mystified until she reveals that her cousin works in the art supply shop in Middleton. Oh my. The network extends.

'I dabble a bit. Just for myself really.'

She wants to know if there's anything I could put up for sale in the gallery at the far end of the store. Jane used to sell her pots there, I remember.

We wander in to have a look and I am struck by the light streaming through high triangular windows and the stained-glass panels in the doors. There's an impressive collection on show – rings and necklaces and other jewellery in glass-topped counter displays, some interesting local landscapes hung around the walls and on wide central pillars, blue-glazed bowls and mugs on shelves alongside hand-carved wooden eggs. Janet takes a small commission, she says, and enjoys the company of city types who wander in to browse. They spend money in the store as well, so it all works out. She is kind, this woman, behind the fierce exterior.

I tell her I'll bring in a couple of my paintings and she can decide whether they're the kinds of things she's happy to hang.

Maybe she knows something about the meditation people – of course she does. They're always polite, she tells me. A bit strange, though, like a lot of those hippie types. Don't eat meat. Don't smoke or drink. Probably don't even have sex. Each to their own.

I copy down the website and phone number, turn to walk down the steps.

'If you're into that kind of thing,' says Janet, 'you might want to meet Sally. She sits at that end table second Sunday of every month and does readings. You know, woo woo stuff. Cards and crystals and the like.'

They put up a screen, Janet tells me, so people can feel a bit private. Sally's always got a queue waiting, mainly tourists, but Janet's friend Pauline had a reading with her once and you wouldn't believe the things that came out. She even talked to Pauline's dead grandmother. Amazing.

I really have to get away. Buy a litre of milk and the paper, and tell Janet I'll drop in next time I'm passing through, to show her my work.

At home, I put the milk in the fridge, then phone the meditation centre. The voice on their answering machine is deep and soothing. I leave a message, enquiring about the retreat.

But my thoughts keep returning to Sally, the woman who does readings. It is only five days till the second Sunday of the month. The second Sunday of this year. Aunty Fran believes in psychics and mystics, has sat with many during her travels. My mind wanders, doing its best to avoid what I'm fixated on – the hope and the fear that maybe this Sally person can contact Bill for me. Janet said she spoke to her friend's grandmother. Doesn't that mean she's a medium? It's exactly what I'm seeking, but now it's on offer, I'm scared. What if she's a fraud? What if she tells me things I don't want to hear? What if she can see too much, see into the dark corners of my secret self?

To distract myself with practicalities, I have decided to set up my files in the corner cabinet. Take all our documents out of their hessian bag, store them away. I make a file devoted to Bill: his academic achievements, a few newspaper clippings, his birth and death certificates. His passport shows a younger Bill, late twenties, just before we headed off to China and Japan. What a trip that was. I can't quite see what he was wearing. A black t-shirt maybe? It might have been the one we bought in Byron Bay, the one with an eagle hand-painted on the back. Soft tears flow as I stroke his face. My heart is broken. But when I rest my hand on it, the beat is steady and strong.

Reproachful memories of Hayden's lean brown body slide across my fingertips. Hayden. Bill. So different, yet in my mind the same. No. That's wrong. There's no comparison. No way or reason to compare.

I slam the cabinet drawer closed, cringe at its metallic clatter, then turn to face another day. Keeping busy. Painting, cooking, gardening, priming the pump.

Some nights I take a torch and walk down to the river to commune with Bill. I slip into its stream in search of solace, come away bathed in lonely dreams. And tumultuous guilt. I will go into the village on Sunday and see how I feel about this woman. Ess probably knows her but I don't want to share these secrets with my sister, at least not yet.

Sally is sitting at the corner table when I walk up the steps at the store. No purple gown or dangling earrings – that's promising. She looks like somebody's mother, a compact woman in a soft grey skirt and singlet top, chin-length wavy brown hair. There is a teenage girl sitting opposite her at the moment, hands clenched, a bunch of tissues in one, listening intently. There are cards laid out on the table, and some crystals neatly lined up in front of the girl. There is no screen.

I have brought three canvases to show Janet – the bowl of roses, a side view of the cottage showing my curving bedroom wall and the extraordinary roof, and a painting of Bill riding his bike. It's a love–hate thing between me and my work. Today I feel critical, seeing angles not quite right and colours that don't represent what I was after. Janet likes them all, though, thinks they'll do well.

We make an arrangement that I'll leave them for six weeks. If they haven't sold by then, I'll take them home. Suddenly, I wonder why I brought the one of Bill. Do I really want to sell it? Janet notices, and hands it back to me.

'Maybe you should hang onto this one for a while,' she says. 'Let's see how the other two go. We don't get many of the bike riders buying paintings – no way they can take them home.'

Again I am aware of her no-fuss brand of kindness, and gratefully carry the canvas back to the boot of my car.

There is no queue for Sally, and the young girl has gone. My turn. It feels too fussy to ask about the screen and there is no one else about.

I ask her how much it will cost, sit down, fidget. She talks a bit about her credentials – years of experience in private practice and at psychic fairs and markets. She sounds reassuringly normal.

'So, Angelica, what can I do for you today? Do you have something specific you want to ask? Or would you like us simply to pull the cards and see what they have to say?'

The question I was dreading. Should I come straight out and tell her about Bill? Or is it wiser to test her?

She senses my hesitation, and hands me a pack of small cards with drawings of children on the back. She explains that she uses these gypsy cards to focus her insights.

I shuffle the deck, and hand her seven, which she places face down on the table between us, her hands hovering just above.

'Before we look at the cards, Angelica, I must mention the man who's come in with you. He's very insistent.'

Wild beating of heart. I can't help it – my hands have flown to my face and there are tears.

'Can you see what he looks like?'

'Oh yes, he's very comfortable about being seen. Not a big man, compact build, with pale sandy hair and a mischievous face. Smile

149

lines around his vivid blue eyes. He's asking me to tell you that he loves you all very much.'

The tears are flowing hard and I realise I am rocking in my chair. I don't know what I expected, but it wasn't this.

'Can you see what he's wearing?'

'Angelica, I'm sorry, I don't want to upset you any further. But he's showing me blood on his clothes. Lots of blood on his coat. It's more of a jacket really – a brown checked jacket. Does any of this mean anything to you?'

I recognised Bob from her first description. Bob. My Dad. Who I never really knew. Who has been waiting all this time to talk to me, apparently. I can't control the sobbing, heaving, trying to speak. Sally reaches out and puts her warm hand over mine.

'It's alright, Angelica, it's alright. He says you're not to upset yourself. The hardest part for him is that the three of you were such little girls when he went. He wants you to know how much he loves you all.'

Slowly the tears subside and the story tumbles out. It feels good to tell a stranger. Sally remembers the accident, of course, the shocking train disaster. So many people died. It occurs to me that my Mum was with him then, but doesn't seem to be here now.

'There's a woman with him, a sweet young thing. She's showing me her wedding ring. Is this your mother? She looks very much like you, but with shorter darker hair, cut in a bob.'

A great wave of heat passes through my belly and I'm afraid I'll wet myself. My insides are letting go. The heat surges up into my gut, bursting from my heart like joy. Gasping, laughing, crying. I thought they were gone, but they're here with me. That old weight of loss and desolation is dissolving as I think of the photo Aunty Fran kept on the dresser all our growing up years. 'There's your lovely Mum,' she would say. 'See how much she looks like all of you? She'd just had her hair cut short the week before ...' And then she'd turn away, hiding grief from her three little girls. 'And your

Dad. Such a natty dresser. It was one of the things Maddie noticed the first time they met.' And she would tell us how he had recently bought a new jacket for travelling to and from work.

There's an entire tribe, Sally says, with grandfathers and aunts and uncles lined up in generations reaching back through time. Sally explains that the spirits of these people have long since passed into the light (I want to ask her what she means) and that they are showing us recognisable representations of their past human incarnations, for my reassurance, to help me believe.

She sounds so matter-of-fact and comfortable with these convincing visions, it's hard for me to maintain scepticism. And there's the jacket and the blood. Maddie's haircut.

'These are not the griefs you carry with you though,' she is saying. 'It's the other young man, the one with the leather jacket. He's the one you really need to hear about.'

The velvety darkness of swoon sweeps through me and I grip the table, drop my head between my knees. It's all too much. Too many of them at once. I am spinning away from the valley, this place, this woman.

Until a deep comforting warmth begins to pulse between my shoulder blades. Sally is standing behind me, one hand on my arm, the other in the middle of my back. I don't know what she's doing but she should never stop. Warmth and peace radiate through me, wave after wave, deeper and deeper peace. My chin raises, eyes open. The store and the table are gilded. Have I died and gone to heaven?

Then Sally is sitting opposite me again, holding my hands across the table. Her eyes are fixed on mine, compassion and concern vying with a radiant smile. 'So, Angelica, tell me about him.'

It all floods out – the nightmare knock at the door, police car ride with sirens to the ICU, the decision to donate Bill's organs. Until she stops me.

'He wants to communicate with you, Angelica. He's been waiting a while – I'm finding it hard to hold him back.'

Her voice deepens, hands fall to her lap, eyelids close. In the next few minutes, as the scent of leather wafts around us, Sally passes on messages from Bill – that he loves me, that he's pleased I've noticed the bird. After the ceremony with his ashes, he understands that he's free to transcend to the light. He shows her an image of me painting, and smiles. And he makes it clear that I have nothing to feel guilty about.

Some of it is cryptic, yet I have no doubt that Bill is with us.

Sally slumps back in the chair, slowly opening her eyes and returning to her natural state. We look at each other, two women on a country store verandah, immersed in awe and gratitude.

'It's unusual for spirit to come through so clearly,' she says, after a while. 'He must have loved you very much, Angelica.'

We don't turn the little gypsy cards face-up. There seems to be no need. Sally gives me her business card, invites me to call if I want to ask more questions or speak with her again. She has written down a short list of books I might find interesting, including one on Reiki, the technique she used to calm me earlier on.

In the space of an hour and for sixty dollars, my world has turned. I have many more questions than answers, yet the feelings of peace and love remain.

22

Liz is home from New Zealand and they want me to go for dinner. She has tales to tell of family members doing it tough, weddings, funerals, innovative programs at the marae keeping the young people on track. The abundant seafood. The best ice cream in the world. But when I glance across at Essie, I sense her distress. Clearly, Liz remains determined to skirt around the real reasons for her regular visits back home.

Ess changes tack. 'What have you been up to, Ange?' she asks. 'Whatever it is, don't stop. I haven't seen you looking this good for ages.'

We are relaxing on their back verandah watching wallaroos feed in the gathering dusk. There has been a slight respite from the heat today and the valley is breathing lighter. So am I.

'Janet tells me you had a reading with that woman Sally,' says Liz, out of the blue. 'I've heard she's pretty good.'

Instantly, my heart is racing – do they know what else I've done?

'She's a medium,' I reply, keeping my voice steady. 'You know – talks to dead people.'

An owl calls on the hill, calls again, haunting.

'She could see Mum and Dad.'

Liz reaches for Essie's hand, offering a safe haven from the impending storm.

'What do you mean, "See Mum and Dad"? Did they say anything? How do you know it was really them?'

Candles glow in metal holders, filling the darkness with citronella scent, keeping the mozzies at bay. I tell them about the blood on the brown checked jacket, Maddie's newly bobbed hair, the messages of love. I describe Sally's accurate description of Bill, and the things he said to me. The way her hand beamed super-human heat into my body and took the pain away. I tell them almost everything, excluding Hayden. Keeping him hidden in a place of precarious secrets, no matter what Bill said.

'We have to tell Aunty Fran, Angel. She'd love to hear all this.'

'And Sage?' I say. 'I'm pretty sure she'd tell us this is the work of the Devil, don't you reckon?'

Essie thinks we should try anyway. That Sage deserves to know. But Liz is adamant it would only deepen the chasm that has already grown between us. I have a sickening feeling that Liz is right. But I'm not up to arguing with Ess right now, and sidestep into reminiscing.

We talk about how lucky Ess and I are to have glimmers of memories, faint lingerings of touch and scent that we think might have been our mother, kissing us goodnight. We reflect on the miracle that is Aunty Fran, who loved us, and gave us the child-hoods that could have been destroyed. Nobody mentions Sage again – there's been enough upheaval for one day.

By the time I'm ready to head for home, we have sorted and filed the stories into some kind of sense. Agreed that I should be the one to phone Fran and tell her about it. Answer her questions. Maybe even fill in a few more details.

Liz mentions that most New Zealanders are at ease with spirit conversations. Not with the tough emotional ones though, I think, silently defending my twin.

Ess holds me close for a long hug before they walk down the steps to wave me off.

I breathe a sigh of relief. My stored secret is safe.

'Oh, by the way, I think I'll give that meditation retreat a try,' I say, as I open the car door. 'Do you know anything about it?'

They tell me Clyde speaks highly of the people who run the place. Maybe I should talk to him.

The laneway into Walden greets me like a portal into other realms. Tashie's tail twitches. A fat crescent moon sits high up in the velvet sky, reflecting into swathes of starlight. It feels as though the Milky Way has bridged itself across this valley just for me.

In the morning, I remember fragments of dream, the feeling of seed pods bursting open in moist black soil, life force pulsing through unfurling pale green shoots, and root tendrils seeking the core of the earth.

There's a message on my phone from the meditation man, whose name is Kieran. He says there will be a beginners retreat this coming weekend. Please call and let them know if I'd like to attend.

In the village, buying milk and the paper, I bump into Clyde. He mentions that he has heard from Hayden who is picking peaches down in the Riverina, doing fine. He sends his best regards to everybody here. And I know then that Hayden will keep his word to me, and travel on. No attachments, no regrets. Bill's wisdom floods me, the things he said through Sally about not feeling guilty. I turn away, shielding my wet eyes from Clyde and the brightness of the sun.

'Do you know the way to the meditation centre?' I ask him later, as we carry mugs of tea out onto the store's verandah.

'Ah. They're a good mob over there,' he says. 'You're planning on going to one of their weekends?'

He draws a mud map on the back of the newspaper, talks about the road. 'You'll be right so long as it doesn't rain,' says Clyde. 'And there's not much chance of that.'

He recommends I check my tyre pressures, fill up with fuel, have a look under the bonnet at fluid levels. Sound country advice.

'The food's great, I've heard,' he continues. 'Best vegetarian nosh outside of the city, so they say.'

He is a strong, easy presence, this white-haired man. No wonder Ess and Liz have grown fond of him.

'Maybe when you get back you can come over and tell me all about it,' he's saying, and I ponder again his interest in mysterious things.

'I'll definitely do that,' I tell him. 'And there's something else I'd like to discuss with you too.'

He raises an eyebrow, enquiring.

'It's about Liz,' I say. 'Whatever it is that she's not telling Essie is really driving a wedge between them. You're good friends with both of them. I'm hoping you might be able to help in some way.'

Clyde leans back in his chair, silent for a while. 'Hmmm. Well, I'll think about it. See what I can do.'

More silence as we finish our tea.

'Best be off,' he says, standing up. 'I have to go into town and sort out some business. You need anything while I'm there?'

I tell him thank you but no, searching his eyes for a hint at what else he might be thinking. But he's a closed book.

Then I head for my car, needing to get home and start a new painting, work with that image from my dream of the sprouting seed. It's a different form for me and my hands are buzzing at the thought of it.

* * *

The road to the meditation centre is more of a track after the turn-off, climbing steadily through dense bush and pale golden outcrops of rock. With Tashie safely ensconced at Ess's place, I am free to focus purely on me. I sense that I have entered a world where natural law prevails, where human intrusions barely exist and my vehicle is allowed passage only by virtue of grace. The air vibrates with the scent of eucalyptus, so fresh that the soft dust from my wheels is a distinct entity. A raven has led me much of the way since I entered this terrain. I wonder whether it has any significance, with its jet plumage and strange white eyes. Far below, the river cuts a silvered swathe through parched fields past cottages and outhouses, bales of hay, occasional livestock.

It is early morning, very still, and not yet hot. The seed painting sits on an easel beside the fireplace at home – emerald greens and rich, dark browns spiralling from a point of shimmering light. I loved painting it, loved the feeling of being overcome, of some other force wielding the brush, blending colour, recreating form. Already there is a series in my imagination, a mysterious progression into life. I don't know yet what will emerge – but I trust that the seed will show me.

The raven's harsh call brings me back to the present and I am shocked that my thoughts could have wandered from the track, from the majestic vista of tall gums glistening in this early morning light. As the car slows to ease around a left-hand bend, I see a clearing up ahead, a carved wooden signpost: 'Retreat Centre'. It's intriguing, this place, spiralling inwards on itself, small neat cottages arranged around a central hall. Hand-painted signs on timber posts direct me towards the office but a couple of hundred metres before I reach it another sign asks me to park the car and walk.

There is no one around, although prayer flags flutter from one of the buildings and a kookaburra eyes me silently from a high branch. The cool fresh air is vibrant with bird calls and the soft ticking sounds of insects hard at work. Even my footsteps take on meaning, quietly announcing my arrival. Sandstone is an integral part of this place, forming the lower walls of almost all the cottages, rough hewn and square cut, solid yet soft.

I am thinking of sitting on the bench outside the office when a door opens and a small man emerges dressed in white. For a moment I think he is an apparition, so silent is his approach.

'You must be Angelica. Welcome. I see the place has already begun to cast its spell on you.'

Kieran asks me to walk as we talk, winding our way around paths that lead past each of the buildings and eventually back to my car, where I collect my bag. The hall at the centre of the spiralling paths is dedicated solely to meditation, with a smaller building set aside for more informal meetings and occasional classes, and other dwellings where community members live. At the furthest end, a cluster of three small cottages offers rooms for visitors.

There are eight of us booked in for this weekend's retreat. Two are already here; the others are on their way. We will be housed in separate groups, the women in the cottage with rose bushes growing by the door, the men further away, a little closer to the trees.

He leaves me to unpack and settle in. Everyone will be gathering at the conversation cottage in about an hour – a bell will ring. Kieran asks me to put away any clocks and turn off my mobile phone. There is no reception here and in any case, we will operate on nature's time, working with the rhythms of the earth, moon and sun.

In the cottage, a quiet woman with pale, silky long hair is standing by the kitchen window. She turns and smiles, nods hello, picks up her cup of tea. I feel a little awkward about speaking but don't want to be impolite. It turns out she is a regular here and has put her bag in the end room. Her husband is over in the cottage with the men. There's a sense that our stories don't matter, that we have truly entered inner realms for rest and contemplation. I choose a room across the hall, the one with pale green walls and a window that looks out into the bush.

In the next few minutes, two more women arrive – one feisty and boisterous, bustling the serenity with her fiery eyes and swishing turquoise skirt. The other is older, walks with a stick and needs our help to bring in her bag and get settled. We will quietly assist her, each of us, over the course of the next day or so.

Lunch is a simple and delicious array of steamed grains, aromatic curries and salads that look like art. It is followed by an awareness walk – no talking – along the creek and past a massive sandstone cave hidden deep in the bush.

Afterwards, we sit in the sacred space of the meditation hall, spines straight, legs crossed, firm pillows underneath our bums, the older lady on a chair. Already we have listened to introductory talks, and engaged in question time. When the bell signals silence, we are guided quietly by Kieran to focus on our breath, to feel the air moving through our bodies, the rise and fall of the chest.

During an early supper, Kieran and other retreat centre residents talk about awareness development techniques – how to lie for hours on your belly and observe what happens in a forest clearing, how to sit silent for half an hour beside a particular plant day after day, observing microcosms. They have learned from indigenous elders, from Buddhists and from mystics, and on this retreat are teaching basic ways they say have worked for them and countless others.

That night, I sleep a deep and dreamless sleep. When the dawn chorus wakes me, I feel refreshed. Calmer than I have felt in a long time.

During our early morning meditation, once our breathing has settled, Kieran's soft voice guides us to visualise brilliant sunlight striking the floor and to breathe it up from our feet and the base of our spine, filling our auras with radiant light that clears and heals. It feels wonderful.

After lunch, when we sit to meditate, I practise this again – breathing the golden light of the sun up through my entire body, feeling a deepening sense of peace as my energy field expands. And I am rewarded in ways I could never have imagined.

As I sit, gently breathing in and out, my aura filled with golden-white light, I become aware of the scent of leather – essence of Bill. And then he is with me, sitting close and facing me, a gentle smile on his beautiful face. I sense more than see his hand reach forward and touch my hair. Watch in awe as he stands, blows me a kiss, dissolves into the radiance and disappears. A feeling of bliss envelopes me; a profound peace approaching ecstasy. No thoughts. No feelings. Breathing in grace; breathing out serenity.

23

Why do I feel so queasy?

I have taken to getting up at dawn every day and meditating as the sun rises, letting its first rays strike the earth at my feet, fill me with radiance and, most mornings, the deep sense of peace and serenity that travelled home with me from the retreat. But today my stomach is playing up, although I can't remember eating anything that could have been off. Maybe there is something dodgy in the water tank.

I have an appointment with Sally for another reading. Need to shower and go. She lives across the river, not far from town. Perhaps the drive will do me good. Secretly, I'm hoping her insights will confirm what I experienced with Bill at the retreat. Tears have come only rarely in the past week or so.

My seed triptych occupies three easels in the living room. I have pushed some of the furniture aside for a better view, new perspectives. Radio National is my new best friend, rhythming my days, keeping me and Tashie inside in the cool with the paintings until the heat retreats at evening and I go out to tend the garden. I still walk down to the river at night and sometimes I swim, caressing my body through the silvery stream, thinking of Hayden and Bill, of love's mysteries, of letting go.

I have not had time yet to catch up with Clyde. Maybe I'll call him when I get back from seeing Sally. Tell him about the retreat, and check whether he has spoken to Liz.

I turn right as I drive off the ferry, away from Lawsons Landing with its pub and shops, and wind my way along the riverside road. Steep sandstone embankments flank me to the left, receding after a while to reveal a cluster of cottages with picket fences and neatly tended gardens.

Sally's place is number seven but I would have picked it anyway, from the rainbow mobile twirling at the door and fairy statues peeping from garden nooks. As if to announce my arrival, the sweet tune of a butcher bird flutes from one of her trees. Surely it must be a sign? I fear I am becoming a superstitious kook – or perhaps there are realities I have never previously explored.

The front door opens as I walk up the path.

'I saw your car, Angelica. How are you today?'

She has her hair swept back, still wet from showering, a few brown curls springing free, and she's wearing a pale green shift. No shoes. A small sign asks visitors to leave theirs on the front porch. I am divesting already.

'I'm excited about being here,' I reply. 'Feeling a bit seedy, but I'll get over it.'

She leads me straight through to the back verandah which is shaded by vines and the rock wall that rises up behind. A small, square table is laid with a beautiful cloth, several crystals lined up on one side, and the cards.

'I've dispensed with the candle during summer,' she says. 'For such a small flame it gives off a surprising amount of heat. And there's the fire risk, of course.'

Sally offers tea, but I settle for a glass of water. And we begin.

'He's here with you again, Angelica. Your husband. Bill. Oh! And he's transcended, glimmering through the light!'

I feel faint. Sip the water. Breathe.

'He's showing me three new canvases you're working on, paintings that explore the emergence of new life. They seem to make him very happy.'

I was sure the tears would stay at bay, but they are running down my cheeks, making me reach for tissues.

'I don't ever want to forget him,' I murmur. 'I'm starting to feel happy again, really happy sometimes. And then I feel guilty. I want him to know he has a precious place in my heart.'

I can't go on. Sally is standing behind me, her hands radiating heat, telling me that Bill needs to immerse in spiritual work we cannot understand. He wants me to live life to the fullest, she says, honouring the love we shared, and letting new loves grow.

Warmth and comfort flow through me, settling to a deeper sense of calm. Reminding me to ask Sally about what she's doing, this Reiki thing.

'It's a simple, pure form of energy healing,' she explains, telling me a little about the history.

We talk for a while about Bill, Sally explaining her understanding of what happens when people die. That their spirit journeys through different realms, progressively letting go of human concerns and emotions as it evolves. We use each interlude in the spiritual realms for healing and learning and growth, she tells me, some of us more effectively than others, depending where we're up to in our spiritual development. Before we incarnate again in human form.

I am surprised how much sense it seems to make. I need to read more widely, to think about it, maybe to paint it out or talk it over with Clyde.

'Shall we pull the cards?' she asks. 'We didn't use them last time, did we?'

I notice that she shifts into a trance-like state as soon as I hand her seven cards from the pack. Although her eyes are open, she seems to have slipped away.

The cards indicate continuity and creativity and fresh beginnings, she is saying, a karmic correcting of some situation dear to my heart. She speaks of positivity, of the spiritual growth that has emerged for both Bill and me out of the devastation and loss. She says the cards indicate major growth on many levels.

As she speaks, a sense of deep peace passes through me. When the last card has been read, I feel serene.

I cannot kick this queasy feeling, no matter what I do or don't eat. There's a GP in town three days a week. He can squeeze me in for an appointment if I come first thing on Friday morning. Perhaps I have picked up a parasite from the water. Or am brewing something nasty like an irritable appendix. The Middleton hospital is a helicopter ride away from Walden in an emergency, and I don't want that kind of drama.

'Call me Frank,' he insists, as he steps forward and shakes my hand. He's a grey-haired man, rangy, casually dressed. 'What can I do for you, Mrs …?' He glances at the form I've just filled out.

'Angelica's fine,' I say, wanting to avoid the telling of my story.

I describe my symptoms, watch him taking notes. He is professional and thorough.

The physical examination doesn't tell us much. He'll take some blood and other samples, do a few tests. Most likely it's a passing bug, but it's better to be sure. He rules out appendicitis, and I'm relieved.

'I'll call you if the tests show anything. Otherwise, see how you go. Come back if you're still feeling crook in a week's time.'

* * *

When the phone rings, I am so absorbed in painting it takes me a minute to engage.

'Doctor's rooms? Oh. Is something wrong?'

The woman assures me there's no need for alarm, that Frank just needs to have a word and would prefer to talk to me directly. He can see me tomorrow, at the end of his day.

Suddenly, I think I know. It's weeks since I've had a period. My breasts are swollen. They sting when the water hits them in the shower. I rush for the diary but there is no need to count up the days, the weeks, the miracle. The dread.

What am I going to do? I have wanted a child almost as much as I've wanted Bill back, but everything is wrong. Single parenting is not on my agenda. My progress of the past few months has vanished, leaving trepidation in my belly and confusion in my mind.

And there's Hayden. I struggle to form the next thought – 'father of my child'. Knowing he is gone. And won't be back. Would I want him anyway? A man so recently a boy, so many years younger than I am. Maybe if I close my eyes and meditate, this will go away. I will emerge to find the nightmare was a dream.

But the seed triptych blazes from its easels. Treacherous fore-teller. I recognise you now. Source of joyful inspiration turned to dust.

Sally's words come tumbling from my memory. Growth on many levels, she told me, and a karmic correcting of something dear to my heart. Bill alluded to it too. Spoke about new love. Assured me that part of him would always be with me.

I must pull myself together. Think clearly. It wasn't long after New Year, all my intimacies with the river. Bill's ashes scattered into the flow, as well as the time with Hayden.

I imagine talking the pregnancy through with Dr Frank, asking questions, making plans. To what? To terminate? But I know I can't. This life is as precious as the glowing seeds around me.

Laughter bubbles up and I am dancing, twirling in slow sweeping circles, hugging my husband's precious promise to my heart, feeling the flat of my belly for signs of new life. I will see Ess and tell her almost everything. No more Hayden secrets now. This pregnancy is a journey I cannot take without her, a journey she will want to share.

But first, a visit to the doctor, to make sure everything's alright.

He is kind and non-intrusive, concerned for my welfare and that of the baby. He ran the test because he had a feeling. And wonders if I want to talk things over with a counsellor, before deciding what to do. I find comfort in telling the bones of my story to this man. Who doesn't judge or ask awkward questions.

'The birthing centre in Middleton is excellent,' he says. 'Great midwives. I'll write you a referral, if you're sure that's what you want?'

It is. I have no doubts now.

I can see Dr Frank for monthly check-ups to begin with. Won't have to travel to Middleton every time, only for scans or if something seems wrong. The pregnancy is real. We have a date, my baby's ETA. A midwife will work it out again, but for now it looks like October 11 – a little Libran. I'll read up on them.

Joy and dawning comprehension have dissolved my earlier dismay. Bill would be proud of me. Now I have to tell Ess. Lizzie. Aunty Fran. Clyde. Does Sally already know? And I suppose at some stage, I will have to tell Sage. Not looking forward to that.

There will be time for serious contemplation, but right now I am thrilled, my mind racing through dietary requirements and exercise plans, musing the mystery of whether it will be a girl or a boy, and of how I will raise this little one by myself.

* * *

Essie is in the garden when I pull into her drive.

As I get out of the car, she looks up. 'Hey, Ange. Something wrong? I wasn't expecting you.'

I am so excited that I fail to notice how subdued she is.

But I feel stirrings of unease as I spill out my news. Reveal the Hayden secret.

Ess remains silent for a long time, after the sharp intake of breath. Turns her gaze to the ridgetop. Shutting off from me.

'I guess I can see why you didn't tell me about Hayden, Angel. I suppose. But I hate that you thought I might judge you. It's Sage who does that, remember? I'm the one who's been holding you together all this time. Why don't you think you can trust me?'

So that's it. The secrecy.

'I felt ashamed, Ess. As though I'd betrayed Bill and even you, somehow. And it was precious too. I just couldn't risk having anyone spoil it for me.'

'Which means you didn't trust me,' she says again, turning her back and walking away.

Tears threaten. This isn't how I wanted it to go.

'Of course I trust you!' I say, exasperated. 'But surely I'm entitled to some privacy? To keep some things to myself? I bet you do. Don't you?'

She strides away along the verandah. Spins around and glares at me, hands on hips. 'You have no idea, Angel! Secrets? You want to know about secrets? Well, here's a big one. Liz's father was a crime gang leader in New Zealand, and she's been keeping it from me all these years. How do you like that for a secret?'

I have never seen Essie so distraught. My immediate urge is to wrap her in my arms and hold her. But her body language keeps me at bay.

'Where's Liz now?' I murmur, realising that she should have been home from work an hour or so ago.

'She's not bloody here! Alright? I think she might be at Clyde's but to be honest, right now I couldn't give a shit where she is.'

I'm aghast. My news, my secrets, my joy fade away in the face of Essie's grief and rage. What's worse is that I know there's nothing I can say that will help. Essie simply doesn't want to hear.

Evening settles over us, valley rustlings barely audible in the hideous silence. We stand mere metres apart but have never been so disconnected from each other, each of us staring fixedly at the far ridge as the sky darkens and stars begin to appear.

Quietly, I walk inside and put the kettle on. Prepare the tea things on a tray. It's pathetic. But I can't think of anything else to do.

And then I hear her voice.

'Better if you go too,' she says. 'I just want to be on my own.'

24

The minute I arrive home, I phone Clyde. Yes, he says, Liz is with him. And no, she doesn't want to talk to me. She's not talking to him either. As far as he knows, she is out with the horses. He feels it's wisest for us to leave Essie and Liz to themselves for a while. Give them both time to process what has happened.

Fresh waves of loss and grief threaten to swamp me. Not Essie too! Please no – don't let me lose Essie too. And please don't let Essie lose Liz. I couldn't bear it.

I don't feel hungry, although I'm aware I should probably eat something healthy. Look after the baby.

Instead, I slump onto the couch, letting the tears flow. Are they for me? For Bill? For Essie and yes, for Liz too? Thank god for Tashie, who curls up against me, concern clear in her eyes.

It is pitch dark when I jolt awake. My first urge is to phone Ess, but Clyde's cautionary advice stops me. She needs time alone. That's what she said. And I need to respect that, no matter how bereft it makes me feel.

My hands wander to my belly. I may not have Ess, but I do have this little one to care for. And Tashie must surely be starving. She whines softly, reading my thoughts.

After I have fed her, and made myself some toast and tea, I check the time. Twenty to three in the morning. Yet I am nowhere near ready for bed.

I ponder what Sally said about reincarnation. I try to contact Bill. But he is elusive. 'Who is this spirit coming back to life inside my body?' I whisper into the cool night air, imagining he can hear. 'Could this little one be you, my darling, or someone else we know and love?'

In the morning, I can contain myself no longer. Cross my fingers and phone Essie's number. And am shocked when Liz answers. She is brusque. Just picking up some clothes and heading back to Clyde's.

Before I can ask her about Essie, she hangs up.

Throughout the day, I keep trying their landline. Curse the fact that mobiles don't work in the valley. The first time or two, I leave brief messages. Please, just let me know that you're okay. Late in the day, Ess finally picks up when I call.

'Piss off and leave me alone, will you? If you care about me at all, you'll do as I ask.'

And the line goes dead. Again.

It is almost a week – six hideous, lonely, grief-stricken days and nights – before I hear from her again. A brief phone call to tell me she has asked Liz to come home so that they can discuss whether there is anything worth salvaging in their relationship. She'll call me again when she's ready.

Tashie and painting and the baby are the only things that keep me going. When I manage to sleep, my dreams are nightmares. So

I avoid going to bed. Instead, I walk with Tashie down the lane or to the river. Cry. Talk to myself. Take daytime naps on the couch.

I call Clyde a couple of times, and he drops by occasionally to check on me, always with the same advice: this is between Essie and Liz; I have to wait until they are ready to let me in again. I feel like screaming, but hold it together, more or less, until he leaves.

Two and a half weeks after I stepped off Essie's verandah and drove away, she phones me. 'Are you free this afternoon? It's time the three of us cleared the air. So if there's anything else you want to get off your chest, now's the time.'

I say I'll be there around two. And she hangs up.

Shit, shit, shit! I still have no idea whether they have patched things up. And no idea whether Essie and I can mend what's been broken between us. I am beyond nervous, but breathe, trying to calm down before I get in the car. This can't be good for the baby. And I am terrified.

There is no one to meet me when I arrive. I close the car door quietly. Walk up the steps onto the verandah. Still nobody. As I open the screen door, I can hear the murmur of voices. Not yelling. Surely that's a good thing?

Essie and Liz are sitting together on the couch, a gap between them. Tea things are set out on the coffee table – they are ready for me. As I take a seat in the armchair opposite, I have rarely felt so alone. Two against one. Is that what this is going to be?

But Liz leans forward, hands clasped together, and begins to speak. She is looking directly at me, so I assume Essie has heard this before.

'My father was leader of one of the main motorcycle gangs on the North Island,' she says. 'I'm going to tell you my story, and I don't want you to interrupt. Okay?'

I nod.

'One day, when I was ten years old, we'd all been out at the pub. That was the way Dad liked it. When the gang met socially, kids and women came along. The kids ran riot while the adults drank. Dad had arrived on his Harley – there was a long row of bikes lined up out the front of the pub. Mum had driven the rest of us there in our old family van.

'We were there for ages. I remember it was dark when Dad decided it was time to leave. All of us kids were hungry. We piled into the van with Mum, me in the front, being the eldest. Dad roared off on his bike and we followed behind, heading home.

'I only remember bits of what came next, it all happened so fast. A big black car came screaming up behind Mum's van, overtook it, and pulled in sharply in front of us, driving straight into the side of Dad's bike. Dad went flying through the air, a dark shape in the headlights. I think Mum must have stopped the van really fast – I remember her yelling at us to lock all the doors.

'Dad's bike was lying in the road, and I could see Dad further up ahead. He was trying to sit up. Then the black car came back. It was speeding. It ran straight over our Dad, screeched to a stop, backed up fast and ran over Dad again and again, then sped away.

'Mum was screaming. We were all screaming.'

Liz sits back. Tears are pouring down her face. Ess and I are crying too. But I dare not say a word.

'Anyway. That's what I've been trying to deal with all these years. All that shit. And all the shit that came after it. I didn't want to tell Essie in case she hated me for it. For being a gang leader's daughter. For all the violence in my childhood. And the mess that is still my community over there.'

She comes to an abrupt halt. Her body language is defiant, yet somehow defeated. As though she has finally laid it all out and is now awaiting our judgement.

The tea has gone cold in the pot. No one moves.

Then Essie begins to speak.

'Liz knows why I'm so angry – we've been talking about it for days. I'm still trying to come to terms with the fact that she kept something so huge from me for all these years. That she didn't trust me enough to love and support her through it.'

Her hand reaches over and touches Liz's. I don't know what to say.

'I love her more than ever now that I know how strong she is. But I'm really struggling with her not trusting me,' Essie says.

'And I'm still trying to help Ess understand that it wasn't lack of trust. I was just wanting to protect her from all that horrible crap.'

Liz looks across at Essie, and I see the love and pleading in her eyes.

'So now you know why I was so pissed off when it turned out you'd been keeping secrets too, Ange,' says Ess.

Silence again. I need to say something, but I don't know where to start.

'Have you told Liz my stuff?' I ask, looking at Ess.

'Yeah, she knows everything,' says Ess.

'It seems pretty tame now that I know what you guys have been dealing with,' I say. 'Hayden. The pregnancy. Good things, really. And I'm sorry, Ess – I shouldn't have kept the Hayden thing from you. You know I'd trust you with my life. Both of you. I'm so sorry – about everything.'

I want to ask what's next for them, but their new-found equilibrium feels so tenuous and raw that I don't dare. Clyde's words echo in my mind: leave them to sort it out between themselves.

Ess looks at me and nods.

'I guess we all have a lot of adjusting to do,' she says, 'and it won't happen overnight.'

We end up talking for hours, each of us making trips to the kitchen to organise food and drinks. Our conversation meanders across many topics – our childhoods, Liz's family, the loss and grief we've all experienced, as well as the bright spots. More of those for me and Essie than for Liz, who did it very tough. Love and trust and respect come up many times. How important they are to each of us. And how easy it is to let rifts grow into chasms when communication falters.

Eventually Liz looks at me and says, 'Hayden has a right to know. You realise that, don't you?'

I sigh. Explain again the 'no ties' agreement we made.

'But neither of us anticipated this, I guess.' I sigh again, weariness blurring my thoughts.

I can find him via Clyde. I promise to think about it.

Slowly an idea begins to emerge. We could raise this child together, Ess and Liz and I. We could make it work, whether Hayden is involved or not. Hearing them say this gives me hope that they are going to be alright. Thank god.

'I guess I'll have to tell Sage sooner rather than later,' I say. 'She's not going to be happy, that's for sure.'

'And that's definitely a conversation for another day,' Essie says, shaking her head. 'It's bedtime for me.'

I struggle to my feet. Give them each a hug.

As I climb into my car, I look up and see them standing at the top of the verandah steps, their arms around each other.

I smile. Decisions can wait.

25

The days are dreamy passages of softness, carrying me and my baby along. Yoga classes twice a week in Lawsons Landing, the garden, meditating at dawn. An end, finally, to the oppressive heat. Long walks down by the river, watching the ducks who have recently arrived, two pairs. Walks with Tashie up the lane and along the dusty road.

Practicalities as well. Making sure I eat healthily. Keeping the gas bottles topped up. Pumping water from the river to the garden tank, a job that always makes me think of Hayden. I still haven't written to him – I know I should. But part of me yearns to keep everything simple.

Whenever I leave the valley to go shopping or for a check-up with Dr Frank, I drop in on Ess on my way home. Ever so slowly, the distance between us is dissolving. It is clear that Liz is still living there, and I take that as a positive sign that they are mending their relationship, although I don't dare to ask. Our connection is still too fragile for me to risk it.

One afternoon, Essie asks me whether I have phoned Sage, and the next morning I do, even though my heart is racing. I never know how to start a conversation with her – it's almost like talking to a stranger.

'Angel. Long time no hear,' she says.

I want to say it's a two-way street, but I am determined to keep the conversation civil.

'I've had a lot going on,' I tell her. 'Settling into the cottage, getting used to valley life ...'

'Yes. About that. What would Bill think?'

Deep breath.

'I think he'd be happy that I'm getting on with my life,' I tell her. 'And I also think he'd be happy that I'm living much closer to Essie and Liz.'

Before she can react further, I explain briefly about how I came to move to Walden, and invite her to bring Mike and the girls for a visit one weekend soon.

'That's a whole day trip!' she exclaims. 'Obviously, we can't come on a Sunday. I suppose we might be able to find a Saturday when the girls don't have sporting commitments. You don't make it easy, Angelica. Then again, you never have, have you?'

I would love to hang up, but am determined to get this task done, so I persist.

'Why don't you get your diary now and we'll work out a date. I'll make lunch. As you say, it's a bit of a drive.'

We settle on a Saturday three weeks away, and I give her my new address along with directions.

'Well, I hope it's not a hovel,' she says. 'What should I bring?'

I assure her I can manage a simple meal, and heave a sigh of relief as we finish the call.

The seed paintings are finished. That point of light turned out to be a magnificent spreading eucalypt offering shade, and a home to many birds, a family of possums and swarming insect life. I have been sitting in the forest every day, all senses wide open, taking in the wondrous miracle of life.

Bill has come to me twice in dreams, the first time that night after I'd seen Dr Frank and Essie. He held my hand and stroked my flat belly, radiating love, emanating his approval, although I heard no words. In the second dream, weeks later, he felt much more physical, sitting on the edge of the bed, talking for hours, or so it seemed. Telling me stories about Bob and Maddie, how much my Mum reminds him of me. Of generations of women in my family, good mothers all, supporting me in spirit through this journey. No answer to my burning question. But reassurance that I should never feel alone, that his spirit will be with me always, although I may not see or hear from him so often as time goes by.

On his way home one afternoon Clyde drops by and I spill out my news. I could swear he already knows. But how much? He mentions again that I should visit sometime. Come at day's end, share a meal, sit and yarn. There are things he'd like to tell me about, he says, and questions I might like to ask.

He gives me a Riverina address for Hayden and I finally write a letter. In it, I say there is news I want to share. I ask him to call or email, wishing now that we'd at least exchanged email addresses before he left.

I write another letter to Neil, too, although I've not had a reply to my earlier one. I suggest that he phones sometime. Tell him I'd like to keep in touch.

On a languid Saturday afternoon a couple of weeks later I sit with my little sister and her husband in my pergola while their girls run through drifts of russet leaves. I observe Sage and Mike closely as I announce my baby news.

'I don't know you any more, Angelica! First you move to this godforsaken place, and now this!'

Mike sits stolidly beside his wife, one hand reaching for hers as she gesticulates.

'You'll go straight to hell for this! You know that, don't you?' Sage says. 'Some passing stranger. I can't believe it. What's wrong with you?'

Mike slips away to play with the children, while Sage continues to rant. So far, I have not said a word.

'Single motherhood's not a game, you know. Let alone with a mixed-race child ...'

My mind shuts down and my body absorbs the pain. Until she rattles to a halt.

'Have you finished, Sage? Because there's something else you should know, even if you don't want to hear it.'

She shudders. 'What else have you done?'

And out it pours. The tale of my readings with Sally, of her seeing Maddie and Bob, of the messages from Bill.

'No doubt this will add to your concerns,' I call her bluff. 'But for me, it's brought comfort, and glimmers of peace.'

She looks away. Reaches for her basket. Stands up. Calls to Mike and the girls.

'You are no sister of mine, Angelica,' she says, coldly. 'Don't expect to see us again. I won't have my children contaminated by your wanton sinfulness.'

As they drive away down the lane, I stand with Tashie beside me, watching another part of my life disappear.

Am I sad? Relieved? Angry? Disappointed? Numb?

Too many emotions to process.

I walk inside and put the kettle on.

26

The wisteria over my pergola has turned to bronze and gold, beginning to bare its branches and let in the autumn sun. I sit out there a lot, reading, writing in my journal, drinking tea, communing with Bill. Coffee has gone the way of other foods and perfumes I can no longer tolerate – it's become a drink I make for Clyde or Ess or Liz when they drop in for a chat.

Many times every day I feel the precious place between my hip bones, running my hands across it, imagining the tiny form inside, caressing the soft little bulge. 'It will be enormous soon enough,' the midwife tells me, laughing. 'In a few months you'll be groaning about the heaviness and constant need to pee.' Meanwhile, they did some extra tests, since I am a 'geriatric primigravida', and in the blurry grey scan I saw a variation on my seed – sweet curve of spine, a dark eye.

Two years ago today I gave the instruction for Bill's life support to be switched off. Two interminable years. The river whispers me stories of how we could have been, living in the city with a happy family and a dog. Living our busy academic and corporate lives, better and worse than this one. It whispers me stories of Jane and Richard, of their earth-nurturing, of Bill's spirit always with me, of a precious gifting from a young travelling man.

I have organised a dinner for tonight, in celebration of Bill's life and the new life coming. My paintings are arranged on the living room walls, telling stories of their own. The angel painting of Bill. Hayden emerging from the moonlit river. A cherub with Bill's face. My seed triptych. And one of me.

Sally is coming, and Clyde. Even Aunty Fran, who will stay the night with the girls. Essie and Liz will help with the food. Already there's a cast iron pot simmering on the wood stove, rich with gravy beef and root vegetables from the garden, herbs, a dollop of tomato paste.

On my walks through the bush I take a wide, sturdy basket and fill it with sticks to keep the kindling box stocked. I throw one or two for Tashie as we walk. It is a long time since I've been this fit. And the first time I've been so aware of the seasons as they turn.

Clyde came last week with a huge load of firewood and spent hours swinging the log splitter and the axe, building high, neat stacks against the west wall of the cottage, underneath the eaves. To the left of the back door are the smaller pieces, cut shorter and not so chunky, for feeding into the stove. And to the right, sizeable logs that will burn long and slow in the fireplace on cold winter nights, spreading the warmth of stored sun across the earthen floor and into my heart.

Janet at the store has insisted on teaching me to crochet, setting me up with the skills I need to make a baby blanket. 'You'll appreciate keeping your hands busy on those long, dark nights,' she said. 'There's a few of us here who'll get the baby wool out and start on booties and jackets as well.' Some of the villagers have distanced themselves from me, I've noticed, but Janet is stalwart. I suspect her friends have been given a good talking-to about not judging people.

I have started making bread as well, now the weather is cooler, pulling out recipes from Jane's old folder. She has written notes in the margins, the name and number to phone for sacks of organic wholemeal flour delivered with the mail. They will pack yeast in with it too, if I want. There is an old ceramic bowl in one of the cupboards, perfect for mixing the dough. And I am loving the rhythm of the lean and fold, lean and fold, kneading with the heel of my hand. There's a wire mesh shelf in the warm space above the woodstove and I put the bowl there, covered with a cloth, to let the yeasty mystery expand. I am carrying out experiments with the stove – what kind of wood, how much, air vents open or shut – the science of getting the temperature just right.

Tonight there is a wholemeal loaf studded with pumpkin seeds to go with the stew. Liz has made rice custard pudding and is bringing preserved plums to serve with it for dessert. There will be bottles of red wine from Clyde, although I've asked him to bring just himself.

The first knock at the door is Sally, wrapped in an emerald green shawl, a posy of exquisite pink roses in one hand and a small gift-wrapped package in the other.

'For you and the baby, my dear,' she says, hugging me before she puts the gifts on the bench.

She is drawn immediately to my paintings. 'Oh my – that's him!' she exclaims, standing back from the portrait of Bill. 'That's how he shows himself to me – minus the wings,' she says. She nods at the cherub and smiles. What does she know?

I'm not surprised any more at her visionary gifts, although vestiges of scepticism remain. Then again, she is so honest, down to earth and real.

The front door opens and the girls and Aunty Fran tumble in with Clyde right behind them, laughing and flushed from the cold.

'Can't believe it's turned so chilly and it's still only autumn,' says Liz, handing me the old-fashioned bottle of preserves. The pudding is warm in its bowl, and can go up on the shelf above the stove.

I love the way the cottage fills with warmth and conversation as coats peel off and wine pours into glasses. Clyde introduces Sally to my family, then he and Sally catch up on the latest news, as old friends do. Aunty Fran insists on feeling for any hint of the precious life growing inside my gently swelling belly. Essie and Liz seem closer again too, thank god.

As we settle around the table, the conversation becomes more personal. I'm surprised to learn that Sally taught at the local high school for several decades. She and Aunty Fran even think they might have crossed paths somewhere, years ago.

As the evening ripens into night, the girls and I talk about Bill – the way he had of making everyone feel special, how he was always there to solve a computer crisis, and his habit of wandering off to the shed when our giggling got too much. We retell the story of those hideous days in the ICU, the heartbreaking funeral service, and how I hid in our house for a year.

Aunty Fran persuades Sally to share some stories of mystical encounters and I'm surprised to hear Clyde chiming in. He seems to know a lot about the esoteric. I notice Sally doesn't drink, just like Hayden, but before I can ask she explains that for her, alcohol clouds the pathways into other realms. Everyone's different in this regard, she says, but she hasn't had a drink for many years.

Hayden lingers in my mind as we savour the syrup from Lizzie's plums – sticky and sweet spooned in with the creamy rice. There's polite restraint, I've noticed, even in this close group, about the paternity of my precious child. Clyde must be in my head, though, because he leans back in his chair, broad hands rubbing his satisfied belly, and looks me right in the eye.

'Did Hayden tell you much about his heritage?' he asks.

'He talked a fair bit about his grandfather, the First Nations man, the one who died recently,' I reply. 'Why, Clyde? What did he tell you? Is there something I should know?'

'Nothing bad, Angel. Nothing like that. No. His grandfather was a Haida man, a respected elder in his community. I'll tell you more about it another time. You'll find it interesting.'

And the door is closed on that. Ess looks enquiringly at me, but Clyde has shifted the talk to other things – who needs more firewood? Is everybody well set up with gas? It's cold for this time of year. Might be a long and chilly winter. Aunty Fran agrees – she's already waking to frosts up in the mountains.

Sally is intrigued with the structure of my Walden cottage, interested in hearing more about the story of Richard and Jane. She'd love to live in a place like this, she sighs.

Everybody has a story, I reflect, wondering what sadness Sally's shadow hides. Putting the question away for another time.

'I see there are red dots on both your paintings at the gallery,' says Ess. 'You must be pretty chuffed about that? A real artist in the family!'

Janet told me last time I dropped in at the store, but I've been a bit distracted. 'There's room for more as soon as you have them ready,' she said. 'Of course you'll want to be careful now, with the turps and linseed in the house, I suppose. Can't expose the baby to toxic fumes.'

She's kind and proprietal. Rough edges and all. People say it takes twenty years to feel like a local in most country towns, but it doesn't seem that way here. It's the valley culture, someone explained. A few hundred people settled either side of a long stretch of winding river, with no way in or out except the ferry, or a rough dirt track at the farthest end. We'll all need one another sometime, is the prevailing wisdom. Best to watch your Ps and Qs. Keep quiet if you don't like something or someone. Stay on the right side of your neighbours. I like it a lot.

'Hey, Angel. Are you still with us?' It's Liz, poking me gently in the arm, smiling. 'You look like you're miles away.'

I'm smiling too. 'I've been getting pretty weary by the end of the day. Baby seems to want me to have lots of sleep.'

We make one more toast to Bill – 'To the man whose love will never die'. There's a lightness in the room, a kind of shimmer, that might be the halo from the fire's flames. Sally doesn't mention anything. But we all feel him here, expansive, radiating love. Contented sighs on this occasion. No tears. And a sweet promise snuggled in my womb.

27

I am crocheting the blanket for my baby, a vivid thing of softest wool in chevron stripes. Janet showed me how to create the zigzags with simple increasing and decreasing, ten half-treble stitches to each rise and fall. Now that my cramped left hand has settled to tensioning the wool, I am finding this a very relaxing craft.

There's a fabulous haberdashery in Middleton where I wandered around the shelves and bins for more than an hour, sussing out colours and textures that Bill would like, wanting the blanket to be perfect for my little one. The lady kept directing me to pastels with apricots, mauves and greens available these days, to supplement the standard lemon, pink and blue. But none of those felt right. Nor did the fine, thin baby wools – I need a substantial rug to wrap this baby in.

I have chosen colours that Bill loved – emerald, ruby, sapphire, amethyst and gold – interspersed with single rows of black. Thick eight-ply wool imported from New Zealand, brushed and combed to chick-down softness, sensuous in my hands. Every night, I curl up on the sofa with the fire blazing and let my fingers fly, hooking and twisting the wool, witnessing new beauty evolve.

Baby is nineteen weeks grown today, a round mound tensioning my skin. He is nurtured in his fluid cradle by the love stories emanating from my mind. And when I link my hands underneath the bulge, it feels like I am cuddling him. It is weeks now since I have heard Bill's voice. Is he still around?

I think of my baby as 'him', but doubt and reason whisper into my imagination, sketching images of red-haired baby girls.

Every morning now the house is shrouded in heavy mist, the surface of the river drifting up in foggy swirls to greet the hidden sun. I set the wood stove for a slow burn all night long, and every morning gratefully greet the warmth as I stumble out of bed to put the kettle on. Jane and Richard paid extra, way back when, to install this wetback model with the pipes and plumbing against the wall, to heat our water at the same time as it cooks the food. On these short days late in autumn I thank them yet again for their dedicated wisdom, their connection with the workings of the seasons and the earth.

I emailed Jane the other day, telling her my news. It wasn't easy. For all our closeness, we don't know each other very well. What if she says a child was not part of our deal?

When her answer comes flying back, I am overwhelmed. This woman is the soul of compassion and generosity. Says she always dreamed of children at Walden, that one of her greatest griefs came from barrenness. There are no awkward questions regarding Hayden. Instead, she writes about the river with its healing waters, the way it measures and nurtures life with its rhythmic ebb and flow. She finishes by saying that she will be staying indefinitely in Nepal, where she feels needed and purposeful, and that I should consider Walden my home. Even if she decides to come back for a visit, she can stay with Clyde.

Sometimes the sun doesn't burn through the mist until

midmorning. Until then, Walden floats on a magic carpet of fog, curling its earthen walls around me, nestling me and the baby in its warmth. Tashie sleeps in the house with us now, on her cushion by the stove. It's too cold at night to have her out there in the kennel. If this is autumn, I wonder what the winter will be like. And have heard stories of minus eight or nine degrees, with frozen pipes and thick frosts hoary on the ground.

Every morning as soon as the sun appears we go for a brisk walk up the lane and out along the road, my breath coming in white puffs, hands plump in woollen gloves, a thick coat keeping me snug. I am walking kilometres every day, keeping myself and the baby fit. Tashie thrives on it too.

There's a miracle happening inside me, this quickening of new life in my womb. Surely by now the baby's spirit must have settled in? As I sit down to take off my boots after walking, there is a momentary tightness that makes me catch my breath. My hand moves to press against my belly and is met by the subtlest of kicks. There it is again, more definite, protruding roundly from my taut skin. A heel maybe? An elbow? Or could it be a bony bottom? It stops after a couple of minutes, and I can move again. Stand up to reach for tissues, hug myself, bursting with this precious news.

Ess and Liz are top of my list – but they will both be at work. I yearn to call Sage, who has experienced all this herself. But she has locked me out. Soured the potential of this fleeting time.

Clyde might be at home. It's probably his morning cuppa time.

'I felt the baby move!' I squeal, the minute he answers the phone. 'I think I could feel its foot or an elbow or something.'

We chat for a while, Clyde sharing the thrill, explaining how he's never had a child of his own, but it's a bit the same with foals and kittens, as far as he can tell. Making me laugh. Letting me cry. Sweet, happy tears these days.

'You still haven't made it over here for dinner and a yarn,' he chides. 'How about we set a time, Angelica? Are you busy on Wednesday night?'

I write it in my diary. Promise to bake some bread. And wonder what secrets and insights he might want to share.

It is the middle of May and the valley is in deep shadow by 4 pm. The sun on its low trajectory slips quietly over the tree-rimmed ridge of rocks. Our lives are governed by the seasons and we get inside early to beat the darkness and the cold. Dinner is at six, but Clyde suggests I come over at around five. 'Remember to watch out for the roos and wombats,' he warns. 'They're likely to be crossing the road.'

His place is set high on the side of the hill, a counterpoint to Walden, wooden with a wide verandah and a view across paddocks to the river on the far side of the road. It is built from local timber, he explains, with a pole frame, perfect for the steep terrain. We wander through the spacious living room – simply furnished, clean – and settle at the kitchen table. He too has a wood stove on which he does almost all his cooking, as well as using it for heating the water and the house. There is a slow combustion fire against the back wall of the living room, its glass face glowing red and gold. No wonder the place is cosy, despite its openness.

'Now, little mother, what can I give you to drink?' He's smiling, already reaching for the cups and saucers on his old pine dresser. 'Tea might be the go, don't you think?'

It's comforting, being cared for by this man. Our surrogate grandpa, we joke. The truth is we still know very little about Clyde's private life. I don't know whether he has ever been married, for instance, nor where he lived before he settled here.

'I haven't meant to set up any mysteries,' he's saying now. 'There's a lot I don't generally talk about, Angelica, as you might have noticed.'

Can he read my mind?

'Those of us who have practised shamanic ways for a long time usually keep pretty quiet about it. There's no reason to make a fuss – it's a way of life.'

So that's his secret. Shamanism. About which I know virtually nothing. He seems normal. Kind, gentle, aware. I thought shamans were witch doctors who conducted ceremonies in the Amazonian jungle.

Clyde begins to talk, his voice calm and deep. 'There is much that we in the everyday world don't see or even engage with, at least not consciously. So much that is invisible or intangible. And yet we have regular experiences that give us clues – tell us, if we're prepared to listen – that beyond the seen world lie mysteries, endless possibilities, vast potential we can tap into.'

He stops, his eyes fixed on mine. It is as though he is speaking with his mind directly into mine, but in a safe way that gives me permission to drift into stillness and peace. My hands are resting on my baby who seems to be asleep.

There are millions of people on the planet who live the shamanic way, he goes on to explain, honouring and respecting all views and systems of believing, deeply connecting with the elements, the spirit realms and the forces of the natural world. Many indigenous cultures have expressions that mean 'we are all connected' – all humans, animals, trees, plants, rocks and water-falls. The air we breathe. Every aspect of creation.

'That butcher bird who talks to you, for example,' says Clyde. 'You have a feeling it's some kind of messenger from Bill, don't you?'

I sit very still. The bird is something I've mentioned only to Ess and maybe Sally. Perhaps one of them told Clyde?

'You told me about it yourself,' he says. 'Not in words. You told me with your heart and mind.'

I am anxious now. What else does he know?

'Sometimes we need to journey into other realms and draw our own conclusions about things. I can teach you how to do that if you want, when you feel the time is right.'

Our conversation travels far into the night, many of my questions met by silence flowing into slow realisation, quiet demonstrations of Clyde's skills and way of being. We eat delicious vegetable and barley soup, dunking chunks of bread and sucking up the goodness.

'You seem to be drawn to this, Angelica,' he says. 'That's why I decided to raise it with you.'

He talks about the way I observe the weather, my love of the river and the sandstone cliffs, how I notice the sun and the moon in their journeying over the land. The way I relate to my baby. The way I paint.

'I'm happy to teach you if you'd like to learn more,' he says, 'and you have teachers in the spiritual realms and the natural world as well. Bill and others, to help you extend your awareness into more expansive states of consciousness and mind.'

I feel exhausted, on the verge of overwrought. We haven't mentioned Hayden but I know he is part of this unfolding picture. We'll talk about him another time, I'm sure. For now, I need to go home and sleep.

'Take this with you,' says Clyde, handing me a small paperback book. 'You might like to read it outside, or by the fire – somewhere where the elements are on display.'

We say a warm goodnight, Clyde's hug comforting and strong, his words cloaking me for the road. 'Take care going down the steep track to the gate. Drive slowly in the fog.'

By the time I get home, the fire has died in the stove and I take time to lay crushed newspaper, kindling, a few bigger sticks, and put a match to it before I go shivering to get ready for bed. I feel very much alive, although it's late and my body is heavy and tired.

Clyde's right – there is something in this mystical path for me. A feeling that I have been searching for these kinds of insights all my life.

Before I turn off the lights I toss a few chunks of wood into the stove and shut the baffle down, setting it to a slow burn to ward off the edge of the morning's chill.

It is a deep and dreamless sleep. When I wake, the first thing I see is a butcher bird, tapping a fat grub against my windowsill, pausing to eye me cheekily. Clyde told me I would be given confirmation of the discussions we had. It would be up to me to recognise it though, he said. My heart beats faster.

28

It's really cold. In the early mornings it is hard to tell the mist from the frost, so white and wondrous is the ground, so thickly white the air. Clyde has made sure we won't run out of firewood and my keep-fit kindling-collecting regime is working, keeping the big box full and my body functioning well.

Essie is coming over today to help me sort through Bill's things. I have baked a rainbow cake for morning tea, and a wholemeal cob loaf rests beneath a tea towel on the rack above the stove. When Ess taps on the door, I have just finished smoothing chocolate icing onto the cake.

'It's open, sweetheart. Come on in.'

Bill's tools and boots and clothes are all in the shed in boxes. I haul on my jumper and coat and mittens and we take Tashie with us.

'Where do you want to start?' Essie asks. 'Should we unpack his clothes? Will that be the hardest part?'

How would I know?

We rip brittle tape from one of the cartons labelled 'Bill's drawers and cupboard' and pull back the dusty cardboard flaps, releasing aged essence of Bill. Inside are neatly folded t-shirts and underpants, and balls of rolled up socks nestled on pairs of faded jeans and well-worn chinos and a small stack of soft cotton shirts.

And now the tears flow, dripping rivulets onto my belly. Essie holds me gently, her own tears running down her cheeks.

I can't bear the thought of seeing any of these things being worn by people I know and ask her if she will take them to a charity store far away. Close the box. But then I stop. I want a memento. A shirt I can wear while I paint. I don't know what I want.

'Should we take the clothes up to the cottage and sort them later?' Ess suggests. 'Just go through his tools and bike stuff for now?'

That's too hard as well.

In the end we trundle the clothes cartons up to the cottage and stack them in the shed near the back door. Essie loads the rest into her station wagon to take home. She and Liz will sort it into piles that I can check.

It's time for tea and cake. We flop into the armchairs near the fire, exhausted although we haven't done much. Talk about the weather, Essie's work, upcoming holidays.

As we begin to relax, I venture into awkward territory.

'How are things with Liz, Essie? You don't have to answer, but I've been worried about you both.'

My sister leans back. Sips her tea.

'Yeah. We're getting there, I think. Liz has told me more about what happened with her Dad. I guess I understand why she kept it from me for so long. None of them trust each other. There's so much secrecy and superstition. Old enmities. I think she grew up not trusting anyone. I'm learning not to take it personally.'

She tells me that Liz has finally offered to take her to New

Zealand and introduce her to her mum. She has brothers and a sister, too. Lots of aunties and uncles and cousins.

'I can tell she's really afraid. But she knows how important it is to me. Kind of a trust test, I guess, for both of us.'

They won't go until after my baby has been born. Sometime in the long school holidays, probably.

I drive every four weeks now to the birthing centre in Middleton. My midwife Michelle is happy with me, and with baby, who is meeting all growth targets, behaving perfectly. I could ask her about the baby's gender. But I resist.

The drive there and back gives me plenty of time for thinking and planning. I'm disappointed that I haven't heard back from Hayden. Perhaps the letter hasn't reached him? Or perhaps he really has moved on and out of my life. The thought of not being able to tell him about the baby hurts my heart. Neil hasn't contacted me either, but that's in character, and not surprising really. I hope he's okay.

The blanket is growing – a gorgeous drift of elemental colours, offset by the black. It bundles on my disappearing lap as I work, hooking rhythmically, pulling and twisting the wool. There are nights when I sit by the fire and crochet and dream, letting my mind journey in through the flames to the possible future. I see a small boy then, with dark hair and olive skin, his eyes like deep pools of light. He is running along the track beside the river, laughing, every so often glancing back at someone. That someone is me. The image morphs and Bill is there, running with Tashie on the same riverside track, throwing sticks into the water for her to fetch, both of them engaged in the game. In that image, I'm not there and neither is the boy. But I don't know why.

I've been reading Clyde's book, about a Native American man known simply as Grandfather, his life and the wisdom he acquired. It occurs to me that I am in perfect circumstances for practising the sacred silence he writes about, the ways of silencing mind and allowing universal wisdom to be revealed. With only a slight change in attitude, I can give it a try. Everything I've explored in the past year or so seems to lead me to the same central themes.

It's been a while since I've seen Sally, who has talked about dropping over when she's finished doing readings at the store. I give her a call, promising nourishing chicken stew and homemade bread. She says she'll be here.

There's something soothing about her way of being calm and comfortable wherever she finds herself. And she loves my baby's blanket. 'This little one is going to have some spunk!' she says, fingering the vibrant rectangle, holding it to her cheek. 'What made you choose colours like these?'

I explain that I went with my feelings, that the pastels didn't suit my mood.

'You're slipping more and more into sync with the universal flow,' she smiles.

I quiz her about how traumas like losing Bill can fit into this view of life. We talk for hours, first at the table and later, curled up on the sofa, adding logs to the fire one at a time, fascinated by the flames.

Sally tells me about a mountain further south, near the coast. Mount Dromedary. Gulaga. An extinct volcano, according to geological history. In another ancient story, a sacred womens place, a place of birthing. The mother mountain, nurturing the land and the Yuin people and the ever-present black ducks.

'I could introduce you to a friend of mine who owns a house

down there. Sometimes the land itself can teach us more than any class or workshop. What do you think?'

A holiday is not on my agenda, and yet I feel drawn to this place. Sally says she will phone her friend tomorrow and let me know if the cottage is free. The baby stirs and rolls, stopping the conversation, a treat for Sally and for me.

'Have you ever felt anything like it?' I exclaim, as we each rest a hand on the wondrous shifting mound.

'I did once, Angelica. Yes, I have.'

Sally sighs. There is such sadness around her that I feel clumsy and insensitive, realising again how little I know of her story.

'I was pregnant a long time ago.' She is dreamy now. 'I was only nineteen. Not much more than a girl. In those days it was different. Shameful to get knocked up when there was no ring on my finger and no man offering me his hand in marriage.'

She was sent by her parents to a place in the country where girls like her hid their shame and worked hard until the time came for their babies to be born. She was not allowed to see her infant, not even told its sex. A respectable married couple had adopted her child, she was told.

'It's a long story, Angel, and it's getting late. Maybe I'll tell you the rest another time.'

She reaches for her wrap and coat and stands to go.

'It's also part of life's mysterious cycle. Relish every moment,' she says, resting her hand on my belly, smiling softly. 'This little one is such a precious gift.'

She calls me at lunchtime the next day to say that her friend down south is going overseas. Would appreciate having visitors come and keep her house alive during her absence. The sooner the better really, as it can get very cold in the dead of winter.

That makes me smile as I throw another chunk of wood into the stove, rub my hands together and feel my toes cosy in lambskin

Ugg boots. Gulaga floats into my inner vision and the bump in my belly rolls. I think Bill approves. I'll mention the trip to Essie and Liz, see if they'd like to make an excursion of it. Ess has holidays coming up soon.

29

I check my emails. There's one from Hayden. Finally. The cursor trembles in sympathy with my hand, hovering over the inbox, desperate yet afraid to double-click. The subject box simply says 'Howdy'. Not auspicious, in the scheme of things.

Got your note, sweet Angel, though it took a while to find me. I'll be passing through Sydney on the 23rd if you want to catch up for a chat. I'll wait at the Opera House steps at 11am, in case you're in town.
    Go easy,
    Hayden

The 23rd. That's tomorrow. Should I pretend I read the email too late? Send a 'sorry I missed you' reply? Or do I go?

It feels like a summons of sorts, off-handed but imperative as well. Is he cocky? Confident he can call me in on a whim? Unlikely.

That wasn't my experience of Hayden. He was sweet and sympathetic and tuned in.

I walk by the river, seeking its counsel. *See the layer of mist on my surface, Angelica? See this illusion? If you come by again at another time, will it still be here? Is it me? Is it real? Then again, am I the water or the bank?*

Rugged up in my thick coat and gloves I hunch on the bank, merging my spirit with the flow, letting go of judgement and fear. Releasing assumptions. Letting go of Hayden, once again. Checking in with Bill. Who seems to rest content.

I will meet Hayden in the morning, and he will see. No amount of clothing will hide my rounded form from him. I am carrying his child. He is a man. Or a grown-up boy. Who will become a father before the end of this year. And has a right to know, I remind myself again.

It feels so intimate, this journey to meet him, that I tell no one, not even Ess.

I have to go into the city sometime soon in any case, to renew the lease with Angelo and Sabina. I make a phone call and we chat. Tomorrow suits them fine since it's Angelo's day to work from home. I tell them I will phone before I arrive, sometime later in the day.

My path is set.

In my dreams that night there is an eagle, soaring close to the sun. I failed at first to see it, but I can hear its cry, transmitting signals from invisible realms to those who hear. In my dream the eagle circles down and down, wingtips barely moving, epitome of oneness with the thermaling spirals of warm air.

Its gaze is fixed on something far below, some kind of prey, something in the long, dull green grass. I am in the paddock directly beneath it. Perhaps it is seeking me. Yet I am unafraid. And stand there, very still. Watching as the massive wings tuck back, talons extended, eye never wavering, and the huge bird drops.

Its plummet takes my breath away, so focused is its fall, its deadeye swoop to catch up in its talons the writhing black snake. As it rises in one fluid motion I see that the snake has a rainbow belly, is rainbowed all over, is expanding and becoming fat.

It rises high into the deep blue of the sky, this eagle snake, twin aspects of majestic creation merging into one, disappearing from sight into the ball of the blazing sun.

When I look again, there is a rainbow arching across the field of grass, pooling at my feet and running through me. Although there is no rain. And although the sky is blue.

At daybreak on the 23rd of May I wake refreshed and peaceful. The warm house welcomes me to the day, enjoys with me my morning cuppa and a breakfast of homemade toast, spread with Janet's luscious strawberry jam.

I have taken to making sketches instead of painting, now that the house is closed tight against the cold. Sketchpads and tins of watercolour pencils live on the table with boxes of pastels. My hand flies across pages and pages this morning, washing in rainbows, tracing fragments of brilliant serpent in the sky. Nothing can capture the moment but my dream has flowed onto the table and peace prevails.

It's time to get ready and go. Check my bag. Fold the lease form for Angelo and Sabina. Shrug into a garnet woollen dress that moulds to my body. Pull on my city boots, rich dark brown, flat-soled but smart. I make sure Tashie is secure in her yard, with plenty of water and a thick blanket to cuddle in her kennel. Throw my good mohair coat in the car. And head for town.

I am up near the front of the ferry, window wound down, breathing in the river's tangy life. I smile. Think about Hayden. I can't imagine how he might react when he sees my belly.

It is one of those fresh, clear mornings when every leaf on

every tree is well defined, singing harmonies with myriad other leaves. The car glides and sways around the bends, waltzing to a melody no one but baby and I can hear. Distance condenses with time to bring us early to our destination.

Old sandstone buildings nudge polished granite and glass, telling the city's story as I walk along the street and wonder how Bill might be feeling about this tryst. At the bottom of the hill, beyond the roundabout, I see the Opera House's eggshell sails pearlescent white against a pale autumn sky – an engineering wonder, still majestic after all these years. I am washed with longing for my old city life, for the carefreeness of weekends bookending frazzled corporate weeks. A different rhythm, from a time when I was young and Bill was here. Tears threaten. But thoughts of the baby growing inside me lend me strength, soothe me.

We will be fine.

It is a few minutes before eleven when I step onto the forecourt's paving, look across at the steps. Hayden is there. And he can see me. Perhaps he has watched me all the way?

He is standing on the landing at the top, backpack on the ground beside him, long hair flowing free. He seems very calm, hands resting by his sides, watching me take the wide steps one at a time, until our destinies meet.

'Angel.'

Wrapping his arms around me, not hesitating.

'Let's walk in the Gardens,' he says, taking my hand and smiling. 'I can see we both have stories to tell.'

It could not be a more perfect day, with the harbour glinting, a few tourists taking in the view. Ancient Moreton Bay fig trees gnarl their massive roots across the lawns, clipped edges of garden beds frame labelled specimens and shrubs.

I feel the firm, gentle grip of Hayden's hand holding mine. The hand of the father of my child.

'When your letter came I had a sense, before I opened it, that my world was about to change,' he says, as we sit. 'Now I see why.' Gently, he rests one hand on my rounded belly.

'I wanted to tell you face to face,' I say, studying his eyes. 'Yes, I am bearing your child.'

Formal words, falling into silence.

This is not how I thought it would be.

'You were right to ask me to visit,' he says. 'Blessings such as this don't come along every day.'

If I had thought he would panic or resist, it's not going that way. I feel embraced, although we are sitting on the soft grass facing each other, his hands enfolding the one he has lifted from my lap.

'I was appalled at first,' I admit. 'Paralysed by shock and disbelief. Until the joy washed through.'

He's nodding, smiling. 'You warned me well. I seem to have missed the appalled state and stepped straight into delight.'

'He – or she – is due in mid October, around the eleventh,' I say.

'I'll be back home in Canada by then.'

So few words. He makes no claims, voices no suspicions or projections but asks what I need, what practical things he can do. If he knows the spirit identity of our child, he has chosen not to say. Both of us skip the dramas, slip straight through to love. The pure form, non-attaching, free from sticky trickiness that clings and clumps and can cause hideous pain.

After everything is settled, we walk to the restaurant by the pond, order soup and fresh bread, sit on the warm verandah and watch the ducks.

'In my tradition, duck medicine is about emotional support and families,' he says. 'You rarely see one duck swimming on its own.'

He tells me he will be making a journey into the central desert with Aboriginal elders before heading home. There is work he needs to return to, stepping into his grandfather's shoes. I should come, when I'm ready, and bring the little one to meet its other world.

We talk about this different way of parenting, our idiosyncratic path of love and care. And pledge shared commitment to the welfare of our child.

Parting again isn't easy.

'I'll keep in touch by email when I can, and send you my number once I'm back in Canada,' he says. 'I want you to know you can always reach me if you feel the need. And if the modern ways fail, hold me in sharp focus in your heart and mind, and I'll get the message, and I'll call.'

No wonder Clyde wanted to teach me shamanic ways. Canny old man.

'I'm refusing to cry,' I tell him, holding him close. 'Why don't you explore the headland while I walk back to my car?'

I don't want to watch him walk away. I don't want him to see the glistening in my eyes.

30

When I pull up in front of Luca's cafe, Andy is stacking the chairs, preparing to close.

'Angel!' she squeals. 'We thought you might have vanished in that valley. Where have you been? How are you?'

I shut the door, click the locks and walk around the car. This might not be easy, and there's nowhere to hide.

'Hey, Andy. Great to see you too. Sorry it's been so long.'

I step onto the footpath, baby advancing before me into Andrea's shock. It's the first time I've seen her lost for words. Her mouth opens and a kind of hiss escapes, and we are stuck. Until I break the ice.

'Do you have time to make me a cup of tea? I need to explain a few things.'

Freeze frames stutter forward. We go inside. She shuts the door and turns the sign to 'Closed'. Walks behind the counter, one hand tightly gripping its edge. I think she might collapse, or explode. But she puts the water on to boil, turns to front me, hands on hips: 'How could you, Angelica? How could you have done this to Bill?'

'Maybe I should leave,' I say, looking towards the door. 'Or are you prepared to hear my story? If you want me to go, I will.'

A blue-cloaked Madonna and her baby Jesus gaze benignly from the back wall of the cafe, probably advocating empathy and compassion, it occurs to me.

Andrea makes the tea on angry automatic. Pot and cups and milk jug all appear.

'Because I care about you, I will listen. But I can't imagine any way you're going to make this mistake okay.'

My meditation practice comes to the fore. Calm, steady breathing. Breathe out thoughts of grace and love. Let the situation settle. Don't judge. Hmmm. Clyde and Sally both mentioned that I would be tested, that life often meets us at the instructional edge.

'Bill's been gone for over two years, Andy. You of all people have some idea how difficult it's been.'

I realise I don't need to justify myself. Start again.

'Last time I saw you, I had just dropped a man at the station. That man is the father of my child.'

Better. Unembroidered facts.

'So who is this man, then, Angelica? Where is he now? Is he going to support you and the baby?'

Slowly and calmly I tell her the bones of the story. How Hayden was working with Clyde. How we spent some time together. How kind he is. How healing it was for me to meet such a lovely young guy. As the story spills, I realise Andrea might not ever understand. I see our worlds side by side, a chasm of ancestry and history and dogma separating us. But I tell it to the end, hoping my contentment and happiness will thaw her, that she will see the peace and joy I have found in carrying this child.

There's a sigh, a leaning back and slumping.

'I don't understand any of this, Angelica. I think you have become someone I don't know.' She pauses. 'But I do see that you are happy, even though you're doing something you will probably regret for the rest of your life.'

Better than it could have been. Much better. We have a way of going forward.

I sip tea and talk to her about the plans I've made with Ess and Lizzie. How we will all spend time with the baby. How well he will be loved.

'So you already know it's a boy?'

'No, I don't. It's just a feeling I have. And "he" slips out now and then. Maybe it will be a girl and surprise me. I'll be happy either way.'

She wants to know more about Hayden. Tut-tuts when I say he will be living in Canada. Then she asks what my plans are about moving back to the city. I realise she is looking out for her cousin's interests, concerned that he and his family might have to move.

'It's okay, Andy. I've brought a new lease for Angelo and Sabina to sign. Right now, I'm so settled at Walden I feel as though I might never leave. And Jane's staying in Nepal indefinitely.'

Andy is struggling to maintain her habitual warmth. But I leave her my number, suggest she and Luca might come out to the valley and visit. The ball is in her court.

'Is there anything you need?' she asks, as I stand with my keys in my hand. 'Something I can make?'

I tell her about Janet and the other women knitting, about the crocheted blanket. How well I am looked after, how well prepared I am. 'Anything you'd like to make will come in handy, I'm sure,' I tell her, in the end. 'A surprise would be lovely.'

We part on civil terms, but the substance of our connection will never be the same.

* * *

Sabina answers my old front door, gazing determinedly at the air beside my cheek. That was a quick phone call, I think. She already knows.

Behind her a shadow shifts, dissolves, re-forms. Could it be Bill? Supporting me?

They have made the place lovely in a different style – cool, elegant, simple. Baby Lucia is crawling, greets me at the kitchen step with a chocolatey smile and charming gurgles.

'Angelo is upstairs. I'll call him. Would you like a coffee? Tea?'

I tell her I've just drunk tea at Andy's and she turns away, calls her husband, invites me to sit at my old table on the solid turned-wood chair.

There's a job for me to do here. To set them at ease. After hand-shakes and his cool welcome, I tell them that I plan to stay at Walden with my baby. Will most likely raise him or her there, at least for the first few years. They are welcome to stay in this house as long as they need.

We are doing business. Sign the lease. I am impressed by their steadiness in the face of my news.

'Andrea called to tell us of your pregnancy, so we wouldn't get a shock,' Angelo admits, as I reach for my bag, preparing to leave. 'We don't agree with what you've done but still we are happy for you, Angelica. Congratulations.'

The ferry queue greets me like a 'welcome home' sign. The tide is out, and the ferry is docked on the other side. I have time to walk down to the river's edge. Look across at the trees silhouetted against a pale afternoon sky. Salute the rocky hills.

31

'Can you both take a full week off?' I ask. We are planning our trip down south. Sally's friend has sent emails with details of keys hidden, when to put out the bin, the idiosyncrasies of the stove, battery backup for the solar system.

We will travel together in Essie's station wagon. It's comfortable, with plenty of space for everything we want to take. The baby blanket with its crochet hook and balls of wool makes a substantial bundle in an old pillowcase. Ess is bringing a stack of novels, a year's worth, she reckons, which she plans to read by the fire or at the beach. And Liz is intent on culinary experimentation, has filled a box with cookbooks and jars, spices, dried herbs, odd-shaped tins and cooking pans.

Sadness sweeps through me as I make everything secure here at Walden, arrange my luggage near the door. Another first. Holiday minus Bill. Equals. Grief. Which I thought had eased. I subside onto the sofa and sob. It's so unfair. Another round of that. And the impatient anger it generates.

Tashie's excited yelping tells me the girls have arrived, just as the last sodden tissue drops into the bin. I'm wearing my Ugg boots and tracksuit for the trip. No reason to sacrifice comfort. Check the list. Turn off the gas and the master switch for the power system. And we're away.

Liz has packed the rear of the station wagon well, leaving exactly the right space for all my stuff. Tashie curls up in her nest on the floor behind Lizzie's seat. They fuss about my comfort and the baby, plumping a pillow at my side in case I want to rest.

We have calculated the drive to be about six hours if we take the inland motorways before cutting across to the coast. Some of these tollways have appeared since the last time any of us drove south, and navigating keeps us occupied for the first couple of hours. Later, we sing old favourites, play children's I-spy games, chat about this and that. The novelty of the journey has all of us excited and slightly on edge. Until the road soothes our spirits, and slowly we all relax.

The house owner's directions are excellent. Turn right a few kilometres past Narooma and follow the Central Tilba signs. You'll see Gulaga, the mother mountain. We cruise slowly along the quaint main street, do a u-turn at the end and head for Tilba Tilba a little further down the road. A few more turns and we are there.

The cottage is nestled in Gulaga's apron, high enough up to give us glimpses of the sea. Firewood is neatly stacked in a shed and we're already laying claim to the sagging old sofas and armchairs that grace the wide verandah.

Over the first few days we acquaint ourselves with teashops and cafes, arts and crafts stores and the pub where locals congregate at night. We laze about, eating delicious treats and savouring languorous home-cooked meals. Paint. Read. Crochet. Sit in silence. Meditate. Often the mountain disappears into the mist of soft, low cloud that rolls in from the west. There's an expansive dream-like quality, driftingly different from the containment of our valley, infused by the ocean and the tree-covered mountain rising at our back.

Captain Cook on his great southern voyage thought she looked like a camel and gave her a new name. But the people who had lived here countless generations knew her far better than that, knew of her procreative powers, of her two sons close by – Najanuga, the little camel, and Barunguba, the island a short distance out to sea.

When we rug up and walk on the windswept crusty beach, we can see them all. And the camel-shaped rocky headland as well. The dull grey surge of the surf sighs in eddies near our booted feet. We pledge to return in summer, when we can swim, and take a boat or canoes out onto the lake. When we will have a baby with us, as well as the dog.

The mound of my belly is substantial now. A solid being in its own right that rolls and turns, rumbles me in the night, nudges my hands and those of his adoring aunties while we sit and talk.

The experts say pregnant women often feel very alive in the second trimester, this waiting and growing time when the baby has established itself. I think that's true, feel like I'm bouncing out of my skin. There's a place near the village with beautiful gardens on the site of an old dairy farm, archways of fruit trees, acres of roses, all manner of perfumed corners and hidden delights. We walk there for several hours, earning our right to scones and jam and cream.

And in the evenings, we talk. After Lizzie's sumptuous dinner, we sit by the fire and reminisce, rewinding memories to the rhythm of my crochet hook. We remember little things about our childhoods, the different perspectives, each unique. Liz tells us stories of her Maori grandparents, the old man who people called *tohunga* – one wise in the ways of healing and the wisdom of land and sea. How disappointed and angry he would have been at the lifestyle his son chose. She talks more about her mother and about programs at the marae, where community elders hope to guide young people towards healthy, productive lifestyles.

In the mornings, after breakfast, we sit on the verandah and watch the sun float above the expanse of ocean in a clear blue sky. Although it is cold and often windy, we cannot stay indoors, want to rug up and breathe the salty air.

We have taken to reading for a while before we venture out, each of us engrossed in a special project, comfortable in silent communion with our momentary muse. I am still reading the book Clyde lent me, and it makes a lot of sense – this story of an old Native American man on his quest for spiritual insight and peace.

The author tells how Grandfather slowly taught him, taking many months for intensive practice, to allow each lesson to sink in. Lessons about listening and seeing in silence and stillness, learning to live humbly in awareness of the-spirit-that-moves-in-all-things – the spiritual realms as well as the physical ones. What was it Clyde said? It becomes a way of life. I realise that's what the author is saying. Encouraging his readers to pay attention. I imagine these are the kinds of things Hayden has been learning from his grandfather. The work he feels obligated to continue.

The mountain is a constant presence, shrouded in mist or heavy in silent repose. A faded sign in the general store's window includes a map, dotting the track that winds up Gulaga's eastern shoulder. I want to go, feel compelled by an inexplicable urge. But Essie and Liz are in holiday lazing mode – to them it looks like a trek.

'Don't you think it's a bit extreme?' asks Liz, glancing at the extra body I'm carrying around.

'I'm fitter than I've ever been,' I say. 'I've been walking every day, don't forget, plus doing yoga.'

We check with the man behind the counter, who says it's a constant climb but I should be right if I take it steady and drink lots of water. 'If you decide to go, I reckon you should head off sometime around midmorning, give yourself plenty of time. And remember to sign the book.'

He pulls an old exercise book from under the bench, shows me the straggly signatures next to dates, times of departure and times of return. Neat columns ruled in blue biro. 'You'd be surprised how many people go missing up there,' he says, shaking his head. 'Can't imagine why. It's a well-marked track.'

'Is it dangerous?' I ask, although I feel no sense of alarm.

'Nah. Don't know what they get up to. Probably wander off the track and can't find it again. The bush up there is pretty dense. Stick to the track, and you'll be right as rain.'

We are here for another two nights. There is time. The weather for tomorrow looks cold but clear, although there is likely to be mist before I reach the top. All I feel is a zing of excitement. I know I will be safe.

I am up early doing stretches, packing a small bag with bottled water, some apples, a banana, an energy bar. My boots are well worn and comfortable, especially over warm, thick socks. Layers are the best idea – I'm sure to heat up as I make the climb.

Liz insists on serving up a substantial breakfast, quizzes me again. 'I don't think you should be doing this, Angel. Anything could happen up there.'

The force of attraction is unarguable, though. I have to go.

They make arrangements to meet me at the store at 4pm. We can have coffee or an early dinner in the cafe there.

'Ah. You're back. There's a group gone up very early,' says the man at the shop when I tell him I'm doing the walk. 'You should meet them coming down. It's a guided tour. One of the local Aboriginal blokes points out some of the sacred sites, explains a few things.'

Why didn't he tell me this when I made enquiries, I wonder. That would have been perfect for me.

'Once you pass them, you'll be the only living soul up there. Apart from the wildlife.'

What is he trying to tell me? I question him again about safety. About the need to sign in.

'Don't worry, love. If you're not back before dark, we'll send a search party to get you. You'll be right.'

The walk starts out gently along a wide dirt road that winds across rolling green paddocks to the base of the mountain. Beautiful, this lush, fertile country where the cold, clear air brushes my skin and winter sunlight hints at warmth.

Rustic tumble-down sheds lean into the side of the hill and a few jersey cattle graze, their cream and caramel bodies painted to perfection. Two willie wagtails flit from cow to cow, picking and twicking at insects.

I walk past an elegant old farmhouse with several citified cars parked outside. Wonder what is happening in there. Visitors, perhaps. Tourists like Ess and Liz and me.

Gulaga is coming to meet me, stretching her strong foundations beneath my feet as the track takes the rise. There are no houses any more, no further signs of civilisation. Just a hand-painted noticeboard outlining the story of the Yuin people in whose custody the mountain rests. A bit about the flora and fauna of the region. Invocations to treat Gulaga and her inhabitants with respect. The notes say the round trip to the top and back will take several hours, depending on the fitness of the walker and their pace. I doubt I'll be going very swiftly, now that I see the incline, but I am not deterred.

A voice cuts my reverie, making me look up along the track. Around the first bend strides a muscular young guy with a walking pole, face ruddy from crisp air and exertion.

'You going up?' he asks. 'Hope you're fit!'

A few more people pass me, each one offering encouraging words. Their faces glow from the effort of the descent and something else – the pleasure of achievement? The last is a man of about thirty, dark-skinned, black curly hair tied back in a band. He stops to speak with me, rests his eyes on my belly, asks me how I come to be making the climb alone.

'I don't seem to have a choice,' I tell him. 'Ever since I saw the mountain, she's been calling to me. Maybe that sounds crazy, but that's how it feels.'

He smiles. 'Not many people have the privilege of spending time alone with her. Enjoy your walk. Both of you.' And he's off, loping after the group.

I turn now to the incline. Breathe long and deep. Clyde drifts into my thoughts, then Hayden. The baby. Bill. I feel a slight tightening in my womb, a readying. And I begin to walk.

Almost immediately, the landscape changes. Gnarly tree trunks and lush undergrowth push right to the edges of the narrow track. I have stepped through a portal into a purer world. The air is cold, but the grade is unrelenting, heating my body and slowing my thoughts until all that remains is the rhythm of one foot stepping in front of the other, climbing up, moving deeper and deeper into the mountain's embrace.

I pause to drop my small pack, take off my jacket and tie it beneath my breasts, sip some water. Pick up my pack and resume.

The forest is vivid with life. Tiny birds dart from tree to tree, flitting across the track. My body has slipped into sync with the heartbeat of the mountain, which is pulsing a stream of life force through my body and my baby. This is meditation of a kind I've not experienced before. There is no 'me', no sense of separation. I am a perfect cell in the vastness of the maternal being.

Every so often, the grade levels out for a metre or two, allowing narrow streams of water to trickle across as they make their way down to the sea. In these rest moments I gaze out to the ocean, see the abundant lake far below, and Najanuga heading for the beach. Then keep on climbing.

Blood sings through my veins. I feel light-headed yet strong. I am a spirit walking in a vibrant, healthy body, at one with the spirit that moves in all things. Later, I will read Clyde's borrowed book with an expanded mind. Read and learn, not only this author's teachings but the wisdom of many others as well.

I am far up the face of the mountain, shrouded in mist. Invisible hands slip into mine, and a vibrant energy surrounds me.

'We are the essence of woman,' the voices sing. 'We are your sisters, your mother, all women. We are happy to accompany you here.'

There are no audible words, but a stream of pure transmission entering my consciousness. Teaching me how to be. The spirit women are youthful and ancient, resilient and strong, demonstrating good humour as a way of addressing life. They are dancing and laughing around me, holding my hands, making the energy light, the walking a breeze. How long they are with me, I could not say. But eventually, I realise they are gone. Were they the spirit of the mountain? Or the spirits of Aboriginal women from long ago?

I don't know. But I know that I have been blessed. That I am safe. And that I am not alone.

The track up ahead is steeper and narrower than the rest of the climb so far. Through the mist I see the dense undergrowth pushing onto and over the path, creating a shadowy tunnel – a birth canal. My breathing is deep and steady as I enter, leaning into the incline, head slightly bowed. There is no room to turn around. The ground is damp, my skin fresh with mist. As I proceed, I come to understand that the spiralling cycles of life propel us forward, compelling us to find our way through the ecstasies, the pain and the joy.

There is a lightening up ahead, a slight widening of the track.

The trees and the undergrowth pull back, and I am delivered. Into a different realm, where the trees grow taller and further apart and silver light filters through the mist.

I have emerged into a clearing not far from the mountain's peak. A space with another noticeboard, a table, and a long bench seat. Women's voices murmur that I am to climb no further. That I am to sit. Then walk into the forest and make a gift. Give thanks to the spirit of the mountain and of the earth, give thanks for life.

Yet I have nothing with me to give. Nothing but a water bottle, some fruit remnants and the wrapper from an energy bar. The clothes I am wearing. My boots. My watch. My wedding ring.

I walk in rhythm with the heartbeat of the earth, in among the trees, keeping note of each fern and sapling, marking a passage for my return. At the base of a massive tree I am required to stop. Look up. Into the canopy of this wise and ancient being. Who invites me to lean. And then to sit. Time and no time passes before I stand, take a step back. The ground beneath my feet is soft with fallen leaves and humus, and I kneel down to dig. Scrape a hole in the damp, dark earth. Into which I slip the ring that came from Bill. This is a marriage of a different kind, committing to love and gratitude. And delight at the promise of joy to come.

I push the soft earth back into the hole, pat it down, cover it again with fallen leaves. My mind registers astonishment at the deed but my heart and my spirit sing.

I retrace my steps to the clearing, and check my watch. There are two hours left before anyone would come searching for me. Two hours to make my descent. I am ready.

Walking down takes more energy than I expect, leg muscles bracing against the slope of the track, pelvic floor muscles cradling tight. The mountain's birth canal widens a little to let me slip through. I am aware of the need to re-enter the world of humans before the day turns to its end.

The mist begins to thin, letting in filaments of light, the bright greens and blues of tree canopy and sky. Freshness and light greet me, and the sweet voices of spirit women drift in and out. My baby in his fluid world feels compact, my body taut and neat. I think about Bill. 'He will always be with you in spirit,' the voices whisper. That message again.

The day is drawing to an end, yet I feel no need to rush. Below me lie lush winter pastures, the roofs of sheds and houses, Najanuga's hump, and a smudged horizon at the ocean's edge. A distant village cluster, where I think I see the maroon shape that might be Essie's car.

A small bird darts in front of my face, startling me. It is unafraid. As I am now to be. Resilient, purposeful, light-hearted, focused on life. The forest is becoming sparser, the track not so steep. As I pass the noticeboard I feel a flush of deep contentment, recall the glow I saw on the faces of this morning's walkers.

Before I step from Gulaga's embrace I pause and turn, face the mother mountain, close my eyes. If this is prayer I feel it as a grateful merging, the profound stillness of understanding that all is one.

As I open my eyes, a slinking dark shape materialises in the trees to my right. I could swear it's a cat. Too large though, and sleekly black. My eyes trace its silent path as it weaves through the undergrowth and for a long moment I forget to breathe. In my wide open mind I can recollect only one creature this cat could be, yet I know that panthers do not live here. And that I feel no fear. And that the apparition is gone. If it was ever there.

The pale gravel road meanders between post-and-rail fences, past the old farmhouse with its cluster of shiny cars, as I walk towards the village store. On either side, cattle graze, some of them flicking me a glance. A crow's raucous caw cuts the air.

Three eagles swoop in from the north, circling low above the grazing cows. They keep pace with my returning journey, wings widespread, gracefully fine-tuning wingtips on the day's last lazy swirls of air. I recollect the snake and the rainbow and that majestic bird from my dream and it is only as I walk past the first of the village houses that the eagles disappear, fading off into the western sky. I shake my head.

My body is ready to stop, thrilled to the point of exhaustion and beginning to cool. The pale skin encircling my fourth finger feels fresh and new and I wonder whether Essie and Liz will notice my ring is gone.

The road turns right and left, arriving suddenly beside the verandah of the store. My sister and her partner are immersed in conversation, sitting at a corner table cradling dark green mugs. Tashie is curled at Essie's feet.

There is a lean, swarthy man sitting at the table to their right, and he lifts a desultory hand.

'Been up the mountain?' he asks.

There's an air of mystery about him. Or perhaps the black floppy hat and straggly dark hair are intended to give that impression.

'She's magnificent, isn't she?' I sigh, as I walk up the steps. 'Better let them know I'm safe.'

He nods, and looks away.

'You made it back alright then,' says the man behind the counter as he reaches for his battered book. 'Give us your autograph here, if you wouldn't mind. So. What do you reckon? Not too dangerous for you?' Now he's laughing at me, we're laughing together. And I tell him I could have stayed up there all night, I felt so safe.

'If you like the old girl that much you might be interested in what that Joseph bloke does,' he says, nodding towards the black-hatted man. 'He's got a mob out at the farmhouse for some kind of retreat. Maybe you should ask him about it.'

'We're going home tomorrow. Otherwise I would. Thanks anyway.'

Essie and Liz are waiting for me when I walk outside, have pulled up a comfy chair. 'You look amazing!' says Ess as she half stands and reaches out for my pack. 'Buggered but radiant. What can I say?'

My body sinks gratefully onto creaking cane, yet I feel as though I could do it all again. Straight away. 'It was worth the effort,' I smile. 'You two should definitely come with me next time we're down this way.' My fingers trail through the ruff of hair on Tashie's neck. 'They'd love it, wouldn't they, girl?'

I'm ravenous all of a sudden and we order three serves of the apricot chicken with rice, as well as a fresh pot of tea.

'Well, are you going to tell us what happened?' asks Liz. 'You look ... different somehow. I don't know ... refreshed?'

Words don't come anywhere near describing the mountain's magic, although I give it a try. 'I'll paint it when we get home,' I promise. 'That might be a better way of explaining it to you.'

I talk instead about the mystery of the cat. 'It was sleek and shimmery, jet black. Way too big to be a feral. Maybe it wasn't even real.'

Ess recalls tales of escaped circus felines and news articles beating up bushland sightings of an elusive black panther. 'It always triggers a hot debate,' she says. 'Some weirdos think it's a bit like the yowie, or the bunyip of Berkeley's Creek. Remember that? From when we were little kids?'

As we laugh and eat I notice that the man in the black hat has risen to his feet and wandered into the store. He's walking towards us now, with a small piece of printed paper in his hand. 'The guy in there suggested I give you this,' he says, handing the leaflet to me.

'He thought you might be interested in joining tomorrow's retreat group. You can call later and let me know.'

His gaze takes in all three of us but he's directing the invitation to me.

'We're leaving tomorrow. But thanks. Maybe some other time.'

He pauses for a moment, shrugs, then turns and walks away. Heading back to that house where the cars were parked, no doubt.

'Strange kind of guy, isn't he?' Ess comments. 'What's his workshop about anyway?'

'Hey. Look at this!' Liz is pointing to some of the drawings on the brochure. 'Did your big cat look anything like this?'

It's uncanny. The panther I saw at the foot of the mountain is staring at me from the page.

'How weird is that?' In my tired mind a thought stirs. A faint buzzing vibration tingles the base of my spine. 'Maybe it means something,' I muse. 'Maybe I'm meant to do this retreat. What do you think?'

Ess and Liz both have to return to work. But I don't. I have no pressing appointments, no need to rush back. It's only three extra days. The fee is hefty, but I'm intrigued. There's a good chance you get what you pay for.

'Do you think it's coincidence?' I ask them again. 'Or could it be a sign?'

Liz laughs and tells me my trek up the mountain seems to have warped my mind. 'I reckon we should get you and your baby bundle back to the cottage before you come up with any more crazy ideas,' she says.

32

In the night I dream of angels and spirits and mountain mists that sing. A slinking black cat. Eagles riding invisible waves. Nothing about Bill. When I stir beneath the doona just past sunrise I feel embraced by peace, a remnant blessing from the spirits of the mountain.

I'm not ready to go home.

Wrapping my warm coat around my precious bulge and pulling my Ugg boots on, I hatch a plan. I will call that Joseph guy right now from the house phone, while Ess and Liz are still asleep.

'Angelica. I thought you might call,' he says.

Joseph tells me he has spoken with one of the women from the group and she would be delighted to give me a lift back to the city when the workshop ends. The circle is happy to welcome me in.

He is using the same kind of language I've read in Clyde's book. It feels right. I have nothing else important to do. And am keen to learn more from the mountain.

I tease Essie and Liz from their bed with aromas of fresh toast and coffee and the crackle of kindling ablaze in the fireplace.

Scrambled eggs, grilled tomatoes and mushrooms are already on the warming rack.

'You're up bright and early,' says Liz as she stretches like a cat and reaches for the milk. 'Baby been keeping you awake?'

Ess curls her arm around my waist – or where it used to be – and plants a kiss on my cheek. 'Morning, darling. Wow! This looks delicious. Thank you!'

As the last of the coffee dribbles into Essie's mug, I sip on a cup of tea and reveal my plan. There's nothing pulling me back to Walden just yet, I explain. If they take my crochet and other bits and pieces, I can get a lift almost all the way home and we can work out the rest from there.

'I don't like the idea of leaving you here,' says Liz. 'He seems like a bit of a weirdo. I can't put my finger on it, but there's something off about that guy. I reckon you should come with us.'

Ess agrees. 'You have the baby to think about, Angel. What do they do at this thing anyway?'

'It's mainly meditation, as far as I can tell. And maybe some energy work. Nothing scary. I don't know what your problem is.'

We argue back and forth, their opposition making me more determined.

'What are you going to do? Drug me and put me in the car?' I say, hands on hips.

When they finally give up, they insist on checking that my phone is fully charged and that I have both of them on speed dial. Here we go again, I think, as we head towards the old farmhouse – lack of trust. Why won't they trust my judgement? I am glad to be doing this deeper work. Maybe it will help us all.

The first session starts at 10am, and we arrive early. When Joseph walks forward to greet me, Essie steps between us, insisting on talking to him. She quizzes him on how many people are attending, whether I will have my own room, and exactly what the program is. Each of his answers is articulate, his voice calm, his body language pacifying. Even so, I can see that she is not completely convinced. But we have already had our debate. When Joseph mentions that the meditation will begin shortly, Ess hugs me tight. Whispers to me to call if I decide to leave early. Liz does the same. And I watch as they drive away.

When I turn back towards the building, I see that Joseph has picked up my overnight bag and is walking up the steps. I follow him onto the verandah and in through the double doors.

The front room is an inviting haven with a fireplace at its heart. From a shimmer of glowing logs, flames flicker up into a suspended chimney hood. Richly woven rugs form a circle in front of the hearth and nests of velvet and satin cushions complete the scene. There are five places set, and by one of them rests a flat circular drum with a rustic drumstick, three small bowls of what looks like dried herbs and leaves, a soft leather pouch and a long bundle wrapped in a woven cloth.

'The others are just finishing their morning meditations,' Joseph explains. 'They'll be down soon. I'll show you to your room.'

A door at the back of the workshop space opens into a country kitchen graced by a timber table and a medley of wooden chairs. On the far side, a narrow staircase leads to a mezzanine loft with small rooms partitioned off. Joseph carries my bag and I follow, sliding my hand up the smooth timber rail.

'It's like a fairytale!' I exclaim as he opens the door on a small but exquisite room. 'Oh! Look at the bed!' The cover is crocheted in chevron stripes, an almost-twin for the one I am making. Through the window I see the beginning of the trail at the foot of Gulaga. Joseph smiles. Drops his chin in a knowing nod.

'The bathroom is at the end of the row. I'll see you downstairs in ten minutes. You'll meet the others then. Barbara will sort out your registration before we begin.'

They are all women, as it turns out. Three of them, who clearly know each other well. Barbara, with long silvery hair, is the one who has offered to drive me home. Sylvia, in her forties or early fifties, carries extra weight and beams a devoted smile at Joseph. Then there's Therese. Whose modest demeanour might mask other attributes.

Yesterday, they tell me, was an excellent day of inner exploratory exercises and sharing of stories. All meditation based. With a focus on the natural world.

Barbara takes me aside into the kitchen where I write a cheque made out to Joseph Eaglehawk. 'In his own culture he's a medicine man,' she confides. 'They eschew all contact with material goods and money, as far as they can.' She hands me a receipt.

We settle into the fireside circle, Sylvia reclining while the rest of us sit cross-legged. The women want to know about my baby – how many weeks I am, whether everything is going well, and do I know the sex? Until Joseph reins the conversation in.

'Great Spirit has blessed us with Angelica's presence,' he says, beginning a soft beating of his drum. 'When I saw her yesterday, I sensed that she and this precious starchild would join us and bring with them many blessings for the group. The nature of these blessings will unfold.'

I want to ask him what he means, and what he might know of Bill, but it feels rude and intrusive to speak. And the other women seem almost reverential. As the drumbeat maintains its hypnotic rhythm Joseph sets up a chant, encouraging us to repeat the strange, simple words and meandering tune.

During the day we practise ways of connecting to Great Spirit, breathing in light that has travelled through Grandmother Earth, and sitting in silence beneath trees, emptying our minds in order to commune. It's quaint, some of the terminology, but the connect-edness feels good. I am content, for now, to go with the flow.

In the evening after a simple, hearty meal we sit around the fire and talk, sharing informal storytelling time. Joseph unwraps his long cloth bundle to reveal a ceremonial redstone pipe, which he cradles when he speaks. He talks about his Lakota heritage, the tribal grandmothers who raised and trained him and his years spent alone living in the bush, immersed in the natural world. He and Barbara go back a long way, she explains in a quiet aside. Way back to when he first arrived in Australia, before he went off on his extended vision quest. 'He's too humble to tell you himself, but he was special even then,' she says, and shrugs. 'One of the chosen ones – a true shaman. The three of us are devoted to him.'

I can hardly keep myself awake. Wonder what Barbara means by vision quest. Wonder how long these women have been studying with this man. I will tell more of my story tomorrow, I promise the group. Each of whom offers hugs and blessings for pleasant dreams. Truth be told, my mind is buzzing with a host of questions and my body feels a slight unease.

We are working with our totem animals today, lying flat on our backs in pairs on the rugs either side of the fire. Joseph has smudged each of us with the smoke from a small bowl of smoul-dering sacred sage, and is softly beating his drum. I hold Therese's cool, calloused hand in mine and close my eyes. Tense all my muscles, take a deep breath and let it go. Feel my body and my swirling mind begin to relax. The mound of my baby is temporarily still. Maybe he is relaxing too. I release that thought.

'Allow your spirit to journey and seek.' Joseph's voice is hypnotic, the drumbeat rhythmic and slow. 'Perhaps it will find itself walking along a path through a forest, or along a golden sandy beach. Perhaps you can smell pine needles, or the salt air of the sea; feel the chill of snow, or the warmth of sunlight on your skin.' His voice pauses, and my body seems to drift away.

'In your spirit journeying, you ask a question: "Please show yourself, beloved animal guide." Focus all your intention on this question, then let it go. Allow the response to arrive in its own time.'

I have no sense of my body. Am conscious only of moving through light. Until glowing yellow-green eyes drift into my spiritual vision and lock to my mind. A deep purring vibration engulfs me, and a velvety dark. The black of the night. The panther is here. She slips in beside me, powerful, lithe, ready to spring. Yet nurturing.

The drumbeat is faster and louder. It's calling me home.

'You are coming back into your body,' chants Joseph, his tone firmer now. 'You can feel the warmth and grip of your partner's hand.' I feel Therese's strong hand resting in mine. And the race of my pounding heart. My baby bump ripples and rolls.

'Without opening your eyes, and without speaking, you might like to share what you've seen. Let your spirit ask the spirit of your partner to open up and merge.'

I can see a wolf. Silvery grey and lean, crouching low in the snow. I can feel the chill of the air as I grip Therese's hand. While my mind, far away on a sceptical edge, asks unanswerable questions.

Joseph keeps up the drumbeat, guiding us back to our bodies, settling us into our toes, our legs and our hips. 'Be aware of the starchild, Angelica,' he murmurs. I feel a pulse in my heavy belly, my heartbeat, my arms, the weight of my head on the floor. And the breath flowing in and out of my lungs.

When I open my eyes and struggle to sit up, I meet Therese's sharp gaze questioning mine. We have time for sharing. I need her to speak first.

'She's the queen of the underworld, Angelica. The black

panther. Ferocious compassion. A bit like Green Tara or Sekhmet. The mother who protects her young and herself against all foes. No wonder you emanate such quiet strength and depth.'

My mind is exploding and yet ... Therese has done this before. And she is waiting for me to speak.

'So did I really see a wolf?' I ask. 'Do you have a grey wolf as your totem?'

I am rewarded by a radiant smile. 'Oh, you're clever at this. You really are. Very open and attuned. You have quite a gift.'

Sylvia and Barbara are absorbed in quiet conversation too. I hear mention of dolphins and bears from their side of the room. And soft, steady drumming from the corner where Joseph has taken himself off to sit, outside our energy fields, he explains.

After dinner, we gather in our circle and talk some more. I hear myself sharing the story of Bill's death, of my lifestyle at Walden, the blessing of being able to work little and paint lots as I let my miracle baby develop and grow.

Later, beneath the warmth of the glorious blanket I sleep and dream, stalk through underground caverns with the panther by my side, and call out for Bill. Is that his voice I can hear in the distance, urgent with love?

'Normally, as most of you know, I would conduct a sweat lodge on the final day,' Joseph says. 'By way of giving thanks, and seeking purification before re-entering the outside world.' But today he is guided to offer a different teaching. Because of me. Because, he says, the sweat lodge might not be wise considering my pregnant state.

I think he should have clarity on whether it's safe or not. But it feels rude to call him on his vagueness. What would I know? Perhaps it's his way of being polite.

Instead, he offers each of us a one-on-one consultation. An

hour of his wisdom and time. And encourages the waiting group to go outside into the grounds in silence. Find a tree that calls us, and sit with it. He suggests a sensory meditation. An opening of one sense at a time, to the exclusion of all the others. Hearing. Seeing. Smelling. Tasting. Feeling. Simply knowing. Some call that the sixth sense, he explains, turning his dark eyes on me. I will be the last of the four to sit with him. Because I signed up last.

I am increasingly aware of the submissive way the other women follow his commands. Couched as suggestions, certainly, but still imperative. Barbara's comment about his humility doesn't quite fit. Maybe that's what's triggering my uneasiness. He counsels ongoing silence after our meditation is done. Says we can reconvene and chat at dinnertime.

From the verandah I spot a rocky outcrop behind the house. A serene place nestled near the edge of the tree line with views of Gulaga. It feels like where I need to be.

There is moss on the shaded southern faces of the rocks and soft grass growing right up to their northern side. That's where I'll sit.

With my back against the solid warmth I close my eyes, focusing on sound. Which laps me with its waves of silence. And then a butcher bird. That liquid melody.

My mind cannot stay still. It has to ask: 'What do you want to tell me? Do you have a message from Bill?' But the melody leaves only a hollow silence in its wake.

I can't stem the flow of thoughts and questions. Why did I not hear messages from Bill? Why can I see etheric wolves and panthers, but not discern my darling? Did I lose him when I gave my wedding ring to the mountain? What have I done?

When I force myself to focus on the sense of sight I am assailed by the image of a panther slinking through the trees, so real that my eyes spring open. And still see her there. Creeping along the tree line in the shadow of Gulaga. I push myself to my feet and prepare to run. Look into the forest again. And she is gone. Was she ever there? I feel like I'm losing it. And have a thousand questions for the shaman.

When my turn comes at last, though, I find myself overwhelmed by lethargy, uncertain where to start. Joseph has a quiet yet compelling presence today.

'You have questions about the spirit you carry in your womb.' His gaze holds mine. 'And many other questions too.'

'Why did you settle in Australia?' I find myself blurting. 'And which one of your parents is Lakota?'

His face is set in stone. 'Your questions should focus on your own issues,' he says, coldly. 'I have told you as much of my story as you need to know.'

I'm feeling very uneasy now. And reluctant to ask him about Bill. If he's so clever, why doesn't he tell me what I want to know?

'You yearn to know about the spirit of your husband, Angelica, but first you must learn to trust. The black panther is a strong totem animal. She has accompanied you through the depths of darkness and has more to teach you if you are willing to connect more consciously with her.'

So he is in my head. Or stating the obvious?

'And how do you suggest I do that, Joseph? I suppose meditation is the way? Or spirit journeying?'

He tells me he knew this would come up for me, because I am sensitive and special. He says he has prepared a space in the bush, just near here, where I can undertake a darkness vigil. If I'm game. Anything could happen when the panther walks at night, he tells me. But he has set up a protection zone to ensure I will stay safe.

What would Bill say? Will his spirit meet me there? Maybe the panther will show me a way to connect with him. Or to settle my questions about baby, once and for all.

Joseph tells me the other women will hold the space for me

energetically, here at the house. I'm not sure what that means, and feel again that sense of unease.

'I wouldn't suggest this if I felt there was any risk to you or your precious starchild,' he says. 'You'll be safe so long as you obey the rules. You must reach deep inside yourself to access courage and trust.'

Immediately after dinner, we rug up warmly in coats, scarves and gloves. The women line up to give me hugs. Joseph hands me a torch and walks silently ahead with his. In the shadow of the night mountain, the bush feels dense. I keep his silhouette close as the track winds through heavy undergrowth and up the hill.

Until we emerge into a clearing where tall gum trees reach into the black velvet sky and shadows surround us. On one side my torch throws its spotlight on some low spreading branches strung with feathers, underneath which is a blanket, folded double, on the ground.

'I've created a sacred women's bower for you,' he says. 'So long as you stay within the confines of this protected space, you have nothing to fear. Although the panther might well visit you.'

It all seems a bit extreme – the set-up and the language he's using. We are only a few hundred metres from the house.

'When the panther walks at night, she can open gateways into realms of wickedness and evil. There's a portal over there.' He indicates a pitch dark area hedged in by trees at the far end of the clearing. Warns me that malicious demented spirits are crowded beyond it awaiting an opportunity to break through. 'But I've put strong energetic protection across it to keep you safe. So long as you don't walk through that portal, nothing can harm you.'

Now it sounds like he's on an ego trip – spouting stories designed to frighten me. But I'm determined not to buy into them. As I shine my torch around I see there is a circle of stones in front of the blanketed bower, with kindling set, ready to be lit. A small pile of firewood is stacked nearby, a box of matches and a candle. Some bundles of dried herbs and wildflowers. It would be almost romantic, if it wasn't so weird.

'I feel fine thank you, Joseph. What happens now?'

'Once you've lit the fire, you must put the torch away. I will leave. I won't go too far. And in exactly one hour, I'll come back to collect you. If you need me before then, all you have to do is call and I will come.'

He sounds so ceremonial and formal, I almost laugh.

As I squat to light the fire, I ask whether he has any guidance about what I should do, or what I might expect while I'm here alone.

He recommends a brief period of meditation. After which I should call on the panther to emerge, then listen and watch for her. He mentions mystery and miracles. Suggests I might also ask the spirit world the questions that have been pressing on my mind these past few weeks. And stresses once again that I must not disturb the evil forces that prowl beyond the energetic portal.

As he bows and exits backwards from the clearing, I hear the twigs snapping and crackling beneath his feet. Hear his footsteps fading as he turns towards the house and walks away. Until I sense I am alone.

The fire casts a cosy circle within my dark cocoon. There is no moon. I sit cross-legged on the blanket in my bower, close my eyes and drift into my steady breath. Where thoughts dissolve.

The moment I open my eyes, I think: This is bizarre. Here I am, in a clearing in the forest, with a sweet little fire to keep me company. And I'm waiting for a panther to appear. Do I need any more proof that I've lost the plot?

My thoughts wander through unanswered questions about Joseph and the work he's doing here. His personal life. He is closed and reticent about all that. But says he roams from place to place, following Great Spirit's guidance, in tune with Grandmother Earth and his totemic eaglehawk. I wonder.

Suddenly, a sharp crack whips through the night air. It came from the direction of the thicket of trees at the edge of my firelit cocoon. My heartbeat is thumping outside my chest. Another crack. A gunshot? Or a portal opening up? My eyes strain into the darkness, trying to penetrate the walls of shadowy blackness, trying to access my sixth sense. Where is the panther now? All my senses are on high alert. Recalling Joseph's words of warning, I am too terrified to stand and walk around. I beg my totem: panther goddess, please, come and help me now. I call on the spirits of the mountain but there is no response. I feel panic on the rise. Feel my body vibrate to the rapid thump of my heart. I sense something else, some massive presence breathing here in the dark. I hold my breath. The darkness breathes in. And breathes out.

Murky shapes sway and shift in shades of blackness at the clearing's edges. If I scream, will demons latch onto me? If I try to leave, will they attack?

I feel the panther sidle into the clearing. Feel her purring strength. Her ferocious, protective courage.

And it hits me. Joseph said he would return. I have been here for much more than an hour. He is playing nasty mind games.

I have wrapped my coat tight around baby, wrapped my arms around him too. I am breathing in the strength and power of the panther.

Adrenaline kicks in. I flick on my forbidden torch, clutch my coat around my belly, and sprint from the clearing onto the narrow track.

'How could you do this to me?' I roar as I burst into the house. 'You bastard! You set me up!'

Joseph is distant though. So cold and distant. Turns his back on me and walks away.

The women are not around.

I rush to the fireplace and huddle beside dying embers, trying to get warm.

'You broke the rules,' says Joseph, who has crept up on me. 'You let yourself become afraid.'

'And where were you?' I challenge him. 'Why didn't you come back when you said you would?'

'Ah, Angelica. Sometimes I use coyote medicine. The tricky teacher's tool. Sadly, you failed the test. I thought you were made of sterner stuff, but I see now that the darkness has you in its grip.

'I asked the other women to leave. They understand you require my full attention.'

Oh my god.

He orders me to take myself and my baby off to bed. Says he will deal with me in the morning. Instructs me to leave another cheque on the kitchen table and he will see that Barbara banks it on his behalf. A donation for the exorcism, he explains. Five thousand dollars would be appropriate. The removal of evil attachments is an exhausting and high-level energy process, he says; he is only willing to do it for me because the starchild is worth saving.

But I am fully awake to his sinister bullshit now. As I make my way up the stairs, I feel a shiver run down my spine. We are both hatching plans.

I have no idea where he is. But the house is in darkness. Now, the voices I hear in my head are the ones from the mountain and they sing me resilience songs. 'We are with you, sweet Angel, and of you. We will support you.' Silently, I pick up my bag and my boots. Creep down the stairs. The breathing I heard in the forest is back.

I don't care. I have to escape. Push open the front door and quietly pull on my boots.

I dare not use my torch, but there's a fat crescent moon hanging low in the starlit sky, newly risen. It could be my friend or my foe. At least it will mean I don't trip and lose valuable time.

Soft grass at the edge of the gravel track muffles the sound of my boots, yet I am too terrified to run. I have made it halfway to the village when I hear a vehicle crawling towards me. In the moonlight it looks like a ute. Its lights are not on. Oh my god. My baby is rolling and kicking and I am afraid for him, too. Can terror bring on labour?

There is nowhere to hide. And barbed wire fences hemming me in on both sides. The ute glides to a crunching standstill beside me.

'Get in, Angelica. Quickly! Hand me your bag.'

Joseph is using Clyde's voice. I scream and take off.

But my friend's stride is longer than mine. Clyde's hands grip my shoulders and turn me around, into his hug. And I burst into tears.

'Thank god I got here in time,' he says, shepherding me into the ute.

33

Our valley welcomes us home with howling winds that whip white flecks of foam from the sullen river. On the long homeward drive I have had plenty of time to reflect on my foolishness. And to wonder again and again at the miracle of Clyde turning up when he did. He says he'll explain later, once I've settled down.

The ferry's engine growls and strains as it hauls the heavy barge across the current, surging us to the shore with groaning ramp and clanking chains. There is a strong scent of home-fires and eucalypt. Trees creak and lean against nature's onslaught, hurling branches at the land. I have never seen the valley in this state, channelling fierce elemental forces, challenging moveable features to cling and batten down.

'Looks like we're in for some rain at last,' I say, ducking nervously as a spray of gumleaves flashes across the bonnet of the ute. 'I'll be glad to get inside.'

Clyde says that Ess and Liz want me to stay the night with them, but I am desperate for my cottage. We debate the issue for a while, until Clyde lets me win. Maybe he is persuaded by Tashie perched on the seat between us, her wiry little presence guarding me. She'll be glad to get home too.

Reluctantly, he drives past Essie's place, then insists that I wait in the ute while he checks my mailbox and opens the Walden gate. The paperbarks lining the laneway are groaning and leaning, tensioning their roots deeper into the ground.

But my cottage that grows from the earth appears unchanged. I will feel more settled and safe once the fires are lit and the windows are glowing with golden light.

'I still don't understand how you came to be there when I needed you,' I say, as Clyde holds the door open and ushers me inside. 'And you brought Tashie with you.' Someone has laid fires in the fireplace and the stove. The girls have been here.

But Clyde is persistent in reserving the details for later. He needs to get back to his place.

All he will say is that he knew I was in danger and repeats that he's glad he got there in time. He knew Eaglehawk years ago, he explains, and had an urgent sense I was in trouble when Ess and Liz said I was with him.

During the night the rain arrives, falling in sheets, soaking the roof and the earth and swelling the river's flow. I am woken by Tashie's insistent whine, her urgent pawing at the side of my bed.

'What is it, girl? What's up?'

I clamber out of bed, pull on my dressing gown, and wander around the house, Tashie at my heels. But I can find nothing wrong. The stove fire I lit last night is still warming the air and the earthen floor, cosying us in. I can't see any leaks. By the clock I can tell that day has broken, despite the gloom. I feel safe. But don't know whether to trust my instincts any more.

I've heard locals tell the story of the last big flood – how houses on the mains electricity grid were without power for days or weeks, residents desperately cooking up curries to preserve kilos of thawed meat, everyone hunkering in. I head for the phone.

'How are things at your place, Clyde? I can't even see our shed.'

'It's bucketing down, alright,' he replies. 'How did you sleep? Are you okay?'

He's concerned about me being twenty-nine weeks pregnant and alone if the rain sets in. He thinks I should drive down to Ess and Liz's place, before the road gets flooded out. Perhaps I am being perverse but I want to stay cocooned at Walden, at least for now. But I tell him I'll call Essie and see what she has to say.

She also wants me to go and stay with her and Liz. Gets annoyed when I continue to resist. 'Even the kids are being kept home from school, Angelica. Their parents know that if the road goes under, there'll be no way of getting them home for days.'

After what I've just been through, she says, and considering the baby's best interests, someone needs to take a responsible stand.

But I am obdurate. I feel unsafe being anywhere but in my cottage. And if I'm wrong, I tell her, and Walden is threatened by flood, I'll call Clyde.

She is far from happy with me. Tells me outright that she and Liz are concerned about my mental state and that they will be keeping tabs on me.

I feel like a naughty child. But I phone Clyde and set up an emergency plan with him. No doubt he will keep Essie in the loop.

'The minute the phone lines go out, I'll be down to get you,' he insists. 'Or if the road to the village gets cut off.'

Ungraciously, I agree. And when I step outside to let my dog do a wee, I get a clearer view of what nature might have in store. Icy wind lashes through the trees and hard, piercing rain stings my face. Tashie squats hastily at the pergola's edge, shakes herself and dashes back inside.

Clyde asked if I would be up to bringing a store of firewood indoors and I do, battling the rain-flecked wind every time I open the back door. I carry small pieces a few at a time in my arms, gardening gloves protecting my hands and a thick jumper keeping splinters at bay. The stack on the floor beside the stove grows to a mini mountain until I am satisfied. Now for the larger chunks of wood. I manage my precious belly with care, squatting to lift, manoeuvring one length at a time into the living room, creating a log dump that I hope will see me through.

Everyone has been praying for this rain, yet in torrents it threatens to sweep away riverside pastures, the winter crops, possibly even small trees. I am exhilarated, though, my breath fogging the inside of the kitchen window. I am hypnotised by torrents streaming down the side of the hill, cutting a deep new creek beside the tree line, rushing to meet the river at its nearest bank.

We are in a world of our own here at Walden – just the baby and Tashie and me. Flames lick up into the chimney and I feel safe. Feel as though Joseph Eaglehawk and his machinations are a million light years away. If they ever existed at all. And decide it is a perfect time for baking bread. I set out the bowl, the yeast and the flour, and knead dough to the rhythm of the pounding rain.

Ess phones again just as the loaf goes into the oven, still trying to twist my arm. She wants to take me and baby to higher ground, although my cottage sits well above the highest known watermark.

'I distinctly remember Jane telling us the cottage has never been flooded,' I say. 'Not even in the floods of '98. If I get scared, or I don't feel safe, I promise I'll jump in the car and come.'

She tries to argue, says that by then it could be too late. Reminds me that it's the road between Walden and the village that goes under water and if the river rises fast I could be cut off.

'In that case, I would go to Clyde's.'

In the afternoon, I look through the mail that Clyde brought in. A couple of bills. Nothing from Neil. I am not surprised, but hope he's okay. Then stretch out on the sofa to feast on warm whole-grain bread with lashings of butter and leatherwood honey.

Licking the sweet yeasty mess off my fingers, I see again the pale band of skin where once I wore a wedding ring.

They didn't notice – Essie and Liz. They would have commented like Joseph and the retreat women did. No wonder I crave solitude. I need to sit in silence in the soft firelight of home and review it all. I have touched the edge of heaven and been singed by the fires of hell, and need to get my thoughts straightened out.

As my breath settles and my mind empties, I slip into a meditative stillness. Fear and confusion begin to drift away and my body releases weight, leaving my heartbeat and that of the baby anchoring me to the sodden land. We are lifting and lifting, rising up. Viewing the raging sweep of the river as it cuts away its desiccated banks. We can see huddles of cattle on hillsides along the road, clutching for solid ground. In the far distance we see an entire shed ripped from its moorings, being dragged askew across the earth. And thin trickles of smoke wisping from chimneys on the dwellings that house other people who are nestling in like us.

The baby stirs and shifts, landing me back on the rose-patterned sofa, into this body that feels solid and fit. Am I being foolish? Will I know if we need to escape?

The sweet strength and resilience of Gulaga's spirit women infuses me as I slip into meditation again, as though they are holding my hands and we are once more walking the ascent. Into the embrace of the mountain I drift, quizzing the spirit women for clues as to who they might be, as my own spirit merges with them. Through my cells flows the essence of endurance, of generosity, of maternal love and spiritual core strength. 'You are woman.' I absorb their sweet song. 'Witness to all births and all deaths, mother of life's unending cycles.'

On the wide screen of my inner vision I view random tableaus of my life. Bob and Maddie around a table with three tiny girls. Bill working with his tools in our inner city shed, and then as a shimmering angel. Myself, progressing steadily through Gulaga's birthing canal. Fleeing in terror from evil in the dark of night. An image of the son I will have. Tall wooden poles painted ornately with stylised eagles, forming a gateway through which my boy and I are walking. A glimpse of Hayden.

My eyes spring open. I suck in air. I hug my arms around my belly and breathe in deeply to calm the frantic beating of my heart. What was all that?

I would give anything to have Bill here, to talk this through with him. To hear him reassure me I am sane.

I gave my wedding ring away to a mountain as a gift. Most people would say that is not a normal act. Now I am seeing and hearing spirits, and walking in unfamiliar places with a child who is not yet born.

I need to think. Or should I talk to Clyde or Sally?

'Don't be afraid,' I hear the spirit women whisper. 'You have had a taste of the way expanded consciousness can be. Settle, and later we will visit you again.'

I stand and walk into the kitchen to put the kettle on. Go to the bathroom to pee.

Do I feel okay? Do I look like myself in the mirror? Yes. There I am, a noticeably pregnant woman in a claret-coloured jumper and black corduroy pants.

I settle with my cup of tea beside the fire. Reach distractedly for the book I was browsing before we went south, let it fall open at a random page.

'Mastery of meditation and the ability to walk simultaneously in both worlds, physical and spiritual, may be acquired via years of dedicated practice. Long-time meditators may experience blissful states in which they feel they have glimpsed other dimensions or spiritual realms. These phenomena are considered normal by those with expanded consciousness; those capable of surrendering individual will to the unfathomable perfection sometimes referred to as god, or the divine.'

Is that synchronicity? There's more, but I am already feeling reassured. Perhaps I'm not going mad? No doubt I've been embarrassingly naive. But that doesn't mean I've lost my mind. Does it?

The wind is hurling soaked twigs and branches through the air. It's wild out there. Rain pours in torrents from the sky but in here the fire is cosy and I feel secure. I am determined to stick it out.

But when Clyde phones, his words are urgent and clear.

'They're forecasting four more days of this. The river's broken its banks. I'm coming to get you while I still can.'

The line goes dead. Whether he has finished speaking, I'm not sure. Either way, my resistance seems to be at an end. I should pack a bag.

I gather my crochet, my Ugg boots, a change of clothes, and the leftover bread. Clip on Tashie's lead. Sit on the sofa like a stubborn child, my dog at my feet, waiting for authority to arrive.

A freezing blast of mist rushes through the door with my old friend. 'Good. You're ready. Come on. I'll take that. You concentrate on getting in the ute.'

Our sloshing, lurching journey up the hill reveals a world half washed away – finally, I understand everyone's concern. I've been living in Walden's cocoon. Broad swathes of sheening water distort the landscape, glinting through rips in the deluging curtains of rain. Where cattle grazed and the occasional horse was tethered there is no longer land. The river is a seething creature intent on misadventure, with a heart and mind of its own.

Tashie dashes for the steps to Clyde's verandah, splattering wetness on the decking as she shakes herself dry. I take it more carefully and my hat and coat are soaked before I make it to the front door. I feel Clyde's steadying hand at my back. A fire welcomes us from behind the glass door of the lounge room stove.

I have lost all sense of time. How extraordinary it is to discover that the day has passed and the night is closing in. The savoury aroma of soup drifts from the stove, making me aware how hungry I am. I have spent the afternoon exploring other realms. It will take a long time for me to get the hang of 'walking in both worlds', that much is clear. If I want to go there at all.

Baby is happy to be in this new place, it seems, rippling an intriguing bump from my left hip to my right. 'I'm sure that must be a foot,' I say to Clyde. 'Don't you think?'

The old man smiles benignly as he ladles thick soup into bowls and serves up chunks of crusty warm bread.

Overnight the teeming torrent intensifies, beating the solid metal roof like a thousand angry drums. Roused from deep drifts of slumber I roll over in Clyde's guest bed, and wonder uneasily whether the valley will still exist at break of day.

Pale light heralds a glimmer of morning and the thunderous rain continues to fall. From the verandah we peer towards the road, but it is a river as well. A wide body of furious water, muddy brown, raging at treetops and telegraph posts. Clyde points out where the fenceline should have been but I see only torn timber and grotesque bloated bodies of livestock being swept along.

'Thank you for coming to get me,' I shout above the relentless din. 'It seemed so safe down at Walden, so secure.'

'And it probably is,' shouts Clyde. 'But what would you have done if something happened with the baby? Or Tashie? What if you had needed help?'

We slip into a rhythm with the pouring rain, flowing through nights and days. Stoking the fire in the lounge room, keeping the kitchen stove fire alight. Cooking simple food. Eating. Reading. Doing yoga. I work on the blanket while Clyde does leatherwork. No point trying to chat. We cannot easily make ourselves heard through the incessant drumming of the rain. Tashie has settled beside the fireplace on a nest of old blankets. She stirs once in a while to lick an urgent itch, or twitches at her dreams.

Hours pass as the dive and twist of my crochet hook morphs colours into substance, hypnotic, setting my mind adrift.

On the third day we hear the roar of an outboard motor, see a bright orange dinghy cutting a frothy vee through the expanse of brown swirling water. Soft rain continues to fall. We have no phone connection, not since the call Clyde made to me. We are concerned about the girls and how they might be faring, but they are well prepared for whatever the elements might bring. And they know I am safely here with Clyde.

A deep megaphoned voice calls out from the little boat that has slowed and is circling in its own wake at the bottom of our drive. 'Need any help up there? We were told you might have a pregnant woman with you.'

We step forward towards the verandah railing, wave wide, exaggerated waves, shout, 'We're okay!' Wave again. Watch the water churn at the stern of the dinghy as its bow lifts to the task of checking the households further upstream.

On the fifth day an eerie silence wakes us. No more rain. Filaments of light filter through gloomy clouds. The obscenely wide river is dirty brown. Clyde says it will be another few days before the water level drops and we can start to survey the devastation, a valley reshaped by nature's imperatives.

Now that we can hear each other talk, rich conversation flows. Clyde tells me more of his personal history – his childhood as an urban boy, wild times at university, a career in the law. He tells me that his life was reconfigured by a slanderous slur – he won't dwell on details – and how that debacle triggered his connection to the spiritual realms, sent him off on years of travelling and eventually led him to his home here in the valley.

It was during his time as a warden in a Northern Territory prison that Clyde met the so-called Joseph Eaglehawk. They certainly weren't friends. Joseph was serving a twelve-year sentence for fraud, rape and grievous bodily harm. Clyde met the man's parents once, a bewildered elderly Maltese couple from Melbourne. No Lakota blood there.

'We often learn most from the teachers who give us the hardest time,' he says. 'Look how much you've learned from your close shave with this conniving charlatan.' He grins.

'But I didn't fully believe him from the very beginning,' I wail. 'Neither did Essie and Liz. I can't fathom why I was so naive.'

'People who use energy for their own dark purposes can be just as skilful as those of us with good intentions,' he says. 'When you think about it, you'll see how that bloke homed in on your vulnerabilities. Your pregnancy. Your yearning to make contact with Bill. Your ability to see glimpses of the spirit realms. That panther, for instance. And eventually, your fear.'

Quietly he talks about the countless teachers he has learned from – workshop facilitators, priests and nuns, lovers, wisdom in books, the spirits of trees and rocks and river and earth. And the occasional murderous bastard who tried to bring him down.

'So you met the spirits of the mother mountain,' he says to me a bit later.

How does he know?

I struggle to describe the way this awakening has been for me. But he doesn't need the words. Points to my naked finger. Nods. 'When you surrender to creation in the way you did with that, life's generosity displays its full potential. Maybe you've glimpsed that already?' There's a smile behind his eyes.

I want to ask him about Bill and the baby, but how will I know I can trust what he says?

'Your son is a special blessing, as I'm sure you already know.' He is in my head again. And he said 'son'. 'Hayden is a Haida man, with ancient heritage to share. You'll see, in time.'

No mention of Bill. I am deeply confused.

Clyde has not heard from Hayden since I saw him in the city. Neither have I. Yet there is no feeling of desertion, no sense of betrayal. We both know he will keep his word and support me and our child in whatever way he can.

Soft light pokes windows of hope in the gloomy sky. A butcher bird lands on the rail at the corner of the damp verandah. Unleashes its fluted melody into the fuggy air.

'Bill is a support and an inspiration,' says Clyde. 'He was a good man, your husband. And he's delighted to see you moving on.'

Similar message to Sally's. I no longer wonder whether they are in cahoots.

'So do you know where Bill's spirit is now?' I blurt. 'If he's happy to see me moving on, what's he up to?'

I didn't intend the abrasive tone. But there it is. Love and frustration imploded.

'How long do spirits drift around out there before they reincarnate anyway?' Out pours a stream of questions, increasingly irate.

'Whoa! Hang on there, Angel. No need to get upset. Questions are good! I hope you never stop questing. It's when you blindly believe that you end up in strife. As you've seen.

'The thing is, Angelica, that sometimes we simply don't know. Some questions don't have easy answers. Native Americans – real ones, that is – talk about the Great Mystery. Meaning all those imponderables that are beyond our human capacity to sort out.'

He sits back. Considers my sceptical gaze.

'Why do you think scientists and mystics keep seeking? If we're so clever, you'd think we'd have all the answers by now. Wouldn't you?'

I can see where he is going with this. Even religious adherents like Sage and Mike give it up to God at some point. Refer to God's love that goes beyond human understanding.

'We can torment ourselves for lifetime after lifetime with discontent and frustration. Or we can accept that there are some aspects of life that simply are. Or that we just can't fathom. Does that make sense?'

I can see that it does. But my heart doesn't want to leave it there. I still want to know about Bill.

'Okay, Angel. At risk of sounding like our shady friend ... would you like to go on a spiritual journey? Safely this time?'

A shudder runs through me. Trepidation? Anticipation? Fear?

'What kind of a journey do you have in mind?'

'Good! It's good to ask questions. If you agree, all you'll do is lie here on the sofa by the fire, and I'll guide you into a meditation where you may find your own healing space in the spiritual realms. Some call it a medicine place. You do the work. I'll just be here to keep you company.'

'You won't leave the room?'

'I'll be here. And you can come back to this consciousness whenever you like. It's important that you feel safe.'

This is Clyde. Ess and Liz's old friend. The man I have known and trusted for a couple of years. The man who turned up to rescue me. I reckon it will be okay. And the curiosity cat is prowling through my mind.

Clyde asks me to get comfortable. Tucks a warm rug over my outstretched legs and my baby bump. Asks me to close my eyes. To take some deep breaths and let all the tension and desperation go.

'With your mind's eye, let yourself look around. Perhaps you see a path leading somewhere interesting up ahead.'

My mind drifts away from my body. I suspend conscious thought. For a timeless while I float in nothingness, feeling a vague sense of wellbeing and peace.

Until a hill rises up before me, with a track winding through long emerald grass to the top. I walk effortlessly up the track, feeling the softness of summer beneath my bare feet. At the top of the hill is a seat. I sit down. Before me is spread a vista of rolling hills, densely treed, blue with eucalyptus haze. When I turn to my left, there is a high escarpment of golden rock, with an opening at its base. I walk down a sandy track noticing, as I draw closer, that the opening is the mouth of a tall cave, curtained by tangles of vines. I push them aside and go in. Find myself on a long stretch of shimmering sand, with the deep blue of the ocean rolling in from my right. My body, still rounded and pregnant, is wearing no clothes. It dips and dives through the waves and emerges radiant with silvery light. There's a shift. My body is clothed in a floaty garment of midnight blue. I am standing in a glade on a plateau from which I can still see the ocean. On the edge of the glade, there is a bench carved out of pale pink crystal rock, overlooking a limpid pool. I sit down. In the shimmering waters of the pool I see a being taking shape. I see that it's Bill. Not in any form I recognise from the past. But I know it's him.

'Where have you been?' I ask. 'What have you been doing?'

He talks about some of his experiences in the spiritual realms, and about the special-interest study groups he has joined. Tells me he has been learning from ancestors and spiritual teachers about the essence of life. About how and why spirits incarnate in physical form on planet earth and countless other planets in galaxies beyond the ones we know.

'Will you reincarnate soon?' I ask.

His image is gone.

And my spirit is back in my cumbersome body, lying on the couch by Clyde's fireplace in his lounge room.

Tears course down my cheeks. Tears of joy and despair and frustration.

Clyde is rubbing my feet. Quietly calling my name.

'No doubt you have more questions than when you began,' he says. 'But first, I want you to rest, Angelica. You've been gone quite a while. You need to integrate everything you experienced. Maybe later we can talk.'

The next time I wake, the lounge room lamp is switched on and soft lights are glowing in the kitchen. There is an unmistakable aroma of roasting chicken and something else – vegetables? Clyde is whistling a tune I don't recognise.

'Ah. You're back,' he says, wandering in. 'More settled now.'

And he's right. I have no recollection of dreaming and my journey to the glade nudges the edge of my memory, peacefully.

'I saw Bill. He didn't answer all my questions. I was upset at the time, but it feels okay now. I don't really understand what went on.'

'And perhaps you don't need to,' he says. 'Check in with how you feel. How are your frustration levels, for example?'

'It's weird. The whole thing's beyond weird. But I feel at peace. Maybe I died and went to heaven ...'

'I doubt that,' he smiles. 'You look very much alive to me. You must be pretty hungry too.'

34

Over the next few days the water skulks back towards the river's restructured banks, revealing devastation and unleashing a hideous stench. Resurrection follows slowly as trucks trundle along the treacherous road. They are loaded with volunteers who clear and clean, provide support, help weary residents set their lives to rights.

Liz drops by to say hello and see for herself that we're okay. She and her team of muddy volunteers sit for a few minutes with us on the verandah, cradling mugs of coffee. There is good-natured banter, frustration, extraordinary tales of determination and resilience, of loss, of survival against the odds.

It's time I went home to survey the damage at Walden. I can revisit the spirit realms some other time. Clyde carries my bag to the ute, hands me in. During the days we have sheltered at his house my body seems to have grown heavier. Thirty weeks. Three-quarters of the way there. My hands rest on the baby, slide the seatbelt straps underneath and over his bulk.

Tashie is acting like a puppy, excited to be going for a ride. She's been a good girl, cooped up for so many days. Clyde takes the gravel driveway slowly, guiding his wheels onto ridges between gullies and washaways. Along the roadside, mounds of twigs and branches and matted strands of grass bank up against remaining sturdy trees, wrap around telegraph poles, line what remains of fences. Everything stinks. In places there are monstrous potholes where the surface of the road has given way. We are travelling at a snail's pace, shocked at what we see.

My gate hangs at an awkward angle off one hinge, a massive tree branch resting across its splintered top rail. 'We'll get that fixed for you in the next few days,' says Clyde. 'Fingers crossed there's not too much other damage.'

By a miracle, the letterbox on its pedestal is standing proud, still in one piece. When I lift the flap I see two sodden envelopes right at the back. I put the formal-looking one on Clyde's dashboard, not recognising the return address. It can wait. The other, the important one, carries Canadian stamps. Hayden. I flatten it carefully onto the dashboard as well.

Shredded foliage and small branches litter the laneway, and we slowly make our way in. Three times we have to get out, move obstacles to the side. So far so good. I have such faith in the house that Jane and Richard built, I have felt little concern. Until now. The general devastation is sobering, and I am holding my breath, waiting for what we might find.

The cottage looks sodden and intact, although all the flowers and most of the shrubs are gone or severely battered.

'Looks like you're going to be okay,' says Clyde. 'Those folks knew what they were doing when they built this cottage. Very much in touch with nature, Richard and Jane.'

I hear respect, sadness. A silent salute. Make a mental note to email Jane. Or try to call her. Once the phone lines have been restored.

'Let's get your things inside and then go for a bit of a walk.'

I lift my precious belly out of the ute, peel the damp envelopes off the dashboard and call Tashie to my side. She can walk with us on the lead, but I don't want her running off to explore alone.

A dank, closed-up smell meets us when we push open the front door. The house has missed being warmed by fires, missed being filled with life. But structurally it seems fine. In a few minutes we have checked thoroughly for leaks or other damage, finding none. Victory for the sod roof. I am impressed.

The damp letters droop in my hands and I say a little prayer that their contents will survive. Lay them on the wire rack above the stove.

'Let's get this fire going before we explore,' I say to Clyde, who is already surveying my stashes of firewood.

'I reckon the rain's gone for a while,' he says. 'I'll take some of this back outside.'

I sort through the smelly fridge, pulling out rank milk and cream. The gas tank connection must be fine, though. Everything is still cold. Check the light switches and the power points. We have survived. Silently, I thank Richard and Jane once again. When I think of the spirit that moves in all things, I cannot help feeling blessed.

The shed and the studio haven't fared so well although they are still standing. The river must have rushed through them, depositing piles of rubbish and mud. Pieces of Tashie's kennel lie ramshackle against the fence, tangled with vegetation. The veggie patch. With a sad shock I realise that my garden has gone, soggy piles of foliage and dank greenery washed up against the wire mesh that was meant to keep trouble out.

The track to the river is gone too, its approaches matted over with detritus and stinking mud. Clyde had the forethought to tell me to wear gumboots and now he holds my arm, steadying me as we pick our way through the mess to see what's left.

Abruptly, we are at the river's edge, a steep embankment that meets us much sooner than the sloping bank I was used to. The grassy sand mound and everything around it has gone, swept downstream to be deposited on neighbouring land or in a re-formed riverbed. Where I once sat with Ess and with Hayden, a swift-flowing muddy torrent churns past our feet, transporting all manner of debris in its urgent mission to reach the sea.

I have never seen anything like it. Clyde's hand holds me steady and I feel his calm energy subdue the shock.

'These ridges and this valley were here long before any of us, with our livestock and gardens and houses,' he says.

'Are you saying we don't have a right to be here?'

'Not that. But it's about balance. About respect. Living in harmony with nature. Being aware.'

The noise of the rushing water makes it difficult to talk, encourages us into quiet. We shake our heads in awe as we survey the damage to the far bank, carved in a sweeping arc from the paddocks that once were there. I feel as though we are praying, to or for what, I'm not sure.

The walk back to the house is slow, weighed down as we are by nature's wrath and indignation. Sobered by her power.

'We have so little power over anything,' Clyde says. 'Life's much easier if we can let go of wanting to control everything, and allow the vital flow to take its course.'

The Great Mystery again. I still have questions about that, but am too overwhelmed to ask them.

'Where do people start with the clean-up?' I ask. 'My house is untouched and yet there's still a lot to be done here to make every-thing right again.'

'It's like anything in life, Angelica. You start in one corner and keep going.' He smiles. Says he needs to get back to his place and check what might have been damaged there. As soon as he can, he'll return. When natural disasters sweep the valley, he explains, the Rural Fire Service and State Emergency Service usually send teams out to help households who can't do all the work themselves.

'Don't you go trying to do too much,' he warns. 'It's not worth putting that little one at risk.'

The cold air has taken on dampness. Time to go inside. Stretched out on the sofa, I think of how Bill would have handled this. A bit the same way as Clyde, most likely. With similar equilibrium and strength. A sad ache flows through me – how different all this could have been. Bill would have loved this place.

I must have slipped into a deep sleep. The fire is reduced to flickering embers, the house is chilly. I rouse myself, drop small sticks one by one onto the ruddy glow, and gently blow. Until a gold-orange flame licks into the air. A few more sticks. Wait. Then a decent chunk of wood. I am fascinated by the flames, drawn into awe at this gift of fire, its generosity of warmth.

There are many things I should be doing, most of them outdoors. But it is beyond me this afternoon. I realise with a small shock that tomorrow is my appointment at the birthing centre, and wonder if the ferry will be operating by then. They unhook the cables during flood, moor the barge securely to the bank, or up an estuary. Too dangerous to keep it going. Too many large bits of flotsam rushing through.

I have no phone. Give thanks for solar power and the gas. For firewood. The radio news makes passing mention of our predicament, detailing more widespread flooding in a better known part of the state. We are the forgotten valley. With all that entails.

Hayden's letter is crispy dry on the rack above the stove. It feels brittle as I pick it up, as though it might disintegrate. The baby stirs, stretches a tiny fist. Or maybe a heel. Weariness overtakes the desire to know. I sit for a while. He is an ethical man. Whatever the letter holds, we will be fine.

Carefully I slide a fine blade along the envelope's edge. Two folded pages slip between my fingers, still intact. I can see clear handwriting even before I flatten out the paper.

He is home safely, he tells me. And has had a lot of time to think about our situation. He reassures me of his commitment to our child: he will send money, and gifts from time to time. The old people of his community have asked him to set up a centre in his town, to work with troubled youth. He is looking forward to that. He has signed off the letter with unconditional love, and a wish that we might travel one day to visit him. Then his name. That's it.

What do I feel? How good am I at non-attachment? Aloneness is a feature of my present life, nudging uneasily against loneliness at times. Yet I know he is too young. That we are worlds apart in ways not only geographic. Sigh. Let the pages drop onto the table. I will begin a file for the baby. A file that shows him who his father is.

The other envelope is of high-quality paper with a company name and Brisbane address printed in the corner. Strange – I'm pretty sure I don't have any business contacts up north. Perhaps it has something to do with Jane? I unfold the single letterheaded sheet, flatten it carefully on the table and begin to read.

Dear Ms Jameson,

It is our sad duty to inform you that your brother-in-law, Neil Arthur Jameson, passed away ...

Neil. Waves of guilt and sadness wash through me as I continue to read. Gorman and Welch are the legal firm acting on Neil's behalf, as executors of his will. Neil had a will? Extraordinary. I would never have thought he'd be so organised.

Letter in hand, I wander into the lounge room, settle my heavy body in the armchair by the fire, and continue to read.

Neil passed away from lung cancer, in a northern Queensland hospice. He named me as his only living relative and has bequeathed to me his entire estate comprising $376,000 and some odd dollars and cents, the proceeds from sale of his share in a cattle station. There is also a box of personal effects and I am to phone at my earliest convenience to arrange safe delivery.

35

Clyde has just pulled up in his ute. I have been awake since early, keeping both fires stoked. Opening windows and doors, inviting the pale sunshine and fresh air to flow through the house. Breakfast was a warm bowl of porridge drizzled with honey and diluted with a dash of long life milk. A cup of tea. My appointment in Middleton is not until this afternoon. Maybe Clyde will have news.

The repair teams are making excellent progress, he says. The ferry is operating and the road is passable again. 'You'll need to take it slow and steady,' he tells me. 'I drove down earlier to check on Ess and Liz – they're fine, worried about you, but fine. Then I spoke to one of the SES blokes who gave me the lowdown on clean-up operations.'

Emergency services have already made good progress on clearing the road, re-establishing power for those who are linked to the grid. The phone is another matter – it could take a few days yet. Tomorrow, if we're lucky. A clean-up crew will come around sometime in the next couple of weeks to do the heavy work in my garden and shed and studio, clean up the mud and muck. I breathe in the stench, and ponder on women who work in paddy fields right up until their babies are born. Feel self-indulgent. I will do whatever I can. Discuss it with the midwife. Take no risks.

'Well, if you're sure you're okay to handle the drive, I'd best be off,' says Clyde. 'I've got a couple of big trees down. Want to get the chainsaw onto them, clear them out of the way. Other than that, not too much damage, thankfully.'

He gives me a hug, reminds me to take it easy on the roads. Says he will be back tomorrow to see how I'm going. 'You'll drop in on Ess, won't you? She'd like to see for herself that you're okay, I think.'

I allow plenty of extra time for the journey. And just as well. Where metres of tarred road have dropped away, bright streamers of orange plastic flutter from detour signs and emergency lights blink a warning from makeshift poles. The black sheen of ravens glistens as they dawdle out of my path, returning immediately to humped carcasses and distorted remnants of fur and bones. The putrid smell of mud and rotting vegetation seeps into my car, although I have the windows closed.

Liz and Ess are outside when I turn up, working at getting their garden back into shape. They're lucky to be high up on the hill. Their house withstood the assault.

'We knew you'd be fine there with Clyde,' says Ess. 'But still …'

She rests both hands on the baby, tilts her head, smiles. 'I can feel it moving!' she squeals. 'Do you think that might have been its foot? Here, Lizzie, feel this.'

I promise to drop in again on my way home, manoeuvre my precious bundle back behind the wheel. It's a slow drive to the ferry, with plenty of opportunity to thank the crews who coordinate stop–slow signs and wave me through with cautions. The growling of chainsaws echoes off sandstone valley walls, releasing the welcome scent of fresh-cut fallen timber into the fetid air, while tangles of barbed wire and fence posts slew across mud-caked paddocks and strips of orange SES tape highlight danger and work to be done.

As I turn the corner to meet the tail of the ferry queue I glimpse the dirty brown river roiling against the ramp. A foul stench assails me when I wind down my window and say hello to the driver.

'Old Mother Nature's given the valley a damn good clean-out this time, that's for sure,' he grins, clanging the gate shut behind me and securing the chain.

As we graunch our tenuous way across the swollen flow, a rotted moss-laden log rolls past the bow of the barge and I spot the legs of a white plastic garden chair floating by. It's a long time since they've seen anything like this, the driver tells me again.

Middleton District Hospital is set among hectares of rolling fields on the far edge of town, its gravel carpark sheening with puddles of water and shadowed by glistening eucalypts that line the boundary fence. My midwife Michelle is relieved and happy to see me. 'I thought you might have been stuck out there. We heard the road was cut on the other side of your village. And the ferry was off.'

My resting blood pressure is perfect, my temperature and urine sample fine. I peel away layers of winter clothing and lie on the narrow examination bench in this heated hospital room, feeling the flat surface of the stethoscope pressing cool circles against my massive belly.

'Here, listen to this,' says Michelle, looping the other end of the device into my ears. 'Beautiful, healthy heartbeat.' My head fills with the super-fast flutter of angel wings and our smiles light up the room. And then tears threaten. If only Bill were here. Well, maybe he is.

But there is no point in 'if only' or 'perhaps'. I am coming to understand that. Bring my attention back to the beating of my baby's heart. And we move on. Weigh. Measure. Write fortnightly then weekly appointment dates in my diary.

'If all our gerrie mums were as healthy as you, we'd almost be out of a job,' Michelle says, her hand resting on my arm. 'It's lovely to see you, Angelica. Take care driving home on those roads. And I'll see you in two weeks.'

Back at Essie's, we drink tea and talk about the flood. Some of our neighbours have been hit hard, their homes full of the stinking mud and rotting debris the river left behind. The girls' horses, stabled on high ground, are safe, but many valley residents were not so fortunate.

We ponder why people choose to build on the river flats. Why council regulations allow it. That has changed in recent years, Liz says.

'There's some other news too,' I say, putting down my cup. 'Neil's dead.'

'Oh my god!'

'Are you sure?'

'How do you know?'

We grapple with the shock of finding the solicitors' letter after the flood. And of Neil's unexpected legacy. I've already decided it will go into a trust fund for the baby, and we talk about synchronicity and mystery, and the apparent sadness of my brother-in-law's life. Once the phone line's fixed, I'll call the Brisbane number and find out what else they know.

Today, I need to get home before dark, especially on the slippery potholed road. This time, they let me go, knowing that I need to be in my own cosy nest. And I have to feed Tashie as well. Something has shifted in the balance of our caring. There is increased mutual respect between the three of us. Look at what we have weathered, we seem to say, although no words are spoken.

All of us are in awe of the baby miracle, of this tiny being that insists on growth and good health. They are more intent on stroking my belly than hugging me. It makes me smile.

'I'll call you as soon as my phone's back on,' I promise. 'Let you know I'm still alive.' Amazing we can make a joke like this. If Bill is listening, I think he would be proud.

Walden is a sad and sorry sight with its battered gardens and the shredded lane. Nothing that won't regrow. But I want to heal the mood with blazing fires, fill the cottage with warmth and the aroma of soups and baking bread.

Every so often I lift the receiver on the phone, check for a dial tone, listen to silence. Eventually, it stutters back at me. There are three messages. An old one from Ess. She must have called just after I left to go to Clyde's. Jane is concerned to know that I am safe. I imagine she would like to hear about her property as well, but is too polite to mention that. Next, an accented woman's voice. Sabina. Do I need a pram? Lucia has grown out of hers and it is stored in the shed. They would be delighted if I want to borrow it for my little one. I return their calls, enjoy telling this story that ends well.

Now that I have an internet connection again, I email Hayden. Thank him for his letter. Tell him about the flood. And the trust fund. And that the baby and I are doing well. This is strange territory. Fond bonds at a vast distance. I am not sure how I feel. But gratitude is part of the mix.

One morning, I phone Gorman and Welch and am put through to a young solicitor who confirms my postal address and offers condolences. She only met Neil once, she explains, when he came in to arrange his will. He seemed to be very distressed at his younger brother's passing, and determined to do what he could to help.

'Was he ill then?' I ask.

'Oh. I'm sorry. Didn't you know? He told me that he'd recently met with you and I assumed he'd discussed it. Yes, Mr Jameson was very ill with lung cancer when I met him. He knew his days were numbered.'

Another small shockwave. Why didn't he tell us? Perhaps we didn't enquire?

'There's the matter of Mr Jameson's remains, as well. His ... umm ... his ashes.'

I surprise myself by asking her to include them in the package she's sending. Feel a need to honour this man I barely knew.

I have started writing a journal, a long letter to Bill. Or is it to myself? The baby? I'm not sure. Neil's story – the little I know of it – weaves its way in. My watercolour pencils illuminate the words, sketching images of cosiness, of the river's devastating rush, of me with my impressive baby bump. It feels like a form of meditation, more than a record. A precious, positive resource.

The two weeks pass in a swift-flowing heavy-bodied dream. Thirty-four-week check. All is well. Michelle asks again who my support person will be for the birth and I tell her we are a team – Essie, Liz and I. She knows that the baby's father is overseas. I am happy with the homely feel of the birthing rooms, glad to see they are anything but ICU white.

We have opted for a one-day birthing class and arrive at 9am on a Saturday morning to join a small group in a meeting room off the maternity wing. Of the eight pregnant women, six are accompanied by husbands, one has come on her own, and then there is us – Ess, Liz and me. Curious glances flicker as we introduce ourselves, and we glimpse the future. And the past. Our family has always been different. I should concentrate on my breathing and how to hold and bathe the baby doll. But my mind wanders back to early childhood, to Aunty Fran, and the three little girls without parents. How much of this carries into a person's future, I wonder. Is there an arcane game of continuity playing out?

Cloth nappies and disposables are debated. Environmentally sound alternatives discussed. The benefits of exercise, yoga and meditation. I have been doing many things right, according to the midwife who is running the class.

Liz is making detailed notes, intent on fulfilling her supporting role. 'I don't think you'll be reading your notebook once I'm in labour.' I smile at her. 'I reckon we'll just go with the flow.'

Others in the group appear to be in awe of my equilibrium, and perhaps a little concerned that I am not taking the formalities and instructions sufficiently to heart. But I feel well prepared, and unafraid.

We head home with our day's booty – a printed booklet, Liz's notes – and our heads filled with a wealth of helpful advice.

'Do you think we should contact Sage?' Essie asks. 'Surely she'd want to know you're alright.'

We toss the idea around, but in the end the girls are clear that it has to be my decision. I don't have to think about it for long. Even talking about her is painful. I won't risk having her judgement hurled at me again.

'She knows I'm pregnant. And she knows where we all are,' I say. 'She'll get in touch if she really cares.'

The August winds arrive late, howling us into September, whipping away torn vegetation and revising freshly hewn riverbanks. For weeks, volunteer heroes have worked like armies of ants through the valley, restoring essential services, repairing property and helping residents get some normality back into their lives. When the main work is finished, red RFS fire trucks convene in the village with the white and orange utes and four-wheel drives of the SES. Weary uniformed men and women are feted with beers and wine and steaming mugs of tea while the air fills with savoury aromas and the barbecue sizzles.

* * *

One Wednesday, the postman leaves a card in my letterbox, sending me on a mission into Lawsons Landing to pick up Neil's mortal remains.

The journey is slow – three stop–slow signs between home and the ferry, with teams of fluoro-vested workers and trucks and graders repairing the road, giving me time to notice the dry mud that coats the bare trunks of poplar trees.

At the post office I hear more stories of miraculous escapes and community heroes. Sign for my registered parcel. And gratefully accept when the postie offers to carry the box to my car.

'It's not heavy, love, just a bit awkward.'

We chat a while longer about Mother Nature and change and the good that can come out of tough times. As I wave goodbye, I hear the same conversation flowing on, the next customer adding colour and exclamations of her own.

The box, when I get it home, reveals sad remnants of a man I wish I'd known. A worn black leather wallet containing a Queensland drivers licence displaying a clean-shaven image of Neil Arthur Jameson. Bill's eyes look out from the weather-beaten face. Three old black and white photos slip from a manila envelope, triggering instant tears. Two studio portraits. A wild-looking, beautiful young woman. June, their mum. A serious young man in a neat, dark suit. Arthur, their dad. And a small, blurry image of a young lad sitting in an armchair cradling a baby, love blazing from his radiant face. Neil, adoring his baby brother, Bill. The only other thing in the box is the container holding Neil's ashes. More than I can deal with right now.

* * *

During the cold windy days of early spring I sit by the fire and let my crochet hook fly. I want the blanket to be finished in plenty of time. When the wind abates, I drive to the village to buy a news-paper and some milk.

'Well, look at you two!' Janet seems impressed. 'Come out the back for a minute, Angelica. The ladies and I have made up a bit of a surprise.'

I've never been into Janet's home before, and feel a little shy. But she bustles me through to her living room where a cello-phaned extravaganza overlaps the coffee table.

'We wanted to make sure you were right for everything,' she says. 'Being on your own and all.' Awkward shuffle. 'So we've added a few extras besides the knitted things. Go on. Open it.'

As the crinkling pink and blue cellophane falls away I am close to tears again. Nested in a cane washing basket are neat stacks of folded miniature clothes, all in lemon and white – impossibly tiny jumpsuits, lacy knitted cardigans and frocks, bootees and mittens and bonnets. Underneath these are two of the softest white towels I have ever seen. Two cream flannel bunny rugs, satin-edged. And a beautiful handmade baby bag with many pockets, plastic lined.

'You'll not be short of babysitters if you ever want a night out,' Janet says, bridling with pleasure at my delight. 'We need more good people here in the valley.'

So. I am no longer considered a tourist, although 'local' might take a little while yet. This gruff woman's kindness has almost brought me undone.

Janet insists on carrying the basket to my car as I follow behind, acceding gratefully. I promise to drop in again soon. We chat about my brief foray into art sales, agree it has taken a back seat but that it will revive once the baby is old enough. Aspects of my future feel solid and real.

Back home, I fold all the baby things into drawers and

cupboards. And decide to deal with Neil's few items as well. The photos I will frame, and set them on the mantelpiece. His wallet goes into a drawer with other must-keep items. And when the time is right, I'll ask Ess and Liz to help me scatter his ashes in the river. Unite him with Bill, whom he clearly loved, despite his long absence.

Angelo and Sabina insist on making a daytrip to deliver the pram. By the time they arrive at Walden they are entranced, thrilled by the adventure of the ferry and the country drive, astonished when they see a cottage with a living roof. Before lunch we walk down to visit the river, Angelo carrying Lucia on his hip. There is a new pathway through the bushes – wider, ending abruptly at the cutaway bank. Nowhere to sit. I might have Bill's bench moved down here. Today the water is murky, still not settled after the flood, eddying in swirls around the remnants of dead trees and fence posts, tangles of wire, rotting bales of hay. We wander back to the cottage and sit under the pergola to enjoy our simple lunch.

I wonder how my abdominal skin can possibly stretch any more, laugh with Sabina at this miracle of elasticity, talk about tiredness, the increasing need to pee. Women's talk. Angelo has taken their little one for a walk along the lane and is wandering back. A scenario I might never see in my own life, I reflect. Don't go there.

I have been searching the Internet for baby names, making lists. Every so often I find a scrap of paper with an old jotting that makes me laugh. Beckett, meaning stream. Would I really have considered saddling a child with that? Native American options seemed appealing for a while, but I can't find one that I really like. Dyami, which means eagle. That might fit. But is it a suitable name for an Australian boy? I can't track its tribal origin either, and blush when I think of the risks entailed in ignorance. I consider asking Hayden. But he has said he wants me to feel free to raise our child in my own way, to trust my instincts and the good advice of other women.

One of the books I've been reading had a character named River. That would fit. But I wonder if it sounds too hippie-like. Keep on searching, making lists.

Jane emailed the other day to see how everything is going. Her life sounds rich and rewarding. Engaged. She says she derives great pleasure from seeing bereft children slowly learning to read and write, regaining joy. She tells me again that she will be staying indefinitely. That she wants me to feel secure. Walden is my home.

Gratitude is high on my list of everyday emotions, where once the list was headed up by grief. How did that change? When did the mourning and deadness begin to dissolve?

There are days when I waddle my heavy body from sofa to comfy chair, pulling out old photos, reflecting on Bill and the life we made. Reflecting on his death. Thinking about continuity and heritage. Sketching likenesses of my parents, of Bill, drawing what I recall of Hayden. It fascinates me, this weaving of DNA and memory, this interconnectedness of imagery and skin.

I progress to weekly appointments with Michelle, take Ess or Liz with me for the drive. Thirty-seven weeks. At night I lie on my side and plump a fat pillow between my knees, trying to get comfortable, trying to get some sleep. My dreams are of wrinkled, dark-skinned elders wearing unfamiliar garb, encircling me with enlivening chants. Sometimes they merge with people I recognise. Maddie comes quite often. Aunty Fran. Occasionally, an angelic form of Bill.

The gnarled, twisted wisteria branches are gleaming with bumps and swellings and the air is balmy. Some mornings, after the mist lifts, I stand outside. Breathe the fresh, scented air. Watch the journey of the golden sun. We are entering spring.

I have a well-organised birthing plan. My bag is packed. Liz and Ess are both on standby and phone me every day, once each.

The moment I feel the slightest twinge of a contraction, I am to call them.

They will come. Clyde will collect the dog. It is over an hour's drive to Middleton. Even the drivers on the ferry have been monitoring the progress of my bump, promise to let us jump the queue when the big day comes.

36

In the pale light of a soft spring day I am eating lunch under the pergola. When I shuffle awkwardly to prise my cumbersome body from the seat, a flood of warm liquid gushes down my thighs.

I am surprisingly calm. Remember to breathe. Give thanks that the phone has a dial tone. Key in the numbers for Ess, who picks up almost immediately. Thank all beings of light, the Great Mystery and the technology gods.

'I think it's coming.' My voice is steady, but my mind is threatening to race. 'Can you come and get me?'

'Hang in there, Angel. We'll be with you in twenty minutes. Just sit down and wait. We're on our way.'

It's my job to phone the hospital, let Michelle know. She will be on duty later in the afternoon. They will be waiting for us. Have I started contractions? No? When they come, I should time the gaps between and note them. And remember my breathing.

Then the first wave hits. A vice is clenching me over, gripping my belly, making me gasp and clutch at the door frame. Walking walking at a steady steady pace. Walking in rhythm with my breath. Observe the second hand sweeping the face of the clock.

Till the wave hits again. Eleven minutes and seventeen seconds. Write it down.

Wheels crunch as loose gravel flies. Here comes Clyde. Who will be looking after Tashie while I'm away. And who is caring for me right now. Calm hands on my shoulders, face close to mine, breathing with my breath. Steady and solid.

'The girls will be here any minute,' he assures me. 'You're a wonderful woman, Angelica, a strong woman who has weathered many storms. You will be just fine.'

I have the strength of his conviction but still the words feel good. In this uncharted territory the stakes are high. I am waiting to meet my baby. To see whether I recognise him.

The wave grips and makes me gasp. I revert to training. Find the steady breath. Breathe it through. Walk. Write down the time.

I feel warmth flowing into me from Clyde's strong hands, feel my breath relax. And then my body. I think I can get the hang of this. Eleven minutes. Still a reasonable gap.

Essie's station wagon wheels to a halt near the front door. Ess jumps out.

'Ready, darling? Let's go!'

She picks up my pre-packed bag, stows it in the boot, comes back for me.

'Are you going to be okay in the car?' she asks. 'Just say if you need us to pull over, if you need us to stop.'

Clyde waves us away, excited Tashie leashed at his side. He will close up the house. No need to give it another thought.

At the ferry, they see us coming, with our lights on high beam in the middle of the day, horn tooting.

'Right then, love. Here we go. Clyde phoned to tell us you were on your way.'

It's a long winding drive to Middleton. I am struggling to find equilibrium within the waves, the all-consuming convulsions of my womb. But we have been practising breathing together, and the girls help me find my rhythm again. There is a wheelchair waiting outside the maternity entrance doors. I am still focused on my breathing, but the gaps between contractions are shorter now.

Brisk steps and smiling faces wheel me away, Liz and Ess trotting at my side. We settle into a pastel pink room with a comfy bean bag and a bed and an assortment of chairs. Our own ensuite. I am desperate to go to the toilet, feel my pelvis is splitting apart. Stagger to walk. Ess supports me. Nothing comes out.

I walk to a dazed rhythm through the resting gaps. Walking back and forth, forth and back. Meeting my body's contractions with my spirit, leaning and breathing into them. Breathing them through, breathing them down. Deep, primal growling echoes around the room, echoes through my body, vibrates to the pulsing of the earth.

'We are one,' sing the faint, sweet voices from the mountain. 'We are here. Breathe in our strength. Be one with us.'

I sip the sweetened water. Lean on the chair. Stand and lean and rock. Peel off the t-shirt, the undies. Rock and walk. Groan and scream. Guttural moaning. Alone on the waves.

Now Michelle is here with us. Asks me to lie down. Listens to baby's heartbeat. Checks my swollen vagina with latex-gloved hands. Delivers good news. Eight centimetres dilated. Almost there. Doing well. Doing everything right. Walking and moaning. Rocking. Leaning on Ess.

Warm hands caress my back. Cool cloth wipes away streams of sweat.

The momentary rests are absorbed in the waves and suddenly I cannot do this any more. I want to go home. I am over it now. Can we go?

I am wild with confusion, pleading. While my pelvis cracks and widens. I think I will die. Breathe and breathe. Soothing hands. Good women on every side. A calm voice. Maybe Michelle's.

'This is normal, Angelica. You're in transition. Not long to go. You're doing amazingly well. Now, breathe with me.'

Rocking and rocking. No strength left. My body is rending into splinters of pain. I need the toilet. Take me there now.

But they lean me over the beanbag, stroke my hair, rub my back. Breathe while I scream.

'Get ready to push. With the next contraction, give a big push.' Michelle.

Hands touching my vulva.

'I can feel the head. Wait for the next contraction. Wait with me.'

One more guttural scream.

'Oh, Angelica, well done. Wonderful. The shoulders are out. Take it easy. Wait for the final push.'

Final push.

And he slithers out.

'Oh, will you look at that! What a little angel! Look at him.'

I hear a baby crying. Someone laughing. Feel strong hands raising me from the floor. Letting me rest on the bed. My body is expanded but, impossibly, intact.

'Would you like to hold your son?'

I have a son.

Sweet, sticky body slides over my belly, rests below my breasts. I can feel and hear him more than see him, feel his perfection in my quivering hands.

They help me sit up. Bathe my face with warm, rose-scented water. Tidy my hair. Three beautiful faces close to mine, all of us gazing at baby. Who has cried a little but has settled now. His miracle fingers are curled. He is coated in blood and creamy goo. Perfection.

'You can put him to your breast if you like.' Michelle. She is an angel too.

Strong, petal-soft tug on my nipple, flooding me with love. More than love. I have no words for it. The tonguing and suckling at life.

'When you're ready, we'll clean him up a bit, cut the cord, get him dressed and keep him warm.'

Ess conducts the cord-cutting ceremony with sterile scissors, Liz on camera, recording our joy. Someone passes me a sweet, warm drink. Milky tea. Too much milk. Delicious all the same. I want to go to sleep. Am wide awake. Am listening to the soothing sounds of attendant women providing care.

Michelle massages the saggy swell of my belly. She is talking to me.

'Come on Angelica, let's push this placenta out. One more push. Then you can tuck up in bed with your baby beside you and get some well-earned rest.'

It is taking too long. But she dare not tug hard at the cord. I have to expel my baby's life support system myself.

The room goes quiet. I can see Ess sitting in an armchair with my swaddled son in her arms. Now the world is fading in and out. The walls are fuzzy.

Someone is doing something to my feet, pressing on acupuncture points. Michelle gives me an injection to encourage the placenta to come. I am drifting in and out. Softening my breath. Several shiny white people are now in the room.

They lift me up. Put my body on a trolley. Wheel me swiftly away. I feel so cold. I feel the fizzing darkness, and the fizzing white.

'BP is dropping. There's an internal bleed.'

My ice-cold body is lifting and falling on the trolley in a white sterile room. Stark white angels surround it. I can see them. I am watching from my vantage point high above the room. Hearing controlled panic in their voices. Urgent calls for help. Call the surgeon. Prepare the theatre.

I am in no-emotion, bathed in golden glow. Swathed in the bliss of heraldic choirs. I have no boundaries, I have no form. Ethereal radiance pervades me, carries me along. My breathing is pure light. In the distance, a glimmer of Bill. My darling.

Far down below me a tragic scene unfolds. A ghost-white body on a surgical pedestal. Blood pressure thirty on fifteen. Barely a pulse. I see glowing white people around it and a corridor outside where two distraught women pace, one with a wrapped newborn infant in her arms. They are desperate, crying. And the baby the woman's carrying is mine.

The baby is mine.

From golden blissful mindlessness I feel his familiar spirit searching for mine. And I am impelled to return. Go back to be with my baby. Go back into living and life.

There is a tube taped to the back of my left hand, a white sheet folded across my swollen breasts. My eyes are having trouble cracking open. My mouth is parched.

Pale faces peer in on me. Essie. Liz. Aunty Fran. All of them have tears running down their cheeks. They look so worried, and so relieved.

Arms wrap carefully around my shoulders. Essie sobs.

'We thought we'd lost you,' she whispers close to my ear. 'Oh, Angel, they really thought you were going to die.'

'Where's my baby?'

I feel her sharp intake of breath. Feel her relax.

'He's in the nursery, Angel. I'll ask the nurses to fetch him for you.'

They bring my beautiful boy. Lie him in my arms. I cannot

fathom what has happened. But I was gone, and he asked me to return.

For the next three days, donated blood flows into my drained body and the colour slowly returns to my skin. Doctors and midwives drop by, speaking of gratitude, of miracles, of courage and other non-medical things. Wondering how I made it through.

The girls and Aunty Fran stay by my side, swapping shifts to wander off and grab food and sleep. And the baby dreams in his crib beside my bed. Suckles my nipples. Has his nappy changed, his tiny body bathed. Lies wrapped and softly breathing atop my swollen torso with his head between my breasts.

His name is William. I have decided to call him Will.

My little angel.

Will has big, round, dark eyes, olive skin, and soft, dark hair that is almost black. Just like Hayden's. And a lot like Bill's.

EPILOGUE

Heady perfume fills the air at Walden. We are settling in. Every morning I tuck Will into his pram with his gorgeous blanket and we go for a long walk, Tashie trotting along beside.

The pergola is dripping with violet-blue blossoms and pale, bright green leaves. Will often sleeps here beside me while I drink tea. Write and sketch in my journal. Regain my physical strength.

I am no longer afraid of death. And I love life, every moment, with every breath. Although there are many things I will never understand.

The river is settling into its newly created channel. In the evenings I carry Will in his cuddle sling against my body and we walk down to stand on the riverbank. Rose-gold light fades behind the western ridge of the valley, and a silver moon rises in the east.

ACKNOWLEDGEMENTS

First and foremost, I am grateful to everyone at Pilyara Press: our publisher, Jennifer Scoullar, who loved this story so much that she invited me to join the collective and has supported me every step of the way; Kathryn Ledson, for insightful, sensitive editing and for making me laugh; proofreader Monique Mulligan for the final meticulous polish; and the entire team for their ongoing collaboration and encouragement. My thanks also to structural editor, Sydney Smith, who gently but firmly coached me on aspects of light and shade.

Daniel Cassar – what can I say? Not only did you take the beautiful image that graces the cover of this book – you have gone above and beyond with all matters technical, my book trailer, new website and Facebook page, and the calm logic that helped me convert manuscript to published book without having a meltdown. Thank you so much. And thank you to Megan Montgomery for my elegant cover design.

My mother raised me with a delight in story, surrounded me with books, recited poetry after dinner, imbued me with a lifetime love of language and its capacity to inspire and inform. She never lost faith in me. When I see or hear kookaburras, and when I write, I thank you and honour you, Mum.

My father worked tirelessly to ensure I could stay at school and receive a fine education, and always maintained faith in me regardless of the unorthodox twists and turns my life has taken. I thank you and honour you, Dad.

The late Sandra Bernhardt, my senior English teacher, instilled rigor and the capacity to reach deeper and further for creative and linguistic integrity.

Leona Dawson forwarded the email that connected me with Joyce Kornblatt and the womens writing workshops and retreat of 2008. Without the inspiration from Joyce and this phenomenal group of women, I doubt my book would even have been begun.

The late Cynthia Cameron faithfully archived each day's first draft offering, reading honestly and sensitively, a constant and much valued support.

Chloe Higgins, you've been a loyal friend and supporter from the beginning and you never let me give up – thank you for the words, thoughts and honest responses that triggered deeper insight and inspiration.

Pamela Robson and Annarosa Berman generously offered their professionalism and their time to review the initial draft manuscript. Thank you both for your honesty, sensitivity and suggestions. And to those who read excerpts and later drafts – Colette Vella, Shelley Kenigsberg, Selena Hanet-Hutchins, Lisa Heidke, Dianne Riminton, Bridgett Elliott, Sandy Yates, Lou Helms, Penny Conlon, Marianne Dodds, Carolyn Walsh, Rachel Moodie, Pat Lehane and Greg Shoemark – each of you has helped me make this book the best it can be. Special thanks to Maisie Keep for her frank evaluation, for sharing Valla and for her exquisite contributions to the tea ritual.

For insights into ICU and organ donor procedures, my thanks go to my friend Ray and to the helpful staff at Donate Life, the

Australian Government Organ and Tissue Authority. Any anomalies are either artistic licence or the result of my misunderstanding.

There have been many non-literary guides and teachers along the way. In particular, my thanks to Liza De Goede for teaching me Reiki, to the Sydney Zen Centre for first teaching me how to meditate, to Thich Nhat Hanh for being a source of wisdom and inspiration for many decades, and to the great mystery of the natural world – that most profound of teachers.

Above all, my children, Sam and Annie Rees, along with their partners Sarah and Matt, are a constant joy and my greatest loves. Their capacity to greet life's challenges with equilibrium and wisdom inspires me, and I am deeply grateful for their ongoing love and support.

ABOUT THE AUTHOR

Desney King writes about love, relationships, death, grief, healing, interconnectedness, the world of nature, and life's unfathomable mysteries. She is a retired book editor, and survivor of several strokes. Born in rural New South Wales, Desney now lives in Sydney in a light-filled apartment with a long view.

Transit of Angels is her debut novel.

If you've enjoyed this novel, please consider leaving an online rating or review. Thank you.

www.desneyking.com.au